Her Greatest Adventure

GREATEST LOVE SERIES BOOK 2

HANNAH COWAN

Special Edition

ISBN: 978-1-990804-21-2

Edited and Proofed by: Sandra @oneloveediting

Cover Design by: Booksandmoods @booksnmoods

Authors Note

Hi, everyone! I wanted to make sure that before anyone jumps into this story that you know Her Greatest Adventure is the second instalment in a second-generation series. This means that there will be a heavy helping of characters involved in this story, both new and from the previous stories. Keeping that in mind, I have written this as a standalone to the best of my ability.

If I am a new author to you and you are interested in reading the books prior to this one, I have included a recommended reading list. If not, I have also added a family tree.

For a list of content warnings, please see my website.

https://www.hannahcowanauthor.com/hergreatestadventure

Reading Order

Even though all of my books can be read on their own, they all exist in the same world—regardless of series—so for reader clarity, I have included a recommended reading order to give you the best experience possible.

This is also a timeline-accurate list.

Lucky Hit (Oakley and Ava) Swift Hat-Trick trilogy #1

Between Periods (5 POV Novella) Swift Hat-Trick trilogy #1.5

Blissful Hook (Tyler and Gracie) Swift Hat-Trick trilogy #2

Craving the Player (Braden and Sierra) Amateurs in Love series #1

Taming the Player (Braden and Sierra) Amateurs in Love series #2

Vital Blindside (Adam and Scarlett) Swift Hat-Trick trilogy #3

Her Greatest Mistake (Maddox and Braxton) Greatest Love #1

Family Trees

CHARACTER ORIGINS

SWIFT HAT-TRICK TRILOGY

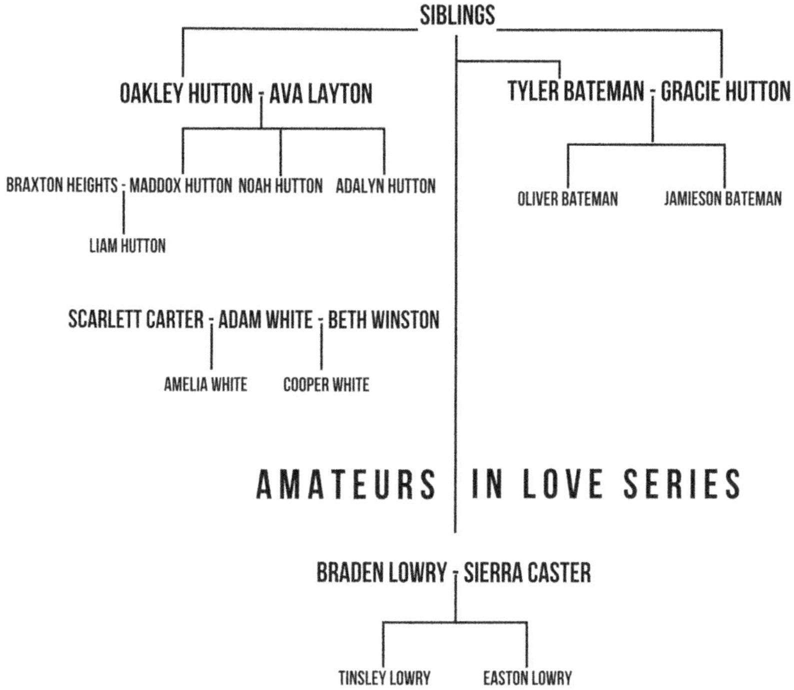

Playlist

You Belong With Me — Taylor Swift	♥	3:51
Take It Slow — Conner Smith	♥	2:43
10:35 — Tiësto and Tate McRae	♥	2:52
Lovers — Anna of the North	♥	3:36
Eleven — Khalid and Summer Walker	♥	3:26
Oceans — Martin Garrix and Khalid	♥	3:36
Sex On The Beach— Iggy Azalea and Sophie Scott	♥	3:01
Uh Oh — Tate McRae	♥	2:50
Not Supposed To Know Each Other — Taylor Edwards	♥	2:42
Until We Drink — Savannah Sgro	♥	3:15
Tattoos — Reneé Rapp	♥	2:53
Memories — Conan Gray	♥	4:09
Kiss You Inside Out — Hedley	♥	3:37
Crazy In Love — Beyoncé	♥	3:46
I Can't Take You Anywhere — Seaforth	♥	3:32
Movies — Conan Gray	♥	3:34
Teenage Dream — Katy Perry	♥	3:48
Feels Like — Gracie Abrams	♥	2:32

For my alpha girls. I'm sorry for edging you so much with this one. It was worth it, though, wasn't it?

1

Adalyn

"If you're going to post a picture of my bare tit online, at least make sure it's the good one," I mutter, kicking my feet out on the couch.

A photo of me soaking wet and climbing onto a boat with my left boob out is blown up on my phone screen. It's from a boat trip I was invited to a few days ago, and while I did truly love the sparkly pink bikini I chose to wear, it turns out that it was made very cheaply despite the hefty price tag. All it took was a quick dive into the ocean for the neck strap to snap and, obviously, for my tits to drop free for all to see.

Having people taking photos of me and posting them online isn't anything new, but I *can* say that this is the first time they've gone this far. The thought of my brothers or, even worse, my father finding this photo is enough to have me sending it to my publicist in an email labelled *urgent*.

"You're the only person I know who would be more upset that someone had posted a photo of the, quote, unquote, 'wrong boob' online than the fact that they took those photos of you in the first place," Ivy says, flipping through the channels on the TV.

The goddess with gorgeous woodsy green eyes, black curly

hair, and smooth dark skin has been my closest friend since we met at a photoshoot for a new line of workout apparel last year. She's also one of the only people who knows me well enough to understand my boob dilemma.

It's not that I don't care that someone felt the need to post pictures of my bare chest online; it's just that it's not really anything that some haven't seen before. I've done photoshoots for a few magazines and billboards, wearing skimpy bikinis and bras that have shown everything but nipple before. This Twitter picture might beat those shoots in the nude department, but a nipple is a nipple.

Plus, if men can walk around with their naked titties out, then I sure as hell am not going to be embarrassed if given the opportunity to do the same.

"I wouldn't care if it weren't for the fact my family could see." Tossing my phone on the plush, velvety grey ottoman beside me, I release a long groan. "My brother's wife sent it to me this morning. Imagine my terror when I thought he had seen it too."

Ivy winces. "If Maddox had seen it, we would be on the way to the hospital right now because he would have had a stroke."

"She promised that he hadn't, but it's only a matter of time. I need it taken down."

"Liv will take care of it. Your pretty, perky titties will be off the internet in no time."

I choke back a laugh. "Pretty, perky titties? Should I say thank you?"

She answers with a wink.

Staring down the loose material of the cropped shirt I'm wearing, I find the titties in question. While decorated with two silver bars through both nipples, my chest is pretty run-of-the-mill. Small handfuls of boob that are perky enough I can go without a bra most days without noticing.

I've always been a tall woman, standing at five seven. But

in comparison to my father and two brothers, who are all well over six feet tall, I'm the shortest of the bunch. I would consider myself the runt of the litter had my family not treated me like the most precious, one-of-a-kind jewel my entire life.

"Are you staring at your boobs?" Ivy asks, sounding as if she's trying not to laugh.

I look up and grin. "You don't look at yours?"

"I do. I have great tits."

"You do," I agree.

She does, and by the hundreds of billboards around the world showcasing her body, it's obvious we're not the only two who think so.

I never wanted to be a model. It wasn't my life plan or my dream job when I was younger. On the contrary, it just fell into my lap. Ivy, on the other hand, she fought for her spot in the industry, and I respect the shit out of her for that.

She's a certified girl boss, if you will.

"Have you finished packing yet?" she asks, switching subjects.

"Almost."

"You haven't even started, have you?"

I gasp in mock offense. "What do you mean? Of course I have."

"You're a crap liar, Addie. I snooped in your room last night, and your suitcase was empty."

"Hold up—you were snooping in my room?"

She swipes a hand through the air. "Forget I said that. Why haven't you packed? We leave in four days."

"Maybe I changed my mind and don't wanna go with a Snoopy Susan like you."

Her eye roll is heavy, annoyed. "I was looking for your blow-dryer because mine smells like fire whenever I turn it on. It's not like I was trying to find your dirty panties or anything."

"Have you ever wondered how much you could sell your used underwear for? I bet you could make thousands by doing that."

"Adalyn." It's a frustrated sound.

I smile timidly. "Right. Sorry. I haven't packed yet because I'm feeling oddly nervous. I'm not sure what's different this time, but I'm almost . . . scared."

This trip has been planned since I was eighteen. And after postponing it repeatedly over the past three years, the time has come.

I'm going to spend the next two months travelling Europe with my best friend.

But just like every day since coming up with the idea, the thought of leaving makes my stomach sour and my back sweat.

Ivy stares at me, blinking slowly. "*You're* scared? The girl who begged for a chance to skydive on her sixteenth birthday and whose idea of a fun Thursday afternoon in Mexico is swimming in a shark cage?"

I frown. "I know. It makes no sense."

"Why are you scared? The next two months are going to be full of sexy European men with even sexier accents and amazing food. We've planned everything to a T. Where we're staying, how we're getting there."

"I know. Trust me, I know. It doesn't make sense to me either, but every time I try to pack, I feel like I'm going to puke."

Her eyes soften with understanding. "Do you not want to leave your family? Two months is a long stretch of time, Addie. If that's it, we can always shorten the trip."

Is that it? Am I just nervous about being gone for so long?

"No. I'll get over it. Maybe I just have to get there, and whatever these feelings are will disappear. We're not changing anything. We've already spent way too much money on this."

And by way too much, I mean *way. Too. Much.* My bank

account hasn't been as empty as it is right now since I was sixteen.

"Are you sure?"

"Yes. This trip is just as much for you as it is for me." With a total fake sense of determination, I push off the couch, plant my hands on my hips, and puff out my chest. "I'm going to pack right now. I'm getting this done."

Then, I spin on my heels and tear out of the living room, my eyes narrowed on my bedroom at the end of the hallway. The door is open, exposing the bare white walls and matching carpet inside. My suitcase is still empty on my bed when my toes sink into the carpet, and I come to a stop with the mattress touching my thighs.

Staring at my closed closet door, I ignore the sore feeling in my stomach and reach for it, tugging it open. The next few minutes are a mess of flying clothes and hangers hitting the floor as I create a pile on my bed of almost every piece of clothing I own. Once that's done, I head into my connecting bathroom and dig my small travel bag out from under the sink and start to fill it with everything I can find, with the exception of what I'll still be needing the next few days.

"Woah. We're going for two months, not two years, sweetie," Ivy mutters as I come out of the bathroom and freeze.

I cringe at the mess. "Help me."

She laughs softly and sorts through the clothes, starting to build piles for different things. When she lifts a heavy wool sweater and looks at me with an arched brow, I laugh.

"Never hurts to be prepared," I say.

"There's prepared, and there's *prepared*. This is too much. Nowhere we're going will be cold enough to need this thing. It's almost July."

"Yeah, yeah. Just toss it on the floor, and I'll take care of it later," I huff, stepping beside her and joining in on the sorting. "What did you pack?"

"Mostly shorts and T-shirts. Too many bikinis. I have this dream of us on a boat in Mykonos, wearing matching suits."

"Hopefully, no broken straps and nip slips occur during this supposed boat trip."

She bumps my shoulder. "Even if there were, who cares? That sounds like a later problem."

That makes me smile, some of the tension in my shoulders fading. "Good point. What happens in Europe stays in Europe."

"At least until we touch back down in Vancouver."

"Speaking of, have you settled on a place yet? I'm assuming you'll want to be ready to move in as soon as we get home."

Ivy's hunt for a new apartment has been a tedious one, with her extravagant ideas and medium-sized budget, but as far as I know, she has the search narrowed down to two places: a mid-size studio downtown only a short walk from her new job or a two-bedroom place twenty minutes west and a taxi ride away.

She blows a strand of curly hair out of her face and drops a neon yellow one-piece suit into my suitcase.

"The landlord for the place downtown won't budge on the rent."

"Can you afford it as it is?"

"Yes, but I don't *want* to pay that much."

I laugh softly, tossing a stack of shorts into my case. "You don't have to move out, you know. I love having you as my roommate."

She's sweet, funny, and cleans up after herself. I mean, really, what's not to like about living with your best friend? I'm going to miss her so much. Living on your own is great for a while, but the buzz wears off when you're eating dinner alone for the fiftieth night in a row.

"You know I wouldn't unless I didn't have another choice. But this place is too far from work. It's cheaper for me to pay more in rent than it is to keep taking the long Uber rides twice a day."

I don't bother hiding my frown. "I know. But I'm still sad."

Her arm slips across my back as she squeezes me. I press my cheek to her shoulder. "We still have two months together before we have to think about it. Put it in the back of your mind. I'm going to get us a drink before we finish the rest of this."

Releasing me, she rushes out of the room, and as I hear her open the fridge and pop the cork on a new bottle of wine, I let myself smile.

Two months of uninterrupted time with my best friend.

Yeah, I think I can focus on that.

2

Adalyn

"What do you mean you can't go?" I shriek, utterly horrified.

Ivy sucks in a breath through the phone. "I'm so sorry, Addie. He said I can have the place at a lower rate, but I have to move in at the end of this month. It's that or nothing."

"Tell me where you are, and I'll be there as soon as I can. This dickwad has another thing coming if he thinks he's going to take you from me. Fuck him!" I shout, not caring that I'm being watched and gawked at by a crowd of photographers and models.

Their judgment can kiss my ass.

"Please understand where I'm coming from here. I need this place, Addie. It's perfect. I can't pass it up," Ivy pleads.

"Of course you can't pass it up! That's why I'm so pissed." My voice drops to a whisper, one that shakes with nerves. "We leave in three days. I can't go alone. I can't do it."

Fear grips me tight, squeezing and squeezing until I'm sure I'll pop.

"Honey," she sighs.

The tenderness in her tone has me waving pitifully at the

lead photographer and scurrying out of the shoot, a sting behind my eyes.

"Where are you going, Adalyn? You're up next!" I hear but don't look back before entering the hall.

"Who tells a possible tenant they need to move into a place with a week's notice? A total ass sucker, that's who," I hiss before angrily swiping at the tears streaking down my cheek, ruining my makeup. "Are you sure that's who you want to rent a place from?"

The door to the dressing room is open, but I close it behind me, wanting—no, *needing*—privacy. Some time alone to think.

I took this shoot last minute, not wanting to turn down a quick payday before leaving, but now I'm regretting that choice. I could have been in my bed right now, alone to wallow in self-pity instead of a hot new gossip topic.

"He's a *total* ass sucker, but need always trumps want," Ivy sighs.

She's right, and I hate it. "What do I do?"

"What about Maddox? The season should be done by now, right?"

I collapse on one of the three faux-leather couches and bury my face in my hand. "No. He's in the playoffs still."

My oldest brother is in the Stanley Cup final for the second consecutive season, and the team looks like they'll win the entire thing again. I'm both proud of him and selfishly frustrated.

Her next exhale is heavy, apologetic. "Your sister-in-law?"

"Doubtful. My nephew is still too small."

"Crap, that's right. Is there anyone else? Could you convince Noah?"

"Convincing the devil spawn to do anything I want him to has never been a wise way to spend my time, Ivy. There's no point in trying."

"What about that other guy you've told me about? The one that's always around your family? Cole?"

"Cooper?"

"Yeah!"

A tiny flicker of hope comes to life at the suggestion. Cooper White has been Maddox's best friend since they were in diapers. There are very few memories I have that don't include him hanging around somewhere. But he's ten years older than me. I'm sure the last thing he wants is to spend his summer babysitting me. Or at least that's what he would see it as.

Babysitting his best friend's little sister as she trollops through Europe.

Yuck.

That flicker of hope is snuffed out in an instant.

"Cooper isn't an option," I mutter.

"You're killing me here," Ivy whispers.

Guilt nips at me. "I'm sorry. I'll figure something out; I can take care of it."

"I could always get another flight in to meet you after I'm moved in," she suggests.

"That's sweet, but there's no way you're paying for an entirely new ticket. We knew it was a risk when we purchased non-refundable tickets in the first place."

Her exhale is stressed. "Please tell me that you don't hate me."

I drop my hand to my lap and take a deep breath. "I don't hate you. I hate your new landlord, but not you. I promise."

The door to the dressing room flies open as a line of women strides inside. Several sets of eyes fall on me before they're looking away quickly, as if the sight of me with smudged eyes and black tears streaming down my face is too gruesome a sight to stare at for long.

My middle finger tingles with the need to say hello, but I don't give in.

"I have to go. I'll see you at home tonight."

"Okay, yeah. Of course. We'll talk more tonight," she rushes out.

"Yeah. Sounds good."

I hang up with a heavy heart and make quick work of getting dressed so I can leave. The feeling of being watched again only makes me move quicker. It's not completely their fault for gawking. I look like a nutcase right now.

Finally, after yanking on a pair of sweatpants and a cropped shirt, I put on my flip-flops and head out, fully prepared to get my ass chewed out by my publicist when she learns I cut out of the shoot.

I hate that I can't find it in me to care.

BEING the baby in a family of five, I was always too small to play with the big kids. By the time I was ten, Maddox was graduating high school, and Noah was realizing it wasn't cool to be seen with his little sister. It made me sad until I realized that meant I could hog our parents' attention.

Because of that, they became my best friends.

I should have been embarrassed to consider my mom and dad my closest friends, but I wasn't. Not in the slightest. I had, and still have, the coolest parents. The ones who knew when to tighten the reins and when to let you out on your own. The kind who never judged and always had a plan to fix whatever it was that went wrong.

That's why I'm here, sitting on the porch swing with my mom, a virgin strawberry daiquiri in my hand because she still refuses to believe I'm old enough to drink.

If there's anyone who can help with what's going on with me, it's Mom.

"Tell me what's going on in that beautiful head of yours,

sweetheart," she says when I continue to keep silent, watching the treeline at the edge of the property sway with the breeze.

"Ivy can't come to Europe."

"What happened?" she asks, voice calm and as soft as ever.

I tuck my legs beneath me and lean into her side, my drink melting in the wide glass from the heat of my palm as I continue to hold it without drinking.

"Things just didn't work out. She found a new apartment, but the landlord is a hard-ass who won't let her move in after the first of July."

She runs her hand up and down my back in a soothing motion, humming like she always does when one of us is upset. "Would you like me to tell Noah to go with you? You know he'll listen to me."

I swallow back my horror. "No, thank you. He'd probably leave me in a dirty hostel and fly back home alone."

"He wouldn't dare," she swears.

A giggle crawls up my throat. "He totally would. But that's okay. That stick in the mud wouldn't do half of the stuff I have planned on this trip, anyway."

"And what exactly are you planning on doing over there?"

She pulls back enough to stare down at me with slightly narrowed, glittering emerald eyes. They crinkle at the corners from years of laughter and smiles, and my heart warms at the sight.

I grin, flattening a few rebel chestnut hairs at the top of her head. "Nothing you need to lose sleep over, Mommy Dearest."

Blowing a raspberry, she nods sarcastically. "Right. My darling daughter has never done anything in her twenty-one years of life that's made that hard to believe."

"Hey, I kept your life interesting," I protest.

"Of course, dear. Whatever you say."

"You suck."

"Yet here you are," she gloats with a cheeky smile.

I sigh. "Yeah, here I am. And it's your motherly duty to give me advice on what to do now. Am I really about to go on a two-month trek across Europe on my own?"

"Absolutely not," Dad barks, his entrance surprising me enough I jolt, some of my drink spilling over onto my hand. I quickly lick it off.

"Okay, Mr. Super Stealth. Warn a girl next time," I mutter, scooting over enough that he has room to sit on my other side. When he only stands in front of the swing with a frown and his hands on his hips, I arch a brow and pat the cushion. "Sit down. You're making everyone nervous."

"You are not going across the world by yourself, Adalyn. I'm well aware of your fearless nature, but please, have mercy on us this one time. I'm too old to be dealing with this stress."

"You're only too old if you believe you're too old," I point out.

He rolls his eyes. "There's no way you actually think it's a good idea to go alone."

"I don't. But I refuse to cancel."

"If it's about money, you know we could always—"

I move my head from side to side, cutting him off. "Not happening. Besides, it's not about the money. Not completely."

It's more my pride than anything else. I refuse to be beaten by a goddamn cranky old landlord.

"Then there has to be someone else," Mom says softly. "What about Cooper?"

Huffing out a breath, I look at the sun peeking over Dad's shoulder. "I don't need to be babysat, Ma."

"I know you don't. But he would take care of you over there. You know that just as well as your father and I do. Right, Oakley?"

Dad's features are pulled tight, his emotions hard to decipher. Is it uncertainty that has him pulling into himself?

"Oakley?" Mom pushes, tone sharp.

The second his eyes fall on his wife, the strain leaches from his face, replaced with a soft, loving smile. "Right."

A nip of what I've come to recognize as envy has me looking away, out at the treeline again. I dream of having a love that pure. That all-consuming obsession with another person.

I grew up watching the way my dad treated my mom and vice versa. I've seen first-hand how my oldest brother loves his wife so fiercely that he can't breathe without her close, and even the way my other brother has silently pined over his best friend, doting on her for as long as I can remember.

I want to be that for someone. Their everything. Their heart and soul. Present and future. But I'm young, which means so are the men that I find myself hanging around, and they don't want what I want. They don't understand the pull I feel for those experiences.

I'm not saying I want to get hitched and pop out a million kids right this minute, but is it really so bad to want to be loved by something so deeply?

"There's no harm in asking, Addie," Mom says, squeezing my shoulder.

I swallow, tipping my chin as I shove those thoughts to the back of my head. "Okay. I'll ask."

3

Cooper

sparrow

"I don't like meatloaf, Mom," my fifteen-year-old sister snarks from across the dinner table, shoving her plate away.

Her mom, Scarlett—or SP, as I always call her—gives her a stern look, the same one she's used to chastise me for years. It still works like a charm because Amelia mumbles an apology shortly after.

"You liked it up until today," Scarlett replies, scooping a heaping of mashed potatoes onto her fork and pointing it accusingly in Amelia's direction.

"Do you ever think about how the animals we kill turn into . . . *this*?" Amelia scrunches her nose at the brown meat on her plate.

Dad's low chuckle pulls my attention. Our eyes meet, amusement sparkling in his before he looks at his daughter. "Are you thinking of becoming a vegan, Amelia?"

"Maybe."

"Vegans don't eat eggs either," Scarlett adds.

Amelia's eyes widen slightly. "What?"

I hum, fighting a smile. "Are you really ready to give up Sunday morning breakfasts of eggs and bacon?"

"You know what? Just stop picking on me," she grumbles before angrily grabbing her plate, digging her fork into the meatloaf, and shoving some into her mouth.

The repulsion on her face as the taste settles is enough to crack me open, my laugh filling the dining room. Her glare is ice-cold.

"You're uninvited to the next family dinner, Pooper Scooper," she mutters.

The nickname makes the corners of my mouth tug. It's one of the most original I've heard, although I've lost count of the number of nicknames I've been given. Almost every person I've ever met has called me some variation of Cooper.

"You can't uninvite him, sweetheart. I'm afraid that's out of your jurisdiction," Dad says, offering her a sweet smile.

Amelia stops chewing and swallows so loud it's audible before darting her eyes to Scarlett. SP only shrugs her shoulders and winks at Dad.

"Sorry, my love. Your dad's right."

Dad's smile is all mischief as he stares at his wife, and something warm settles in my stomach at the exchange. It's good seeing him like this.

Blissful.

From the moment Scarlett fell into our lives when I was twelve, it was obvious she was going to become a huge part of our family. Our Scary Spice fit into our duo like she was meant to be there, and I've never regretted the matchmaking I did that nudged them together when they were both too stubborn to do it themselves. Not once.

I've always loved my family, even when it was just Dad and me and my mom, Beth. But now it's complete. Even after my little sister came along, turning our lives upside down, I wouldn't change a thing.

"What happened to girls always sticking together, Mom?" Amelia cries.

Scarlett laughs. "Who said we weren't?"

"Why don't you tell us about school, Amy," I say, nudging the conversation in a different direction.

She lifts her glass of iced tea and brings it to her mouth, holding it there as she exhales a blunt "Pass."

I arch a brow. "Why?"

When she busies herself with slowly drinking from her glass instead of replying, I look to Scarlett for answers. She smiles bleakly at me.

"Amelia hasn't been getting along well with her English teacher. There was an . . . incident yesterday." She pushes loose red hair behind her ear and dares a look at her daughter. Amelia ignores her, posture suddenly stiff.

"What kind of incident? Did something happen?" I push, worry burning a hole in my stomach.

I know the majority of her teachers from my time at her school. My employment at the middle school wasn't overly long before I moved over to high school, but I'm not a forgetful man.

"I really don't want to talk about this. Can we move on? I know for a fact you wanted to talk to Cooper about something, Dad, and it wasn't my education," Amelia blurts out.

Dad ignores her. "Your sister stole a can of spray paint from the garage and decided to give Mr. Wright's car a makeover during her last class."

The name doesn't sound familiar, so he must be new.

"Dad," she groans, hanging her head.

"You did what?" I croak, blinking away my disbelief. "Did it at least look good after?"

"Cooper!" Scarlett half scolds, half laughs.

Amelia peeks up at me, mouth twitching. "Of course."

Dad blows out a long breath. "Well, I guess this is on me. I should have known your brother wouldn't lecture you when it came to something even remotely artistic. That's why you're grounded for the next year. I have to be the bad guy."

"It *was* his spray paint," SP says, muffling her laugh with her shirt sleeve.

"What did you paint? And was it deserved?" I ask.

Amy rolls her eyes. "Trust me, he deserved to find a beautiful graffitied dick on the side of his fancy SUV. Now he can have his personality on display for all to see instead of just in his classroom."

I wince. "He's that bad? I don't think I know him."

A shrug, and then she finally sets her cup down and says, "Put Cooper in the hot seat now, please, Dad."

"Fine, but this talk is not over. Tomorrow, you'll offer to scrub Mr. Wright's car until there's not a speck of paint left. Got it?"

"Yeah. Fine."

I lean back in my chair, the collar of my button-down suddenly suffocating. My palm breaks out in a sweat as I reach for my beer and take a swig. "What's going on?"

Dad doesn't beat around the bush. "Adalyn needs someone to go with her on her trip. I told Oakley you would join her."

The beer burns when I swallow it wrong, coughing violently. Tears form in my eyes that I try to blink back. *Surely I heard him wrong.* He wouldn't say yes to me joining my best friend's little sister on her trip across the world without at least mentioning it to me a *single* damn time.

"You did what?" I rear back.

He at least has the nerve to look the slightest bit sheepish. "As far as I knew, you didn't have any plans besides holing up in your basement studio all alone and painting until your fingers bled."

"But you didn't think to ask me first? This isn't like when I was a kid and you could volunteer me for babysitting duty."

"Is this the part where I tell you I told you so?" Scarlett cuts in, her amusement obvious in the crinkles beside her eyes as she watches Dad.

"Only if you want to pay for it later." He winks, and I swallow my gag.

"Can I be excused? I think I might vomit," Amelia groans, already pushing away from the table.

Scarlett laughs softly, shaking her head as she drains her glass of wine and stands. "Yes, but help me take some of these plates and put them in the dishwasher first."

My sister doesn't bother with a reply before she jumps out of her seat and hurries to help SP clear the table. Once they've collected everything besides the glasses in front of Dad and me, Scarlett brushes a kiss over the top of my head and ushers Amelia into the kitchen.

I pin my father with a pinched look. "Did you even think to ask me about this before you agreed on my behalf? What if I actually did have plans?"

"Did you?" he asks, two thick brows slipping to his hairline. Despite turning fifty-one this past year, he's almost wrinkle-free. It probably has something to do with all of the facial creams his best friends have made him try out over the years.

All it takes is one look at him to know he's not going to let this go. The stubborn man has never been afraid to be the bad guy, and I've always been too compliant.

I'm quick to steel my expression, hiding how annoyed I am. Not at the idea of going with Adalyn, but the fact I'm a thirty-one-year-old man being *voluntold* that I'm about to spend my entire summer off trying to keep up with her.

Adalyn Hutton is the Webster definition of a wild child. She's loud, bossy, fearless, sometimes out of control. There's no cliff too high or cave too deep. I think she came out of the womb with her middle fingers up and a point to prove to the world.

My spine aches from being snapped so tight. "I spent ten months straight waking up early, following a schedule to a T, and barely getting a moment alone. I wasn't planning on doing the same all summer long."

"You're being bullheaded."

"I'm frustrated, Dad," I breathe, running a hand down my face and jaw, over the stubble I've let grow out since school ended last week.

Guilt flattens his lips. "I'm sorry. You're right. I shouldn't have agreed to anything on your behalf. I'll call her father back tonight and set it straight."

I let my head fall back on a tight exhale and stare at the bumps on the ceiling. I've always struggled with dealing with the aftermath of disappointing someone. That tight coiling in my chest when I catch the first glimpse of it right on their face always makes me feel unsteady. It's why I'm so compliant. The guy who's ready to throw himself on the sword if it means I don't have to live with the pinch in my gut at the knowledge I've let someone down.

That's the only reason why I'm blurting out my next sentence, even when I know this decision is most likely doing to bite me in the ass down the road.

"It's fine. I'll do it."

My porch light is on when I step into the warm evening air. I shut the car door behind me and do a double take at the figure waiting on the front steps, a Tupperware of leftovers in my hands.

When I recognize the visitor, I release a breath and say, "You're lucky I didn't mistake you for a burglar."

"And you're lucky I couldn't find a spare key, or I would have been waiting inside already. Do you not have one? It's not in any common spot. I checked pretty much everywhere."

I give my head a shake, blowing out a low laugh. "Do you check a lot of houses for their spare keys?"

Adalyn stands when I reach the steps, her smile wide,

white teeth gleaming even in the dark. She places a hand on the porch railing and moves aside to let me pass.

"I tend to stick to the houses without porch lights, but I decided to make an exception tonight."

"Under the right cushion on the porch swing," I say, swinging open the screen door and unlocking the deadbolt on the main door.

"I'll make a note of it in my phone for next time," she replies smoothly, not missing a beat.

"Or you could just call."

The cool air from my newly installed air conditioner washes over me as I hold the door open and nod for Adalyn to move inside first. Once we're both in, I leave the heavy door open but let the swing door slam shut behind us.

The tall blonde moves past me, strolling right into my home like she owns the place. I shake my head, slipping off my shoes and following her.

"I figured if I called, you might have turned me down. But a surprise visit with your favourite dessert? I figured my odds were better off," she says, and for the first time, I take notice of the small cardboard box in her hands.

Despite just having dinner less than an hour ago, my stomach makes a loud growly noise. "Is that what I think it is?

Her blue eyes spark, the colour so light they nearly appear clear. "Double chocolate cheesecake with fresh raspberries from the Sweetery downtown. You bet your perky ass it is."

Her bluntness doesn't affect me much anymore, not after being on the receiving end of her ridiculous banter all these years, so I ignore it, choosing to place a solid hand on her back and move us toward my kitchen instead.

"You didn't have to bribe your way in, but I appreciate the gesture. I'm certain you're here for the same reason I was planning on calling you tonight. We can talk while we eat."

4

Cooper

sparrow

Adalyn flicks on every light we pass on the way to the kitchen until I'm sure the entire house is fully lit and then slides onto one of the leather dining chairs surrounding my small table off to the side of the kitchen.

The dining area is on the smaller side as my house isn't big. There's enough room for myself to live comfortably but not much else. With only the master bedroom, a spare room small enough that if it weren't for the window, I wouldn't even consider it a bedroom, and one and a half bathrooms, I tend to get out of hosting family dinners more often than not.

The only time I can fit the number of people we consider to be family at my house is when I can shove them all outside in the backyard.

The cardboard pastry box falls to the table seconds before Addie peels back the top. My mouth waters as I dig around in the cutlery drawer for two forks and hand one over before sitting across the table.

We dig into the cheesecake in silence, a familiar buzz of nervous energy in the air. Addie slips her gaze around the kitchen as she places her fork between her teeth and gently bites down. I flinch, the sound of teeth scraping metal making my muscles tense.

"Do you want me to start? Or do you want to?" I force the words out.

She flicks her eyes to mine, letting her fork slip from her mouth as she carefully sets it on the dark wood table.

"I need you to come with me on my trip. My roommate—or I guess she's not really going to be my roommate for much longer now that she has to move. You know what? It doesn't matter. What does matter is that she can't come anymore, and I don't think I can do it on my own. Actually, I know I can't. I would either get lost and end up kidnapped and held in some creepy basement, or—"

"Addie," I interrupt softly. It becomes abundantly clear to me that she doesn't know about her dad talking to mine, so I decide to keep it to myself. I doubt telling her would do much besides embarrass her.

She sucks in a long breath, her cheeks flushed but not from embarrassment. It's something else turning her face the colour of her lip gloss, and when she grits her teeth, I realize it's frustration. Anger that she can't take care of something on her own.

"I know you have a life and that this probably throws a wrench in your entire summer. You don't owe me anything, but I really need you this time," she rushes out, fingers tangled in the streaks of blue and pink that highlight her light blonde hair again, after a year of having it dyed a pastel purple.

Without thinking twice, I snap a hand out in her direction and carefully envelop her fingers in mine, pulling them from her hair. I offer a small smile as I set her hand down on the table and lean back in my chair.

"Don't pull out your hair, Adalyn. Take a breath."

She taps her nails to the table and tips her chin. "Shit, sorry. I'm freaking out."

"You are, but it's okay."

Her eyes find mine again. I laugh at her minuscule glare. "Please tell me you'll come."

"Tell me about the trip first," I say, as if I haven't already made up my mind.

Some of that frustration ebbs away from her features, making room for a sliver of excitement. "We'll be starting in Spain, then working our way to Ireland, Paris, London—"

The details of the trip continue to spill from her lips at an alarming rate, and by the time she's finished, I know my bank account is about to take a serious hit. My years of saving money like a man terrified of falling into early retirement are about to pay off in a big way.

Her voice lifts an octave when she goes into details about the spots we'll stay and the trains and planes that will take us there, and a soft wave of pride hits me at how prepared she seems to be. Everything is planned to the letter, and I won't pretend that doesn't appease at least some of my uncertainty.

Adalyn has always been an act first, think about the consequences later type of girl. I've dealt with the repercussions of her reckless behaviour more times than I can count over my life.

With her being the youngest Hutton, by the time she was old enough to be making silly mistakes and reckless teenage moves, Maddox was in the NHL, and Noah was always off doing God knows what. That left me, Maddox's best friend, as the closest thing to a real friend she had at the time. I was her first call when she needed a ride to the hospital after taking a fall at the skate park or to leave a party that got out of control.

I never minded because I'm a fixer. The guy you call when you need someone to bail you out of jail or pay the tab when you forgot your wallet at home. Being that person—whether it was for my family or my best friend's little sister—has never felt like a burden. But two months of chasing after this woman day and night across the world, making sure she doesn't get lost or wind up in a foreign prison . . . *fuck*. It terrifies me.

My chest tightens so badly I actually reach up and rub it in slow circles. "You seem like you have everything ready, Adalyn. But I won't lie and say I'm not skeptical. We both know how you can get—"

She narrows her eyes, looking offended and ready to defend herself when I shake my head, not done speaking.

"And while there's *nothing* wrong with your bravery or your love of the thrill, I'm going to need your word that you won't get me on your family's shit list by getting yourself hurt. Or worse, married to some guy you barely know after a night out on the town. Everyone is trusting me to watch out for you, but I can't do that properly unless you help me out. I don't want to go on the trip and be a chaperone. If I'm going, it's as a friend who just also wants to keep you safe."

There are a few beats of silence as she takes in my words, her glare gone as quickly as it came, leaving her features smooth and kind. Her plump lips are not shiny like they were when she arrived, the classic Adalyn gloss having been wiped off as she ate her few bites of cheesecake. The dimple in her left cheek that always seems to pop, even with the simplest smile, is trying to do that now, making the one in my right cheek do the same.

"You want to be my friend, Cooper?" she asks slyly.

I tilt my head. "I thought I already was."

"How about best friends, then? No chaperone or bodyguard. Just best friends."

"Maddox might get jealous," I warn teasingly.

If anything, I think that idea excites her. "You make it sound like the idea of that would send me running."

I lean forward, elbows resting on my table as I fall into the banter. "On the contrary. I think a bit of competition will do him good."

"What do you think he'll do when I end up stealing you from him?" she croons.

My throat threatens to close at the drop in her tone. At the sheer confidence. I drop my cheek to my palm, chest rumbling with a hum. "Have you ever feared your odds at accomplishing something once in your life?"

"No. There has never been something I wanted that I couldn't find a way to get." It almost sounds like a dare.

A dare I don't know if I should be encouraging right now. Suddenly, I stand and clear my throat, my fork and half-eaten cheesecake scowling at me from the table.

"Text me all of the flight information. It's late, and you shouldn't be driving at night without your glasses."

"Your worry is adorable, but they're in the car. Do you have a laptop? We can go over the details right now. Plus, I want to help with the cost of your tickets since I'm the one dragging you there with me. We can try and find a way for your seat to be beside mine that way." She says it so casually, either missing my hint for her to leave or just not caring. Probably the latter.

I fold my arms across my chest and lean my hip on the kitchen wall. "You're not doing that. I can buy my own tickets."

She blinks at me. "Why would you spend your money on something you could have for free? I thought you would be happy to hear you didn't have to dish out thousands on plane tickets, you penny-pincher."

"I'm not a penny-pincher."

Her laugh is bright, unrestrained. "When did you get such a fantastic sense of humour?"

"I'm frugal. Not cheap," I defend myself.

"There's a difference?"

"Don't make me throw you out of my house, Addie."

"Ooh, I do love to be tossed around from time to time." She winks brazenly at me, barking out a laugh when I fumble over her words.

"I actually think I'm busy this summer," I mutter, quickly slipping out of the room.

Her laugh bounces off the walls as I move to the living room and flop down on the couch. My head falls back, hitting the back as I close my eyes. Seconds later, the cushion sinks beside me, a flowery, sweet perfume floating up my nose.

"No take backs. You're stuck with me," she says, letting her hand fall to my knee, gently squeezing before pulling back. "I appreciate this, you know? A lot. Thank you."

I roll my head along the back of the couch and meet her waiting stare, smiling softly. "You're welcome."

"So, where do you keep your laptop?"

5

Adalyn

The next time I see Cooper, he's pulling up inside an Uber outside of my parents' house the morning we're set to leave. With a warm smile and an easy wave, he steps out of the car and moves to greet us.

His chestnut-coloured hair is shorter than it was when I saw him two days ago, the sides cut close to his scalp and the top just the slightest bit longer. Deep brown eyes wash over me as he strides up the driveway, and the calmness in his stare has me smiling back at him, a few of the knots in my stomach falling loose.

I didn't sleep worth a shit last night. For the first time in my life, all I could think about was how genuinely scared I was to leave. All of the excitement and giddy buzz that I'd been feeling during the years-long lead-up to this trip was gone, hidden behind a genuine terror that rocked me to my core.

The cold night air was a shock to my system when I stormed out of bed at 2:00 a.m., collected my suitcase and carry-on, and drove out of town to my parents' acreage. It was as easy to sneak into my childhood bedroom as it used to be to sneak out, and the confusion on my mom's face when I appeared at her dinner table this morning would have been enough to make me laugh had I not been on the verge of throwing up.

But as Cooper comes to stand between my father and me, the sun rising above the hills behind him and his shoulder softly bumping mine as they shake hands, my nerves begin to settle. The tension fades from my muscles, and I inhale my first full breath in what feels like days.

"Good morning," he says, bending at the waist to give Mom a hug.

"Good morning, Cooper. Do you have time for a quick coffee? If not, I can send you off with a to-go cup," Mom offers as they break apart and Cooper moves to stand by me again.

He doesn't tower over me like my brothers do, but the height difference is still glaringly obvious, with him being over six feet tall. That, combined with his wide-set shoulders and thick arms, makes me look small in comparison.

"A to-go cup would be amazing, Ava. I'm not much of a flyer, so I think we should get to the airport a bit early."

Mom's smile brightens. "Be right back!" she says before rushing inside.

"Well, shit. Addie isn't a flyer at all. You sure you two will be okay by yourselves?" Dad asks. He's almost glaring at Cooper now, that protective, fatherly look in his eye.

I force a laugh, wrapping my fingers around my travel companion's wrist, the warmth and thickness of it startling me as I try to tug him toward me. When he barely budges, I roll my eyes.

"We'll be fine. Stop worrying before you give yourself an ulcer."

Dad scowls at me. "I'm allowed to be worried. No offense, Cooper, but the only people I fully trust to take care of my daughter are myself and her mother. You're the only option I have right now."

I glance up, half expecting to see Cooper looking

offended, but when his expression remains calm as he nods in agreement, I realize I should have known better.

"I understand. I'll do everything in my power to keep her safe. You have my word."

"Thank you," Mom says, joining us again. She moves from behind Dad and extends a Styrofoam cup toward Cooper before snuggling into Dad's side. "We appreciate that. Right, honey?"

Dad's green eyes wrinkle at the corners as he pulls her beneath his arm. "Of course."

As Cooper grabs the cup from Mom, I tug on the wrist I'm still holding. There's understanding in his eyes as he looks down at me, watching me fidget by his side, anxiety flowing off me in thick waves.

"We should be going, yeah?" he asks.

"Yeah. You know how busy the airport can get, Dad."

Dad frowns. "Yeah, I do." He swallows hard. "Are you sure you don't want to cancel?"

"No can do. Cooper already paid to join me. It's too late to get a refund." I step down the first porch step. "I'm not sure I want to test that Uber driver's patience either."

He has the nerve to shrug as if it doesn't matter. "Your mother and I could drive you to the airport."

"We wouldn't want you to make a scene there, Daddio. Now, come hug me before I leave without—"

He doesn't let me finish my sentence before he's scooping me up and holding me tight. It's an *I'll miss you* hug, and tears sting my eyes before leaking out, coating my lashes. I lean into the embrace, trying to wrap my head around the fact that this is the last hug I'll get from my family for the next two months.

Maybe it's childish to be so emotional over this. It's not as if I'm moving across the world and will never see them again. But family is everything to me. It feels wrong to be leaving them for so long.

I wonder how Maddox does it as often as he has to for

work. Is it as hard for him to leave Braxton and Liam? Is it harder? If so, does it ever get easier for him?

"Pass her over, Oakley. It's my turn."

Dad slowly withdraws his arms and steps back. I only get a brief glance at his face before I'm tugged toward Mom, but I think his cheeks are wet. My heart scrunches painfully.

Mom holds me close, one hand stroking up my spine while the other smooths the hair at the back of my head. Her vanilla-and-orange scent is like a soothing balm over my worries, and I sigh into her T-shirt.

"You're going to do amazing, Adalyn. You were never meant to stay in one place your whole life. I can't wait to hear all about your trip when you get back. We'll call often too, okay?" Mom whispers for only me to hear.

"Okay, Ma. Thank you."

"And don't be too hard on Cooper. Let him have fun instead of just watching over you. I have no doubt he can keep up if you give him the chance."

A giggle escapes me. "I'll believe it when I see it."

"You do remember who taught you how to skateboard, right? And risked his life skydiving for you?" Cooper asks from behind me.

Stepping back from Mom, I spin and grin at Cooper. "Yeah, after I begged you to take me."

"Begged or not, you wouldn't have gone without me. You know, if I wasn't such a nice guy, I would say that you actually owe me."

I snort. "Owe you? More like you owe *me*."

"Are you feeling okay? You're not making any sense. I swear I just heard you say that I owe *you*." He brushes the back of his hand across my forehead before snatching it back when I rear back and nip at it.

"Don't patronize me, Cooper. You won't like what happens when you poke too hard," I warn.

He gasps. "I'm terrified."

I jump when a car horn blares through the air, drawing our attention. The Uber driver has the passenger window rolled down, his glare prickly as he watches us impatiently.

"Sorry! We're coming right now!" I shout with a subtle wince. Dad is giving the driver a stare down when I look at him again. "I'll see you in two months. Try not to miss me too much. And don't forget to spend some time outside of the house. Go for a walk or something, you homebody."

Dad tries to scowl at me, but it doesn't last. His lips tug into a soft smile as he grabs me and kisses the top of my head before ushering me off.

"For the record, I'm not a homebody. I've just given the public enough of my life. I'm making up for lost time with your mom. Now, get out of here before I lock you up inside and refuse to let you out again."

"Good luck with that, Dad." I step onto the circular driveway with Cooper at my side and blow a kiss to my parents. They both blow one back as Cooper walks past with my bags in his hands and softly nudges my shoulder on the way to the car.

I straighten my spine, spin on my heels, and follow after him, away from my family.

"Did you know that I didn't have a passport until two years ago?" Cooper blurts out a few minutes later.

The Uber ride has been silent for the most part, if you don't count the annoyed grumble our driver let out once we climbed inside and the random bits of small talk Cooper and I have shared thus far. I won't say it's been an awkward drive, but it hasn't been the most relaxing one either.

Despite growing up with close families and spending a big

chunk of time together when we were younger, Cooper and I aren't overly close. Life is a busy, fleeting thing, and ours are *very* different. They always have been.

There isn't anything besides our families that brings us together much anymore. He's fighting for a teaching job at the university he graduated from, and I'm still trying to figure out what I want to do for the rest of my life.

I turn my body toward him as much as I can and lean my elbow on the back of the seat, resting my cheek in my hand. He's already looking at me, copying my positioning.

"You've never been out of the country before?"

He shakes his head. "Not once."

"How did I not know that? Adam never got you a passport once in your life? Even as a kid?"

"There wasn't a need. My mother had no interest in taking me out of Canada, and by the time I was a teenager, Amelia was just a baby, so there wasn't much talk of vacations. Then I was in university for eight years and working right after. There wasn't much time for travelling."

"I can't tell if I should feel sad for you or even more excited that I get to take your travel cherry." My lips tug at the corner.

He smiles back, eyes bright. "You should be excited. Definitely excited."

"I'm very excited. So, that means you don't know if you hate planes yet, right?"

"I've been in one before. It just wasn't for very long before I was jumping out of it."

I laugh. "True. Okay, well, the time that you were inside of it, did you love it or hate it?"

"It was fine, I suppose. What about you? Do you like planes?"

I shrug. "It depends on the flight and the plane. The small planes I could do without, but the bigger ones are usually fine.

I tend to get a bit nervous on the smaller ones. Need a bit of a cuddle and a shot of cheap vodka to relax, you know?"

He nods slowly, understanding playing on his features. "And which do we have to take to get where we're going? Big or small?"

I flash him a devilish smirk as I say, "Both."

6

Adalyn

The flight attendant hands Cooper two shot-sized plastic bottles of vodka before dashing up the aisle toward a woman who's currently holding a barf bag to the mouth of a young boy. I cringe toward the window when the boy releases a low gurgling sound, and the paper bag shudders in her grip.

"I like you enough, Cooper, but I refuse to hold a bag to your mouth if you puke, so for the love of God, please swallow it back down if the urge arises," I mutter.

"I'm not going to puke."

"Are you sure? You look a little green."

He doesn't. Not really, but his discomfort is obvious as the plane continues to fly. We've been in the air for about twenty minutes now, but for some new flyers, it'll take a bit of time for the nausea to pass.

Cooper keeps one hand on his thigh, fingers curled into the dark denim the same way they were when we took off, while the other grips the alcohol tight. His cheeks are a bit pale, his forehead clammy. I almost feel guilty that his second experience on a plane will be followed by a short layover at LAX.

Poor guy.

"I've jumped *out* of a plane, Adalyn. Staying inside of one has never been my issue. I just don't like the takeoff part."

"Did the gum help, at least?"

He nods and stiffly twists off the caps of both tiny bottles before handing me one. "Not as much as this will, I'm sure."

"I like the way you think," I reply, grabbing the bottle and extending it out for a toast. "Here's to a fucking fantastic trip."

There's no sound when our bottles collide, but it doesn't matter. In near perfect sync, we down the contents, my face wrinkling in disgust while Cooper's remains calm, as if the flight attendant had swapped his for water when I wasn't looking.

"Let me guess, you're a whiskey on the rocks guy," I mutter while setting the empty bottle on the tray in front of me.

Cooper chuckles softly. "Close. I usually reach for a bottle of rum before even thinking about whiskey."

A memory of watching Jack Sparrow dump out a bottle of rum during one of our family movie nights has me saying, "Ah, that must be why the rum is always gone."

He cocks a brow at me. "What?"

"Don't tell me you haven't watched the *Pirates of the Caribbean* movies. You know Jack Sparrow, right? 'Why is the rum always gone?' Ring any bells?"

"I know *Pirates of the Caribbean*, Adalyn. Maybe not line for line like you, though." The corner of his mouth tilts into a—is he *smirking* at me?

"If you're going to make fun of me for my love of one of the greatest series of movies in existence, you can kiss my ass."

I watch the other side of his mouth lift as he grins, flashing me a view of his perfect teeth and a deep-set dimple. He never even had to have braces when he was younger either. They just popped out of his gums all shiny and straight and oh-so pristine. *Lucky him.*

I wasn't so lucky. I got braces when I was thirteen because the kids in my class used to call me Beaver Teeth.

"Have I ever made fun of you before?" he asks.

I tilt my head, blinking slowly. "Is that a serious question?"

"Yes, because you know I haven't."

"That depends on what we're counting as *making fun*."

"You never make anything easy, do you?" he asks on an exhale.

My smile drips with satisfaction. "Nope. But neither did you or Maddox when you both used to harp on me about the posters on my walls or complain about me trying to get you to invite me to places with you."

"It would have hurt our street cred to be seen with you. And those posters were creepy. I still shudder thinking about the one you had of Tony Hawk beside your bed."

I gasp, jabbing my finger into his bicep. My nail hardly digs into the muscle there, but I blink that thought away. "Take it back."

His gaze falls to my finger briefly before lifting again. "Not going to happen."

"Tony was everything to me, Sparrow. You can't talk shit about the love of my life and walk away unscathed."

He shrugs his shoulder, and I drop my arm to one of the armrests between us. Humour makes the green flecks in his eyes brighter amongst the dark brown.

"You didn't just nickname me after a pirate."

"Would you prefer something else? Amy calls you Pooper Scooper, right?"

"Amelia is allowed to call me that simply because I don't have a choice whether or not to accept it. Special sister privileges and all. But you, Adalyn, can*not* call me that."

"Fine. Sparrow it is, then. You should take it as a compliment."

"Would you like me to thank you?"

"I mean, it wouldn't hurt," I tease.

He moves a hand to the armrest beside mine. The thick, dark hair on his forearm tickles my skin as the veins in his hand bulge with the movement. I stare at the silver watch cupping his wrist, my interest blaring when I catch the quote engraved along the edge beneath the face.

Even miracles take a little time.

I remember when his mom got him that watch. I'll never forget the grin he wore when he showed it off to all of us the day after Christmas a few years ago.

"How's your mom been? Does she know you're off to travel the world?" I ask, changing topics.

"She's good. Loving her job at the school. It's still a bit odd seeing her so often, but I like being able to keep an eye on her."

Warmth fills my chest at that. I've heard enough about Cooper's mother, Beth, to know that she's had her fair share of struggles when Cooper was young. With how hard she's worked to overcome every challenge put in front of her, it's amazing to witness her accomplish so much in life. Starting a new teacher's assistant job at the high school where her son teaches has to have been a bit intimidating for her. But I doubt her concern swayed her much when it came down to it.

I don't know her all that well, considering she wasn't around a lot when I was growing up, but Cooper loves talking about her, and we all love to hear what he has to say. I'm sure getting the chance to spend the weekdays catching short glimpses of him and having brief conversations in the hallways makes her far happier than Cooper knows.

"She's been working there for how long? Three months? And you still aren't used to seeing her there?" I ask, glancing up at him.

He flexes his wrist. "It's an adjustment."

"Do you worry about her seeing you flirt with all the pretty teaching staff, Sparrow? Is that it? Because I think you're probably taking away some of her fun. At this rate, she probably thinks you're purposely trying to die alone just to spite her."

His laugh is deep, and my stomach flops at the raspy sound of it. "My mother is perfectly content with my current relationship status, thank you."

"That makes one of your parents, then. Last I heard, Adam was trying to convince my mom to start shopping you around to some of her colleagues from the foster centre." I make a low humming noise in the back of my throat, settling further into my seat, acting eerily at ease. "Of course, I stepped in and told her that retired singles probably weren't who you were looking to settle down with, but I can always retract my statement if I was off base."

Cooper grimaces, unsettled brown eyes focusing on me. "I'm not surprised that he's started meddling. As if he's one to speak. Thank you for stepping in, though. You were right."

Thinking of Adam not meeting Scarlett until he was thirty-three makes me giggle. It's hypocrisy at its finest for him to give Cooper a hard time for still being single at thirty-one. And going to my mom, knowing that the only women she knows are those who spend their grandchildren-free weekends volunteering with her at the foster care centre . . . he must be desperate for some grandbabies.

It's a rush of curiosity that has me blurting out, "Why *are* you still single?"

Even as he flinches slightly at the sudden question, I don't let myself regret asking. I could count on one hand the number of things I've said that I actually regret. Asking something that will give me more insight into the guy travelling with me across the world isn't the time to add to that tally.

Cooper might have been around constantly while I was growing up, but he's still an enigma to me. There are things you never ask your brother's best friend, especially one ten years older than you. Up until now, I can't say I was ever even interested in gaining the knowledge, anyway.

Maybe it's the idea that for the first time in my life, he might learn to see me as more than a child and as a real friend instead that has me suddenly changing my tune. I've seen how great of one he can be to those he cares about, and *maybe* I'm a bit jealous. Sue me.

"I'm not purposefully single if that's what everyone has been thinking but not saying," he says, fiddling with that gleaming silver watch. "I've just been so focused on my career that I guess dating has never been at the forefront of my mind."

"Understandable. I'm the opposite, but nobody really cares enough about my dating life to pester me about it. They just let me do my own thing in peace."

"You're the opposite? So, you're focused on dating?" He asks it with a weird note in his voice, like he's confused by what I'm saying. Like the idea of me wanting a relationship above all else is mind-blowing to him.

I nip at my lip, contemplating how to explain what's running through my head without sounding like a fool. "Not exactly. I don't know how to explain it, but I guess I just don't really have a career that I care about as much as you do, so I've been exploring other things. Like dating, romance, and all that jazz. Or at least, I've been trying."

"Been trying to . . . to explore," he echoes, nodding once.

I risk a look at him and find his cheeks splotchy. "Oh, shit. Is this awkward for you? We can talk about something else."

He avoids my eyes, staring at the seats diagonally across the row instead. "No, it's fine. I'm just surprised. I had you pegged as a girl who would want to stay commitment-free for as long as possible."

"Why? Because I'm young?" It's an honest question, and I keep my voice level as I ask it.

His tongue darts out to swipe at his lips before he looks at me again and says, "No. Because you're wild and free, and I can't imagine a man alive who would be worthy of getting to share that side of you for forever."

7

Adalyn

"Oh. That's very . . . sweet of you to say, actually," I mutter, taking in Cooper's red cheeks and the awkward darting of his eyes as he fidgets beside me. It's almost like he's embarrassed.

Would it be weird to coo at him adorably like I do my nephew? *No shit it would be.*

The genuine tone of his voice is almost unsettling now that I think about it. He said something so honest and sweet but made it sound like the friendliest sentence on earth.

"It's true. I admire you," he says softly.

"Admire me?" I guffaw. I'm a twenty-one-year-old Instagram model with over a million followers and three real friends to show for it: Ivy, a close family friend who lives five hours away by plane, and my sister-in-law. I had to bribe someone to come with me on this trip with a cheesecake instead of rising up to the challenge and going alone like I should have. Of course, I don't tell him all of that. Instead, I say, "I find that hard to believe."

"It's true. It takes balls to be able to do half of the stuff you do. I was lecturing a bunch of rowdy preteens in a muggy classroom while you were out getting your cave diving certificate."

I flush cold at the memory of being in that black water, nothing but a tie-off to a guy I had only known for a handful of days and a tank of air strapped to my back keeping me alive.

"Cave diving scared the living hell out of me, Sparrow. I can confidently say that most of the things I've done in my life I'm happy to have experienced. But I could have lived to be a thousand and been perfectly content never having dived into those waters."

He frowns slightly, concerned. "It was that bad? I don't think you ever spoke much about it when you got back."

"That was kind of the point. I thought I knew what I was getting into when I signed up, and while I was doing my courses, I put on a brave face, but even that wasn't nearly as scary as the real thing. Something about how dark and quiet it was just freaked me out. I chickened out before we made it past thirty feet," I admit, letting the secret tumble out of my mouth all in one breath.

A laugh bubbles in my chest, and I let it out, my shoulders shaking in my seat. "I've never told anybody that before. My dad brags about his daughter the cave diver all the time, even though he almost crapped his pants when I told him I was going to try it. As far as everyone is concerned, I made that dive my bitch."

"I'm scared of the ocean, Adalyn. Anything that has fins or gills is an immediate no for me. And when you can't see what's beneath you? No way. Just thinking about it makes me want to cry. There's nothing wrong with having fears. If not a single thing scared you, I would worry you weren't human," he says, a slight smile tugging at his mouth.

His hand covers mine on the armrest, the weight of it heavy and warm and reassuring. I return his smile and turn my hand so I can squeeze his fingers.

"Careful—keep talking to me like this and I might refuse to return you after we're done." With a sudden yawn, I glance out the small window at my side at the endless dark sky. Who knew exposing something about yourself could take so much out of you? "Is it okay if I use your shoulder as a pillow while I take a nap?"

He laughs. "Sure. Just let me grab my laptop first. Do you want me to wake you at a certain time?"

I shake my head, fighting off another yawn. In what seems like one quick movement, he brings his shiny silver laptop out of the carry-on beneath the seat in front of him and sets it up on his tray.

With drooping eyes, I turn my body toward him and snuggle in, not giving a damn about much of anything besides my sudden need to sleep. He smells woodsy, with hints of sandalwood and amber peeking out. It's like he bathed in my favourite scents this morning.

Naturally, I take a giant sniff while I rest my head on his shoulder and release his hand to wrap my arm around his elbow. He ignores my creepy action like the gentleman he is.

"No, just shake me off if you need to go to the washroom," I mumble, closing my eyes.

"You got it."

It takes me a few minutes to fall asleep, but with the quiet tap of his laptop keyboard and the steady rise and fall of his shoulder, I don't wake again until breakfast is offered in the morning.

The ride from the Madrid airport to our rental is turning out to be a blur of mopeds, old, traditional architecture, and crowds of people who aren't the least bit scared of walking into the middle of busy streets.

If culture shock is a real thing, I think I'm beginning to experience its effects already.

From the way Cooper is staring out the window of the cab, his head twisting every which way as we move down the street, it's possible he might be feeling the same as me.

"Everybody is dressed so nice," I note, suddenly thankful that I didn't wear a sweatsuit on the plane like Ivy suggested.

There isn't a single person we've passed so far who isn't dressed like they're planning on going to a nice dinner. A spark of excitement flares inside of me at the idea of dressing up every day. Clothes are a comfort for me, and getting the chance to show them all off? *Fuck yes.*

Glancing down at my outfit, I hum in approval. White high-waisted, straight-leg jeans, a pale green top that falls just a centimetre above my waistband with ruffled, short sleeves, and an adorable tie above my boobs. A pair of beige wedges with ties around the ankles and a simple gold chain around my neck finish the look. It's the closest thing to a sweatsuit anybody will ever get from me.

Cooper hums in agreement, not tearing his eyes off the window. "I like it. Makes it easy for me to dress every day, considering most of the clothes I own are dress shirts, polos, and slacks."

"Stop flirting with me, Sparrow," I sigh, waggling my eyebrows when he looks at me, alarmed.

"What? I wasn't—"

I snort a laugh. "Relax. I'm teasing. Men who know how to dress themselves nicely tickle my . . . *brain*. That's all." I throw in a wink for good measure, already obsessed with making this man squirm.

He makes it too easy.

"You're going to send me into cardiac arrest."

"God, I hope not. I haven't had to use my first aid training, and I'm warning you right now, I don't remember a damn thing."

His laugh is loud, carefree. It makes me grin, joining in as the cab driver glances at us from the rear-view mirror with an amused roll of his eyes.

Cooper sniffs, composing himself after another few moments of laughter. "Note to self: make sure not to need medical attention if I'm alone with you. Got it."

"You're a quick learner," I tease. "And what about you? Do you know first aid?"

"Yes. I wouldn't have felt comfortable teaching without it. Especially with young kids."

"Ever had to use it on someone?" I blurt out.

He doesn't look surprised by my question, but he does frown, the slightest haunted look travelling across his features. "Only once, back when I was teaching at the elementary school. A third grader was dared to see if he could swallow a loonie, and no surprise, he couldn't. The coin got lodged in his throat, and by the time I got it free, he was passed out. Luckily, CPR worked fast."

"I'm sorry."

His frown flips slightly as he smiles appreciably. It's totally for my benefit, but I accept it without a word. "Thank you, but it all turned out okay. I'm happy I was able to help. We had a school nurse, but at least we didn't have to wait for her to get to us."

Because I can't seem to leave anything alone, I keep pushing for information. "Was it scary?"

A beat of silence and then, "Yeah. There's nothing comforting about holding somebody's life in your hands, especially a child's. Amelia was so small back then, and all I could think of was *what if this were her*?"

"You're a good man, Cooper," I tell him, reaching across the carry-on bags between us to pat his knee. "I've always known I was safe with you. You exude this protector type of vibe."

He chokes on a laugh. "Is that so?"

"Mmhmm. It's like a mutually known fact about you. Tinsley once called you Big Daddy C, but Noah told her if she ever said it again, you would be Dead Daddy C."

Brown eyes focus on me, humour making them look a few shades lighter than usual. "No surprise there. I'm assuming she never uttered that name again."

"Not in front of my brother, at least," I say slyly.

Tinsley and I have been calling him that for years behind closed doors. It's one of our most well-kept secrets. My closest friend from childhood is three years older than me, but our ages have never meant a damn thing to either one of us.

As the only two girls in a massive group of friends and family, we stuck together. I used to wish she were my older sister. Of course, that was before Noah decided to butt his big head in and try to take her from me. It only worked to some extent—much to his displeasure. My brother hates to share, but when it comes to Tiny, I took that choice from him with my tongue out.

It's been a couple of months since I've last seen her, but as soon as I'm back from this trip, I'll be going out to Ontario to see both her and Noah, considering the douche moved out there to be with her two years ago.

In a perfect world, she would have joined me on this trip when Ivy cancelled, but with her boxing career taking off, it wouldn't have been a good fit time-wise.

Maybe that was a blessing in disguise. I can't say I'm regretting bringing Cooper with me so far.

"You and Tiny have always been a dangerous pair," he says.

"I'm sure she would love the compliment as much as I do."

Dropping an arm to his bag, he shakes his head, smiling. "I'm sure she would."

The small cab comes to an abrupt stop, and I startle,

surprised to find us already at our rental. My lips spread into an excited grin when I look out the window.

Our rental is a small house with a burnt-orange brick porch and two sets of glass patio doors leading inside. Potted plants line the walkway, and a sunshade hangs over a small portion of the front lawn. The roof is sloped enough to showcase the two skylights that, from the pictures I saw, should be directly above the main living space.

Cute and quaint. That's what I thought when I saw it online. Well, that, and *is that a pool*?

Tearing my eyes from the house, I find Cooper staring past me, doing the same inspection I just was.

"Ready to go?" I ask.

He flicks his eyes to me, and he grins, making him look boyish for a change. I make a silent promise to myself to see him smile like that a hundred more times on this trip.

"I'm ready. Show me what you have planned for me, Adalyn."

8

Cooper

The first thing Addie does when we step inside our rental is abandon her bag on the tiled floor by the door and take off through the back. She's a blur of pastel hair and loud giggles as she folds her arms around her front, and before I can get a grasp of what she's doing, she has her shirt pulled off, sending it soaring through the warm Spanish air.

Stunned, I blink at the pale skin of her back and the lacey pink strap wrapped around her middle. Her tall, slim frame flies toward the pool before sinking deep into the water with a loud splash.

As if hit with a gush of water, I snap out of it, diverting my gaze with a turn of my head. I stare at the wicker armchair in the living room instead, at all the pale yellow and red pillows and abundance of green plants spread along the room. The handles of our suitcases are slick with the sweat from my palms when I lean them against the wall and move through the house.

The main room is snug but has been decorated to enhance the space. A TV rests on the stand at the front of the room, with two swinging doors adorned with a lattice design. Along with the wicker chair, there's a sofa with wood arms and soft green cushions, a tall floor lamp tucked in the corner, and a rug with blue and orange tile designs.

From the living room, I move to the kitchen, taking in the bright colours and small sitting table with two chairs. Down the hall, two bedrooms sit opposite one another. I give the bigger of the two to Adalyn and then bring our luggage from the entry. As soon as I set my suitcase on the edge of the double bed, I exhale a long breath and sit beside it.

The suddenness of this trip has stunted my ability to think any of this through the way I usually would. Hell, I don't even remember where we're going next or what comes after it. I tried to pay attention to what Adalyn was telling me that night in my living room, but I couldn't grasp more than a few words. In one ear and out the other.

She worked out my tickets and everything else I needed. All I did was hand her my credit card and wince at its silent whimper.

But now, sitting alone in silence for the first time since I left my house, my mind is running laps. I want to scold myself for agreeing to this so easily, knowing just how busy my summer was supposed to be. Dad was wrong when he said I would have been spending it in my basement painting, and I guess that's on me.

I was supposed to be creating a syllabus for my first year as a university professor, but I'm here instead. Sitting in a closet-sized bedroom in Madrid while my best friend's little sister swims out back in the pool. Nobody knows I was offered the art professor position at my old university, and I'm not sure why I haven't shared that with anyone yet.

Maybe it's fear at the idea of it being taken from me if I get too excited, and that's a guarantee once I tell my family. They'll hype it up to the point where I won't be able to keep a level head about it. It's too risky to tell them so soon, as if I'll have the chance to do so now with an ocean between us.

Teaching art at this high of a level has always been my

dream. The goal I worked toward my entire life. Art isn't just something I like to do. It's a living thing inside of me. It's my passion, my heart and soul. For as long as I remember, me and art have been a joint entity.

It kept me company when I would hide in the unfamiliar room at my dad's house the first days after my mom left me. Everything was so new back then, and while I don't remember too much from the early days, given I was so young, I remember drawing.

Art was my escape back then, and even after I had begun to warm up to the man I came to know as my father, I could never get myself to let it go.

That's the beauty of it, though. Art doesn't have to be tied to one specific emotion. One problem in your life. It's something that can heal any wound. Excite any soul. Simply put . . . it's magic.

"You look lost in your thoughts."

I snap my head toward the door and find Adalyn leaning in the doorway with a towel wrapped tight around her body, her arms above her as she grips the frame. A laugh rumbles through my chest when she notices my staring and pops a hip.

"Did you know that standing in a doorway like this is one of the hottest things a guy can do?" she adds.

"Can't say that I did. It looks uncomfortable."

She rolls her eyes and flexes her biceps. "That's only because I'm barely tall enough. My calves have never been stretched so tight."

Her pink towel is hanging on for dear life as she continues to keep her arms outstretched, and I refuse to look down at said stretched calves. For my own sanity, I hope she kept her bra and underwear on after she went into the pool on the off chance the towel slips.

"Did you have a nice swim?"

"Yes. The water was warm. I was waiting to see if you'd

join me, but when you didn't, I figured you might have decided on taking a nap. You didn't sleep much on the plane."

"Surprisingly, I'm not tired. I am hungry, though."

Her eyes spark. "Wanna go explore? We can find somewhere to eat while we're out."

Her excitement makes it impossible to say no. It's beautiful how open she is with her feelings. Every emotion is always on display for those who know what they're looking for. My fingers itch to sketch the way she's looking at me right now, like I just gave her her new favourite gift.

"Sure. Just let me change," I tell her.

I'm unprepared for the kiss she lays on my cheek before slipping away and heading out the door as if it never happened.

I PULL my fist to my mouth and force a cough to hide my laugh for the third time since the waiter arrived at our table. Adalyn has the poor guy fumbling over himself trying to make conversation with her. Wide, infatuated brown eyes watch her closely, so focused I wonder what it would take for him to look away. A fire at his feet, perhaps?

Adalyn is smiling brightly at him as she waves her hand animatedly and tells him all about our plans for tomorrow, but her cheek is dimple-free. That's the only reason I haven't told him to leave and let this conversation continue.

I promised Oakley I would keep her safe, and no offense to this guy, but as innocent as he may look, I'm not naïve.

"I'm serious. Give me your favourites. I didn't come all the way here to eat something safe. Step outside of the box with me tonight, Adrián," she says.

He turns a deep shade of red. "Okay, if you're sure. I'll put that through for you."

Addie giggles, shaking her head when he turns around to leave. "Do you want to ask my dinner companion what he wants to eat tonight before you go?" she calls, drawing his attention again.

"How generous of you to remember I'm here, Adalyn," I murmur for only her to hear. She nudges my foot beneath the table.

"Right," Adrián breathes, looking at me for only the second time since we sat down. At least he seems apologetic. Or maybe it's just embarrassment that has him so fidgety. "What can I get you, sir?"

I make a show of slowly closing my menu before extending a hand to Addie, taking hers as well. As I hold them out for him, I hear Adalyn's soft laugh and smirk to myself. If she gets to have her fun, then so do I.

"Give me whatever my date is having. Please and thank you."

He blanches, coughing to hide his noise of surprise. "Right. Right away."

I glance at Adalyn, curious as to how she's planning on reacting to my comment. When I find her grinning at me, dimple out, I notch a daring brow, surprising myself.

"Date? Don't tell me you forgot about our conversation already. We are over," she tells me, grin replaced by a look of fake annoyance.

"I didn't forget. I'm simply pretending it never happened."

"*Of course.* Pretending is your specialty, after all," she hisses.

I swallow a laugh and fight to keep my lips flat in a scowl, curious as to how far she'll take this act. "How could you say that, pumpkin? I never pretend with you."

Her mask almost cracks right then, but somehow, she keeps her amusement locked down enough to up the ante. "How can you say that when you haven't asked me to role-play in months? I *know* you have problems getting hard unless

I'm in my bunny suit, so what gives? Are you sleeping with someone else on the side?" She gasps, fingers tapping her lips. "Did you find someone else to call Little Wabbit?"

My breath explodes out of me, spit getting lodged in my throat. The sharp inhales from the people around us and the crash from someone dropping a glass nearby don't help any as I cough, face suddenly on fire.

It's Adalyn's laugh that I focus on in the midst of my coughing fit, and I narrow my eyes on her, even as I find it hard not to laugh along. There are tears wetting the skin beneath her eyes, but she's quick to use a napkin to dab them away.

"You don't want to go up against me, Sparrow. I was born without a filter, and I haven't wanted one once in my life," she says.

"You make it seem as if I don't already know that."

She sets her elbow on the table and rests her cheek in her palm. "I'm going to loosen you up on this trip. That's a promise."

"Should I be scared?"

She doesn't hesitate. "Yes."

Nodding, I lean back in my seat and look away from her. Adrián is long gone and we're no longer the centre of attention. I should feel guilty for the scene we just made, but it's hard when I have Adalyn across from me. She's not the least bit concerned about the judgment of others, and I can't help but think that maybe she'll make good on her promise after all.

9

Adalyn

The next morning, I wake to the smell of strong coffee and the sound of someone dropping something heavy onto the floor. Groaning, I turn onto my side and block out the sun trying to bleed through my eyelids.

I'm not a morning person. I never have been. And today is no different. My mood immediately sours as I wake further and check the time on my phone. 7:00 a.m.

"Cooper!" I shout before burying my face in my pillow.

Soft footsteps and then, "Yeah?"

"I'm going to kill you." The words are muffled mumbles.

"What?"

I flop onto my back and give him a withering glare. He looks far too put together for so early in the day, even if he's dressed casually in a pair of dark jeans, a stained White Ice Training shirt, and bare feet. There's this whole casual yet sexy look he's got going on, and I'm kinda digging it.

Wait, *what*? Cooper's *never* been sexy. I scrub my eyes with my hands and look again. Shit, still sexy. This is exactly why I don't wake up early.

"I said that I'm going to kill you. We seem to have forgotten to talk about some ground rules last night. Let's fix that right now." Batting away all other thoughts, I haul myself into a sitting position and cross my legs beneath the thin blanket. "I need the house to be silent every morning until at least nine. I get grumpy when I wake up before then."

He stares back at me calmly but folds his arms across his chest and leans a shoulder against the doorframe. *So close. Now just lift your arms and grab the—* "Is that negotiable?"

"Not overly."

His laugh is a deep grumble as it fills the room. I lift my chin defiantly.

"I've been getting up at six every morning for the past ten months. It's going to take some time to break the habit. Are you wanting me to sit in silence for three hours while I wait?" he asks bluntly.

"That would be preferred. I'm sure there are things you could busy yourself with that don't include dropping pots and pans on the floor at seven and waking the entire neighbourhood."

"Are you planning on dictating my every move during this trip, Adalyn? I don't handle being controlled very well."

I drop both my chin and my glare as guilt slips like cold water down my back. Ignoring the way his face fills with immediate regret, I say, "No. I'm not. Eight is as early as I'll go unless we've made plans to do something earlier. However, I am going to warn you now that I won't exactly be a doll if that's the case."

He nods. "Alright. Eight it is. Do you want me to make you some coffee while you get ready?"

My mouth quirks. "Please. I like mine pale."

"Got it," he says softly—as if he wasn't just annoyed with me a second prior—before slipping out of my room.

I stare at the empty doorway for a few beats longer, trying to gather my thoughts. Maturity is something I appreciate like nothing else, and Cooper has it in bundles. I've been spending far too much of my time entertaining douchebags my age because for a minute there, I was worried he was going to take that brief disagreement and blow it up into something bigger.

It's obvious we have a lot to learn about each other over the next couple of months. Dinner last night threw me for a total loop. I had no idea he could be fun like that. Even Ivy wouldn't have entertained me to that extent. I couldn't help but keep pushing in an attempt to find his limit. But I don't think I came close to it, and that only makes me want to try again and again until I do.

Rolling my neck, I slip out of bed and head to the shared bathroom across the hall to get ready. Half an hour later, I find Cooper out back by the pool. My steps slow as I take in the peaceful image of him stretched out on a patio chair, legs crossed at the ankles and arms folded over his chest. He's changed into a pair of salmon-pink swim trunks and a white tee, and I blink a few times to make sure I'm seeing him correctly.

It almost seems like a crime to interrupt him right now, but I can't help myself. "How have I never seen you in swim trunks before?"

"You probably have. It was just a long time ago," he replies, not looking back.

"Well, I like the look. You should stand and give me a spin so I can see the whole thing." This time, he does look over his shoulder at me, and I grin at his heavy eye roll.

"Or you could just come over here and see instead," he offers quietly, looking forward again. Clearing his throat, he points to the small patio table off to the side of the patio. "Your coffee is there. I tried to time it right, but I wasn't sure how long it takes you to get ready, so it might still be too hot."

"Thank you." Appreciation warms my chest as I head for the table and grab the mug. A quick test sip proves the coffee is the perfect temperature, and I sit in the empty chair beside him a moment later.

"You're welcome."

I wrap the white cup in my palms and take another sip, soaking in the bubble of serenity that's formed over our small rental. We're not close to the ocean here, but that wasn't a big deciding factor for me when choosing where to go in Spain. Ivy wanted to come to Madrid for the nightlife, and I easily agreed, not putting too much thought into it. There are plenty of other places to see the ocean.

"So, what do you want to do today? I was thinking we could start by exploring the markets a bit and then take a look around the city?"

"I'm good with that," he agrees.

"Are you much of a shopper?"

"Not overly, but I don't mind it."

"Yeah, me neither. I get bored easily when I do the same thing repeatedly, so I prefer to do most of my shopping online when I can." I feel his eyes fall to the side of my face and laugh under my breath before drinking more coffee. "Don't be cliché, Sparrow. Didn't Adam teach you not to judge a book by its cover?"

"I don't mean to judge you. I've just always assumed because of your job that you must have a lot of clothes. I'm sorry."

I nudge his knee with my toes and wait for our eyes to connect before saying, "It's alright. I do have a lot of clothes. But there's a difference between loving clothes and loving the experience of buying them. Plus, crowds aren't really my thing."

He pushes out a long breath, sitting straighter as he hangs his legs off the side of the chair and faces me fully. "You don't like crowds?"

"Nope. Not big ones. It's one of the reasons I don't do runway shows."

"I feel like I know nothing about you."

"Why would you?" It's an honest question. There has

never been a need for him to know these things about me. It's not like he was *my* best friend.

"That just feels like something I should have known."

I shrug. "I've never told anyone but my parents about it. Could you imagine if Noah or Maddox found out? They would never let me live it down. I have a reputation to protect, you know?"

My lighthearted words only make his naturally pouty lips curve into a frown. I straighten my shoulders, prepared to command he not feel bad when my phone starts to ring from the pocket of my shorts.

"It's Tiny," I tell Cooper when I pull it out. He nods, not pushing our last conversation.

Tinsley's smiling face fills the screen as I quickly answer the FaceTime call. Her skin looks shiny, like she's all sweaty, and by the glitter in her silver eyes, she must have just finished a boxing session.

"There's my precious world traveller," she mewls.

"Here I am. Miss me?"

"Been missing you since the last time I saw you."

"I'm fully prepared to come steal your ass as soon as I'm done here." It's a threat and a promise.

She grins wide, the walls behind her moving as she walks through the gym. "I'll be waiting. Now, tell me Spain is as beautiful as it looks online. And be careful how you answer because I don't want to be disappointed."

"I haven't even been here for a full day yet, but it is just as beautiful as I thought it would be. The food is amazing, and it's so warm."

She makes a loud moaning noise, and Cooper barks a laugh beside me. "*The food.* I can't handle talking about food right now. I'm starving, and the only thing waiting at home for me is a fridge full of chicken and broccoli."

I wrinkle my nose. "At least tell me it'll be worth it."

"Oh, it'll be worth it. The fight wasn't scheduled, but she

brought it on herself when she called me out online. I have to cut about fifteen pounds to hit her weight class, though. Dad's been watching my diet like crazy. Noah has been sneaking me snacks between sessions."

Imagining my brother sneaking anywhere makes me laugh. He's probably been shoving past her father, Braden, and openly handing her food, knowing it'll piss him off. Those two haven't gotten along since . . . well, *ever*.

Tinsley's retired boxer dad is intimidating to damn near everyone. My brother might be the only person on this earth who doesn't give a damn that Braden could knock him on his ass before he's taken a single breath.

"Jayna doesn't have a clue what she's done by provoking the great Tinsley Lowry. You'll mop the floor with her," Cooper cuts in, cheeks slightly pink as he stares in my direction.

Jayna Crown is Tinsley's biggest competition and self-proclaimed enemy. In reality, she's just a bitter woman who thinks bringing their beef to the public eye will somehow make her a better fighter.

I turn the phone toward Cooper so he can see my best friend, and he lifts a hand to wave. Tiny makes a kissing noise that I can only guess means she's kissed the screen.

"Thank you, Big Daddy. I wish you both could be here to watch, but you can make it up to me by bringing me back a present," she teases.

Cooper chokes on the word "Deal."

Laughing at his reaction to the nickname, I turn the camera back toward me. It takes a second for my eyes to adjust to the screen as it grows brighter when Tinsley steps into a new room. The locker room at Knockout Training is easy to recognize. I've been to Tiny's family gym often on my trips to Toronto.

Chatter filters through the speakers, and I arch a brow when a girl with spiky black hair and a plug in her earlobe comes into view and narrows her eyes on me. My habit of internet stalking proves most useful as I recall her from one of Noah's posts a few weeks ago.

"Hello, Sparks. It's nice to finally meet you," I introduce myself.

The hint of a smile. "Hi."

"I gotta go, Addie. But please call me soon," Tiny says, eyes pleading.

"Of course. Love you."

"Love you more!" she calls before her picture disappears, leaving me staring at her contact. I immediately miss her.

When I slowly slip my phone back into my shorts, Cooper's at my side, his hand outstretched. His fingers are long, and his palms are smooth. I grab it and let him help me up.

"Fancy a quick swim?"

10

Cooper

It turns out that our quick swim wasn't quick at all. My fingertips resemble raisins by the time we get out and dry off beneath the late-morning sun, but seeing her happy again makes it hard to care that I may have a bit of a sunburn.

I rub my sides with a towel as she bends at the waist and starts to dry her hair before folding it up in the towel the way women do after a shower. Her eyes bore into me as she stalks around the patio in a strappy bikini, bare feet slapping the tile.

My self-control hasn't been stretched so thin in my entire life. I've never had a desire to look at Adalyn like this, but keeping my eyes from exploring is becoming a struggle as curiosity urges me to take one long look down her body, just to see what she looks like right now. Does that make me a bad person? Maybe.

Respect for Maddox has me draping my towel over my shoulders and heading inside.

"I'm going to get changed. Do you want to head out in like half an hour?" I ask, pausing at the patio doors.

"Yep!" she calls, voice higher-pitched than normal. I shrug it off and move inside.

In exactly thirty minutes, she pops out of her room

dressed in a thin-strapped, flowy white dress with red and pink flowers all over it. There's a pair of chunky pink, loosely tied Converse on her feet and a matching clip holding some of her hair out of her face.

"You look handsome," she notes, fiddling with an earring. Her words are so genuine I fumble with a reply.

"Thanks. You too. I mean—you're not handsome. You look pretty," I mutter, trying not to focus on the flush creeping up my chest and neck.

She beams at the compliment. "Thank you. Shall we go?"

Nodding, I pull open the front door and usher her outside a second later, praying I don't look as out of my limits as I feel.

"You have to try this," Adalyn gushes, reaching up to shove a small wooden spoon toward my mouth.

The gelato starts to melt against my lips as I part them for her. The tastes of vanilla and raspberry hit my tongue, the added sweetness helping to cut the bitterness of the fruit. A moan builds in my throat, my body seemingly uncaring about the number of people around us on the street.

Adalyn's eyes flash with approval. "It's so good, right?"

I lean back when she doesn't pull the spoon out of my mouth. "Really good."

"Do you want to try a different kind before we leave? We can share it."

There's something almost fairy-like about the way she moves around in front of the gelato stand. She's carefree and so damn happy. I notice the curious eyes that can't help but take her in as she pushes through the crowd, pastel hair bouncing with each enthusiastic step.

I sympathize with those who can't look away because

despite how hard I try to tell myself to do exactly that, I can't either.

There's a gentle tap on my shoulder, and I spin around to see an older gentleman behind me, a green apron looped around his neck and over his front. A single word is sprawled across his chest. *Valeria's.*

Behind him is the hint of a flower stand, hidden behind dozens upon dozens of fresh flowers. White and yellow and blue. Every colour possible. I take a deep breath and fill my lungs with the smell of them.

"*Eres un hombre afortunado*," he says, a pair of tired green eyes focused on me.

"I'm sorry, I don't speak Spanish," I apologize.

His smile is soft as he nods, running two shaky palms down his apron. "You are a lucky man." My confusion must be obvious because he nods toward the gelato stand and adds, "Her. You are lucky to be with someone so free."

"Oh, we're not like that," I rush out.

He tilts his head and stares at me disbelievingly. "Maybe not."

"Hello! Are you trying to convince Cooper here to buy me some flowers?" Addie's voice cuts through the noise of the busy street.

I shift toward her as she moves to my side and grabs my forearm. It's an innocent touch, but our friendly flower salesman's eyes light up like he's just witnessed life's greatest miracle.

"What is your favourite kind?" he asks her.

She doesn't miss a beat. "Hibiscus. My dad used to order them in bundles for my mom and me when we used to vacation in Mexico."

My interest piques as I stare at her, noticing the sudden pop of freckles over her nose from the sunshine. The Hutton family used to vacation in Mexico yearly, but Maddox only told me about the shit he got into over there. Not about his mother or sister and their traditions.

"A beautiful choice. And a sweet story," the man says, glancing behind him for the briefest second.

Adalyn juts her chin and grins. "Thank you . . ."

"Luis." He extends his hand, and she grabs it.

"I'm Adalyn. And yes, that's my father for you. He's the sweetest man I've ever met. Well, besides Cooper's dad. They make good competition, those two."

The man's eyes dart between Adalyn and me, a smile tugging at his mouth. "And his son? Is he sweet too? Does he treat you well, my dear?"

"We're not—"

She cuts me off. "Oh! Of course he does. Although he's never asked my favourite flower before," she says, glancing up just long enough to wink at me. I reach behind her to pinch her side, and she jumps, belting out a laugh.

"My apologies, pumpkin," I retort.

"It's okay, as long as you order some flowers for me from this gentleman." She leans into my side, her cheek against my arm. Slim fingers slip from my forearm down to my hand, latching on and squeezing.

"If that's what the lady wants." I look at the man. "Do you have any hibiscus flowers?"

He almost looks offended. "Sí. I will be right back."

"Thank you!" Addie calls.

We both watch as he walks slowly back over to his stand and speaks briefly with a younger man selling a bundle of daisies to a woman with short silver hair. The exchange only lasts a moment before he's moving along toward the back of the stand.

"You're going to make that old man fall head over heels for you, you know?" I ask softly.

She tightens her grip on my hand. "He's sweet. But I think he's lonely."

"How do you figure that?'

"He has sad eyes."

My brows dip. "I didn't notice that."

"Maybe you just weren't looking."

"Yeah, maybe." *Why were you?*

"Oh! I almost forgot your gelato. It's totally melted by now, I'm sorry." She pushes a small cup to my chest, and I stiffen as her knuckles brush my sternum. Her brows lift when I don't immediately take it from her. "Are you wanting me to feed you again? Because I can, but it will cost you."

"Cost me?" I grumble.

"Mmhmm. Better make your choice quick."

If I've learned one thing about Adalyn Hutton over the past few days, it's that she loves to push. She did it at the restaurant, and she's doing it now. The question is whether I give in and let her have her fun or shut it down.

One look at the glint of excitement in her eyes is all it takes for me to decide.

I open my mouth and blink down at her, waiting. Her lips tug into a massive dimpled grin as she scoops some brown gelato onto the spoon and slips it into my mouth. It's coffee flavoured, the taste as strong as sipping a cup of it fresh out of the pot.

"I took a guess at what kind an old man would like. Was I right?" she teases.

I fake a scowl. "We both know you just picked your favourite."

"Not a chance. Do I look like a plain-coffee girl to you?"

Again, the question feels like a dare, but this time, I back down.

I'm grateful when Luis joins us again, this time holding the stem of a perfectly grown hibiscus flower between his fingers. It's a pale orange colour with a burst of pink in the centre. The length of time it took for him to find that must speak to how hard it was to find among the jungle of flowers surrounding the stand.

Addie's attention falls on Luis, and she takes a step back. "Oh, my God! That's for me?"

"Sí. Sí. One of a kind, this colour."

She's quick to take it from him, bringing it to her nose. A sheen slips over her eyes, making my stomach tighten.

"You're too much. Should I put it in my hair? It even matches my dress."

"Yes," I blurt out. "If you want to."

"My wife wore flowers in her hair," Luis says lowly, the pain Addie was describing early now becoming obvious to me. "Not hibiscus but lilies. Her favourite."

"Let this flower honour her, then," Adalyn murmurs. She slides the flower behind her ear and lays a comforting touch on the man's forearm. Her smile is brittle but genuine.

My chest grows warm as I watch an odd yet beautiful friendship grow between the two of them. They'll most likely never see each other again, but right now, it doesn't matter. Adalyn has given him something that he probably hasn't had in years.

Companionship. Even for a fleeting moment.

Each day we spend together exposes another part of her that I've never seen before. She's intuitive and caring, even to those she barely knows, like it's second nature for her.

Luis sets a shaking, wrinkled hand on top of Adalyn's and says, "*Nunca dejas que nadie te haga sentir ordinaria. Eres cualquier cosa menos.*"

The adoration beaming from Adalyn's face is enough to tell me she doesn't care that she doesn't speak Spanish and has no idea what he just told her. His words slither themselves inside of her heart anyway.

11

Adalyn

Our rental in Dublin, Ireland, is small. By the time we get inside and drop our bags on our beds, it's half past one in the morning, and exhaustion makes my bones heavy. The flight was quick from Madrid, but I think I left a part of myself there after our four-day stay. The tiniest piece, but one I can feel missing. I wonder if Cooper feels the same or if Madrid is already in his rear view.

"You can use the bathroom first. I'm going to check the place out," he says. His tall frame is perched by the bedroom window, one arm holding the long curtain to the side so he can see out.

"Alright. Thanks."

I unzip my suitcase and dig around for everything I'll need before entering the bathroom. It's small, like the apartment. A standing porcelain sink, a small mirror above it, a toilet, and a bathtub with a showerhead. The shower sputters when I turn it on, but the steam that follows is euphoric.

My eyes are heavy as I wash the plane ride away, and by the time I drag myself out of the water and slip my pajamas on, I feel like a zombie. After brushing my teeth and applying my moisturizer, I push open the door and make my way to the single bedroom.

"Tell me you're as tired as I am, because I swear I could have fallen asleep in the—*oh!*" I gasp when I come face to face with a bare male ass. Perky. Round. *Christ, it's so round.*

Any normal person would turn around at the unexpected sight, probably embarrassed or downright mortified to have seen something they definitely weren't supposed to, but I've never been normal. And Cooper's ass is far from normal. It's a fucking masterpiece.

"Do you do squats? You have to. There's no way an ass like that came naturally to you," I ramble, finally forcing my eyes away from his backside and up to the pair of wide, panicked brown ones watching me from over his stiff shoulder.

"I'm so sorry," he mutters quickly, yanking the heavy-looking quilt from his bed and draping it around his waist like a towel. "I thought I had more time to change. You were quieter than normal."

"Are you calling me loud?"

His laugh is unsteady, almost unbelieving. "Yes. You stomp when you walk. It's like a warning call."

"I don't stomp," I defend.

"You do."

"Maybe I do it so you can hear me with your old man ears."

He sits on the edge of the bed, blanket still around him, the hem of his soft blue polo shirt tucked inside. Our eyes stay locked in a silent battle that neither of us wants to lose.

"So, you're admitting it, then," he says.

"What? No. I said maybe. As in, maybe if I did stomp, that would be the reason why. I'm not admitting anything."

"Ah," he hums with a one-shoulder shrug. "Right."

I narrow my eyes. "What does that mean?"

"There's no better time to learn how to accept defeat than

right now, Adalyn. I'm a good teacher. I won't rub it in your face."

I scoff. "Yeah, right. There will be no accepting of anything besides a win."

"If you say so," he sings while pushing off the bed and walking toward me.

The way he moves drips with confidence. There's an aura to him right now that makes my heart skip despite myself. I freeze when he gets so close I can smell his cologne, that perfect woodsy mix slipping over me.

"I need past you. I'm going to get dressed before this blanket gives me a rash."

I find myself nodding, but no words come out. There's not enough room for him to walk by from where I'm standing at the end of the beds, blocking the way. *So move, Adalyn.* The warmth from his body seeps into me, drying my mouth. *What is happening?*

"Adalyn." There's humour in his tone. "You okay?"

I nearly burst out a quick *thank you, God* when my senses come back to me, and I jolt to the side, creating more than enough room for him to pass.

"Yep!" I squeak, staring down at the clothes in his hand. His grip looks tight, his knuckles slightly white.

"Be back, then," he says, and then he's gone, the air suddenly cold on my skin.

At the sound of the bathroom door closing, I leap into bed, not caring that my silk pajama shorts give me a wedgie as I tuck myself beneath the scratchy quilt. He wasn't lying when he said he didn't want to get a rash. This thing feels like it was made from sandpaper.

Nevertheless, I close my eyes and try to push the mental picture of a naked, peachy ass and whatever else just happened back there from my mind. I don't behave well when I'm tired, or at least that's what I'm going to blame my unusual reactions just now on.

The sputtering sound of water filters through the apartment as I try and fail to think of something—anything else—besides the image of Cooper in the same bathtub I was in just minutes earlier, naked and soapy.

For the first time in my life, I let my mind wonder about Cooper. Let myself conjure up things that I never would have before today. Before this trip.

Suddenly, there are questions I want answered. Like what is his dating history? How many women has he been with? Is there a reason I have yet to see him bring anyone to big family dinners?

I swallow, flopping onto my back and folding my hands on my stomach. The shower is still running, and as I open my eyes to look over at his empty bed, I exhale heavily, almost disappointed in myself.

"Don't start, Adalyn," I whisper, turning my back to the extra bed and locking those thoughts up and away where I hope I'll never find them again.

"You're not seriously going to kiss that," Cooper sputters where he stands, watching me in disbelief.

I grin wide and continue lowering myself to the stone castle floor. The Blarney Stone is directly behind me now, and I sneak a peek of it over my shoulder before waggling my brows at Cooper.

Kissing the stone is known to give you the power of eloquent speech. I don't think I believe that, but I want to give it a go anyway. Cooper, on the other hand . . .

"Are you really going to make me kiss it alone?" I ask.

"You're going to get a disease if you put your lips on that wall, and one of us needs to be able to go home and explain to our families what happened."

"Maybe you'll agree once I kiss it and get this alleged eloquent speech that's supposed to be bestowed upon me after. I'm already a great smooth talker, so I'm about to get a lot more dangerous.

"It won't work. I agree to a lot of things, but this? Not a chance."

"Is it the kissing that has you worried or the fact you could fall through the space in between the floor and the stone?"

"Both," he states.

I huff. "Fine. Will you at least hold my ankles so I don't plummet to my death?"

"Of course." Stepping up beside me, he waits for me to recline until my back meets the stone. "Don't try to test the limits with this and just hold on to the bars like you're supposed to."

"Give me some credit here. I'm a risk taker, but I'm not dumb." With a wink, I wait for him to grip my ankles and then dip my neck over the ledge, reaching for the bars on the wall.

My abs engage as I pull myself closer to the wall, and Cooper tightens his hold on my ankles. Apparently, I trust him even more than I thought because I don't have a single worry about falling as long as he's holding me up.

"I'm gonna kiss it now," I sing.

"It was nice knowing you," he mutters back.

"Loosen up a bit, babes. You're too young to have such a massive stick up your ass."

"I thought I was old."

I roar a laugh. "You got me there."

My lips meet the stone for less than a second before I'm pulling them away and hauling myself back into a sitting position. Cooper is by my feet, and his hands linger for a moment before he snatches them back.

"Feel accomplished?" he asks.

"Very. Now it's your turn."

He stands, glancing around nonchalantly at the people around us. "Funny. But I think it's time to go. I'm quite hungry."

"I'll let you choose our dinner spot if you kiss the stone."

"How many more times are you going to ask me to do this?"

I shrug. "A million, give or take a few."

His expression is far less serious now, as if he's beginning to give in to me. My pride swells as I push harder. "It would make a great photo op."

"For you?"

"For you and me. I'm sure your dad would love to see you stepping out of your comfort zone."

"My dad is far too easy to please."

"This is a once-in-a-lifetime opportunity, Sparrow. You might regret it if you don't do it now."

My smile starts to grow when he sighs and, albeit reluctantly, switches places with me. It feels like an even bigger win than it should be, but I don't care. I sit at his feet and wait for him to lower himself into the same position I was in before wrapping myself around his shins. It takes a bit of careful maneuvering, but I manage to snap a few photos of him dangling over the ledge as well.

"Don't let go," I warn teasingly.

He doesn't reply, just leans back and kisses the stone. When he pulls himself up again a beat later, his face is scrunched.

"I need some mouthwash."

"Let's go find you some, then. I'll even buy it as a congratulations for taking a risk."

"How generous of you, Addie. Thank you."

I smirk, helping him onto his feet. "You're welcome."

"I expect you to share these photos with everyone you know so I get my money's worth of this experience."

A laugh escapes me as I loop my arm through his and say,

"I'll share it with a few people, but I want this moment mostly to myself if that's alright with you."

His next words are gentle. "Yeah, that's alright with me."

A CELTIC TUNE mixed with excited, loud voices fills the pub the next evening. The energy around us is like no other. From the clanging of beer glasses and whooping hollers from every direction, I haven't been able to stop smiling since we walked inside. Joy makes my blood tingle beneath my skin.

After a day full of exploring, this is exactly what I needed.

"Sweet or spicy, Sparrow?" I ask, setting my elbows on the table and curling my hands beneath my chin. Cooper glances up from his menu.

"What exactly are we discussing?"

"Chicken wings, of course."

"Then spicy."

I smirk, an idea taking shape in my head. "How spicy? Like mildly spicy or *really* spicy?"

He leans back, draping one arm over the back of his booth. The black button-down he's wearing parts where he's left the top two buttons undone, exposing a light dusting of brown hair over pale skin. I'm so used to seeing my brothers covered in black ink that it seems odd to stare at untattooed skin.

"Really spicy. Go hard or go home, right?"

Dropping my hands on the table, I grin. "I'll be right back."

Then I'm moving through the pub, my smile unwavering, even as I find a small opening at the bar and squish between two burly men. Their conversation drops as I lean my fore-arms to the counter and wait for the bartender, but I don't pay them much attention. Cooper's eyes burn holes in my back as

I stand here, and for a moment, I wonder if he'll stalk over here and pull me back to the table with a lecture, but he doesn't. When I steal a glance at him, I find him waiting in the booth, looking ready to leap up at any moment, but he remains where he is, even as the seconds continue to tick by.

He's giving me room to breathe. Watching but not involving himself where I don't need him to. That realization shakes something inside of me, and I glance away.

The bartender is quick to take my order once he notices me, and even as his eyes stray to my minimal cleavage, my good mood doesn't fade. I grip the two heavy mugs of frothy beer and slip back out with a muttered *excuse me* to the two still-silent men at my sides.

"I hope you like your beer extra frothy and your chicken wings on fire, baby cakes. I think we should have a little competition tonight, and we're not leaving here until one of us has tapped out," I say once I sit back down and slide Cooper his mug of beer.

He blinks at me, his expression giving nothing away. "You want to have a beer-drinking and chicken-wing-eating contest?"

"Damn right I do. Whoever eats and drinks the most by the end of the night wins. Are you in, or are you too scared I'll wipe the floor with you?"

I don't miss the way his eyes drift over me with subtle disbelief. My size might be my greatest advantage right now. He truly doesn't know how serious I take my food, even after this past week together. I may have a small figure, but my stomach doesn't always get the memo.

"It should be an easy win for you, right?" I add, goading him.

"It should be," he agrees.

"So? Are we on?"

He brushes a hand through the air. "Hold on, you haven't even told me what we're competing for."

I shrug. "What do you want?"

"I don't know. That's your job to decide. It's your competition, after all."

"Ultimate bragging rights aren't enough?" I ask.

"Not if I'm going to have to take care of your drunk ass tonight, they're not."

"Fine. You make a good point. How about the winner can claim a favour from the loser at any time? I'm sure I could find some use of that someday."

He rolls that over in his mind for a few silent beats before those soft brown eyes sharpen. "Deal."

He extends his hand over the table. I shake it eagerly, and fifteen minutes later, two plates stacked high with hot wings are set on the table, along with two more tankards of beer.

Cooper stares down at his wings excitedly and holds his glass in a firm grip. I do the same before saying, "On three."

He nods. "One."

My knee bounces. "Two."

We both lift our mugs in the air and press them against our lips. "Three!"

A few onlookers glance curiously at us as we shout, but we go unnoticed by others. If anyone else chose to stare, I don't pay them attention. They all fade to the background as we tip our glasses back and drink.

Cooper's throat bobs with each swallow, those pouty lips curling at the edges. I fight off a giggle at how silly I must look gulping down this giant mug of beer while he manages to make it look like one of the most attractive things a man can do.

As my belly fills, I soak up this moment, even as he finishes his beer off first and sets the mug down with a smug smile, waiting while I finish mine.

"Off to a slow start," he pokes at me.

With a final, long pull, I set the glass down on the table

with a bit of force and wipe my mouth with the back of my hand.

I give him a toothy grin. "Slow and steady wins the race, old man."

"Call me old again, Adalyn," he rumbles. I freeze at the drop in his tone before belting out an awkward laugh.

"Or what?"

His expression shutters before he's reaching across the table and pinching one of my chicken wings between his fingers. The next thing I know, he's pressing it to my lips and winking.

"Eat. There's a lot more where these came from."

12

Adalyn

The ground spins as I eagerly take Cooper's jacket from his extended hand and tuck it around me. It smells like him and is still warm from inside the pub. The goosebumps on my arms disappear as we walk down the street, a soft hum of music chasing our heels.

I'm deliriously drunk. And happy. Happy with a hot mouth. A burning one. Even after forcing a tall glass of milk down my throat before leaving the bar. I cup my hands around my mouth and blow, expecting to see fire. I'm disappointed when nothing but warm air escapes.

"My taste buds aren't budding," I shout into the street, eyebrows curling in at the squeaking sound of my voice. Eight tankards of beer and three plates of hot wings is what it took to beat Cooper. More beer and fewer wings than I was expecting, but a champion I am.

A warm hand grips my elbow, steadying me as I stumble in my wedges. *Why did I wear these shoes?* My pinky toes hurt like a bitch.

"They're going to be gone forever now," Cooper replies, sounding just as drunk as I am but a lot less squeaky.

Shit, his voice isn't squeaky at all. It's deep and gentle but also surprisingly commanding at times. I wonder if he uses it in bed. Is he secretly bossy? The idea of it is hard to wrap my head around, considering the man blushes when he compliments me. I can't imagine him speaking dirty commands.

A giggle slips out before I can stop it. Cooper asks, "What's so funny?"

"I was imagining you in bed giving filthy commands."

He's the one stumbling this time, and with his fingers still wrapped around my arm, I move with him. Suddenly, we're falling, falling, falling. Cold air strikes my arms as his jacket slips from my shoulder and tumbles to the ground seconds before we do.

"Cooper!"

"Fuck my life." The wind steals his drunken curse.

The grass is so green. So long and thick and damp against my skin. Hard too. *Hard?* I blink until my vision clears, and my body hones in to the feeling of somebody beneath me. Arms are coiled tight around my waist, and a solid chest rises and falls rapidly in time with mine.

"Oh," I blurt out. My fingers curl in the grass beside Cooper's head as I hold myself up above him, my hips pressed to his hips, my legs tucked between his. "Hi."

Mouth pulled in a tight line, he squeezes his eyes shut and releases my waist, arms falling to the yard we've stumbled onto. His back must be wet, and I half expect him to jolt up and set me aside, but he only blows out a long breath and carefully peeks up at me. Eyelashes fluttering, he slips his stare over my face from bottom to top.

"You okay?" he slurs.

"Maybe I should have given you the nickname Prince Charming instead," I reply.

Confusion fills his stare. "Why?"

"You sacrificed yourself for me."

"Dramatic. I just didn't wanna hear you complain about grass stains on your clothes."

I hiccup and sag against his body. It's been a long time since I've been in a position like this, but my mind is too loose to focus on that. Once my fingers uncurl from the grass, I move them over the length of his shoulders and bite the inside of my cheek at the solid feel of them.

"What are you doing?" he croaks.

"Feeling whether or not you're husband material. What does it look like I'm doing?" The words sound ridiculous coming from my mouth, but alcohol has dissolved me of a single care.

My flirty joke turns serious when he says, "I'm not husband material."

"Why not?"

"I don't know how to be like that for someone." He says it like it's obvious.

The smell of rain comes so suddenly I tip my head back and stare at the previously bright evening sky, finding it painted with endless dark clouds. I look back at Cooper and frown, my thumb slipping inside the open material of his shirt and stroking the tip of his collarbone.

"I don't know how to be a wife to someone, but I don't care. I want to try."

He shakes his head. "You don't need to be anybody's wife yet."

I tilt my head. "How is it that you think you know what I need?"

Tipping my chin, I watch as his fingers bite into the grass at his side, just like mine did moments prior, only for some ungodly reason, my drunken mind takes offense to the action. *He would rather get dirt beneath his nails than touch me.*

"It's obvious that I don't know, so why don't you tell me, Adalyn?"

There's that commanding tone again. This time, it drags a line of fire down my spine, and I arch in an attempt to get away from the burn.

It only brings me closer to the blaze in front of me.

"I need . . ." I trail off. The alcohol in my blood begins to sing with terrible, problem-bringing ideas. A flash of lightning fills the street as thunder rolls over us in one long, thrilling rumble. It's either a sign of spectacular proportion or a warning. I choose option number one.

"You need . . . ?" he echoes softly.

"I need to do something. Something I've never done before. Something completely crazy and idiotic."

"Everything you do is crazy and a bit idiotic," he says, somehow without judgment.

I nip at my bottom lip before saying, "I want to go farther than all those things."

"What are you talking about?"

The devil on my shoulder pounds its fists to its chest while the angel sighs, turning away and covering its ears.

Cooper would never agree to what I have in mind. But what if he did? What if I *could* convince him to do something totally fucking bonkers? The idea of beating odds set against me is like dangling a steak in front of a wild, hungry dog. The warm thumping of blood beneath my skin is near rabid as adrenaline comes racing in.

"Marry me. Tonight."

His eyes go wide, surprise and alcohol making them appear glossy. He blinks slowly, watching me like he's waiting for me to jump up and say, *Just kidding!* I don't move a muscle, still lazing over him like a human blanket.

"You're not serious."

I roll my eyes. "Is it that funny of an idea? Marrying me in Ireland?"

"Funny? No. Scary? Fucking hell, yes."

"Live a little, Coop. Take a risk." I drop my voice to a whisper and lean closer, flashing my teeth. "Be wild."

His Adam's apple bobs as he stares at me, unblinking. "We're drunk."

"That's why we should do it."

"It is a bad idea."

"Bad ideas are the fun ones," I argue, refusing to back down.

"We'd regret it in the morning."

"Not for long before we got . . . what's the word?"

The corners of his mouth curl into a dopey smile. "Arnold?"

It still doesn't sound right, but I don't care. "Sure. That."

"It won't ever go away, though. Even after. Forever."

"I wouldn't regret it. What if I never got married again? At least I could say I did it once."

"We're drunk."

"You already said that."

"I'm older than you. Others might think I forced you into it."

That makes me laugh. A bird-scattering, chest-aching laugh. Cooper doesn't find it as funny as I do, but that doesn't stop me.

"Then they don't know me well enough. That means they don't matter." I jab a finger into my chest. "I don't get forced into anything. Plus, it will be a secret." I move the finger to his lips and press. "Shh."

I flush when he takes my fingertip between his teeth and softly bites down. His eyes grow dark, his stare heavy. "A secret?"

"A dirty one."

His laugh is strained as he releases my finger. "You could never be a dirty secret."

"Okay. Make me a clean one, then."

My nipples rasp against my bra as my chest heaves. The part of my brain that has any sense is shouting for me to back up and pull myself together, but all the beer in my bloodstream dulls that voice until it disappears completely. *Shit*, he feels good beneath me. Strong and secure. Forbidden.

This is the last position we should be in. These are the last thoughts I should be thinking. But when you're three sheets to the wind, everything sounds like the best idea.

That's the only explanation as to why I take advantage of his loose bite on my finger and push it further inside of his mouth, curious as to what he'll do now. A shot of electricity moves between my legs when he takes me by surprise, pulling my finger in deeper and sucking.

My throat grows tight as I swallow a moan and whisper, "Well? Do you need me to beg?"

He shakes his head a single time as I pull my finger from his mouth. His eyes refuse to release mine as he rasps two words that turn me to mush.

"No. Not yet."

I'm woken by the churning of my stomach. Everything I ate and drank last night spins like it's inside of a washing machine as I fling myself out of bed and run to the bathroom. I drop to my knees and barely have time to pull my hair from my face before retching into the toilet bowl.

A whimper escapes me as the bathroom tiles cool the hot skin of my legs and knees. My shirt sticks to my sweat-slicked back, and if my arms weren't so fucking heavy, I would rip it right off.

Soft footsteps on the carpet outside make me stiffen. I hide my face in my elbow and close my eyes as the room continues to spin. I've never liked people seeing me when I'm not feeling well, and I don't see Cooper being an exception to that.

"Are you okay?" Cooper asks softly. By the rough sound of his voice and the fact I was awake before him, it's probably extremely early in the morning.

"No," I say into my elbow.

"Do you get sick after drinking often?"

"No."

"Do you want me to leave?"

Anxiety grips me as I blurt out a surprising "No."

"Okay."

Shuffling noises have me looking up from my arm to find him sitting down beside me with his back against the tub and his knees bent, arms slung over them. I take in the bags beneath his eyes and his curly hair standing up every which way and let out a breathy laugh.

"How do you feel?" I croak, closing the toilet lid and flushing.

"Like you look, but without the throw up."

"Lucky you."

He hums, eyes darting around the room as he wipes a hand down his face. There's a nagging feeling in the pit of my stomach when I watch him do it. Like he knows something I don't but is too afraid to say it.

"What are you thinking about?" I ask.

Something like disappointment darts across his face before it's gone, replaced with an impossible-to-read expression. "Do you remember what we did last night?"

"Not really."

I remember beer and wings and how hot my lips burned after finishing my second plate. There was even a crowd beside our table, cheering us on as I finished my fifth beer just seconds before Cooper did.

"It's all kind of black after the bartender cleared our table and announced me the victor. Even that's a bit fuzzy."

He tips his chin and swallows. There's guilt in his eyes when he looks back up at me. My brows tug inward.

"Why? Do *you* remember what we did last night?"

"Not much more than you do. It keeps coming in waves, but I think I'm starting to put it together," he says.

"Okay . . ." I drawl. "So, why do you look like Liam after he's used marker on the wall and been scolded?"

Not even the mention of my adorable nephew is enough to crack through whatever is going on in Cooper's head. It isn't until he lifts his left hand in the air that he breaks, taking me with him.

Horror grips me. "Is that a—"

Slowly, he dips his head in confirmation. Then I watch as his eyes move to my hand.

"We didn't," I whisper, tucking my fingers into a fist as if that will hide them.

It doesn't work. As soon as I follow his stare and find the matching tattoo on my ring finger, I'm flinging back open the toilet lid and disposing of anything left in my stomach.

Fuck.

13

Cooper

sparrow

Adalyn Hutton is my wife.

It's safe to say I'm utterly fucked.

My streak of perfect behaviour has been demolished in a single night. Reduced to rubble. To ash.

I'm never drinking beer again. Even the thought of chicken wings makes me want to run to the bathroom and join Adalyn in throwing up until my stomach no longer feels full of lead.

I stare at my hand and glare at the black ink circling my finger. *Tattoos*. Wedding ring tattoos, at that. I'm ninety-eight percent sure they were her idea. I've never been one for tattoos. *Apparently, that didn't matter last night*, I remind myself. Not much of anything seemed to.

Twisting my hand in front of me, I groan at the name written on the inside of the ring. *Adalyn*. If I had to bet, I would say my name is on her finger as well. Even better.

"Maddox is going to kill me," I mutter to the empty room.

He's going to torture me first. Then kill me and bring me back just to do it again. Over and over until Oakley joins in. Maybe Ava will want a turn. Scarlett too.

I flop backward on the bed and stare at the ceiling, guilt

zipping through me. The toilet flushes in the bathroom, followed by a low, pained moan that's soon washed out by the faucet.

My memories of last night are weak, hazy. I don't remember leaving the pub or finding a place to get hitched. Brief flickers have been coming since I woke up, but nothing substantial. Like the image of blue-and-pink hair brushing my cheeks as Adalyn stared down at me, her lips parting on words I can remember, my back wet and sore. Then there's the photo I found in my camera roll of a blurry marriage certificate taken in the early, *early* morning.

I should have been the responsible one last night and said no to our contest, but how am I supposed to regret something that made me feel so good? So damn happy and light. Like during our time together, there wasn't a single thing weighing me down or making me feel like I needed to be the grown-up. The one making the hard decisions and ruining everyone's fun.

Adalyn pulls out that side of me. She pushes me out of my comfort zone and makes me feel like a kid again.

Our friendship is growing quickly. So quickly that it's almost terrifying. We've been spending so much time together that it's become second nature to blurt out the most random facts about ourselves and share things that we never would have under different circumstances.

This accidental marriage threw a wrench in everything. Now I have no idea where to go from here. Not a fucking clue.

At the sound of the bathroom door opening, I push up on my hands, clearing my throat. Adalyn doesn't so much as look at me as she crosses the room, heading right for me.

"Can I lay with you?" she whispers, voice sounding raw.

The question is innocent. That much is clear when she lifts her eyes and stares at me with tired eyes. Her lips are drooping into a frown, and I fight the urge to use my thumbs to lift the corners up.

"Yeah."

I get off the bed and move around her to pull the blanket back, exposing the sheets. She all but dives beneath it and rubs her cheek over my pillow like a kitten trying to get comfortable. My chest grows tight at the sight.

"Lay with me," she says, watching me watch her.

"Are you sure?"

She nods and pats the mattress, eyes fluttering shut. "We should talk."

"We can talk when you aren't half-asleep."

"Just get over here, Sparrow. Maybe I want to spend my morning cuddling my husband."

"It's too soon to make jokes about that," I mutter but slide in beside her anyway.

She sighs when I squeeze onto the double bed before tossing her leg over mine and folding her hands beneath her chin. I'm stiff as that warm, smooth leg of hers moves up and down along my shin, but she doesn't say anything about it.

"It wasn't a joke. Not completely. I get clingy when I'm hungover."

I fold my arms across my chest and nod. "Alright."

"My family is going to be really upset when they find out," she breathes.

"Mine too."

"We need to keep it a secret for now. At least until we find a way to get it taken care of."

"You want an annulment?" I look at her and catch her already watching me curiously beneath blonde lashes. Turning onto my side, I trap her leg between mine and push up on my elbow. "I can call my father's lawyer and see if he knows of anyone who specializes in this kind of thing."

"I think that would be best. At least then it might not be such a big deal when everyone finds out. Just a drunken mistake we took care of like adults."

The term "mistake" sounds wrong, almost dirty, but I shove that thought away.

"We still have a lot of time left on the trip. If we're lucky, we might be able to get it figured out before we get back."

"What do we do about these?" She lifts her hand and wiggles her ring finger. "Adding our names seems like something you would ask for, you big softie."

I snort a laugh. "Big softie?"

"Your heart is the size of a dinner plate; I just know it. You've gotta have a sentimental side."

"I can. Depending on the situation."

She gives me a sleepy smile and shifts closer, her face just inches from my shoulder. I release a tight breath when she gets the nerve to lift her head, setting her cheek over my ribs. She smells like mint toothpaste and lingering perfume. Flowers and mint shouldn't go together, but when it comes to her, they do.

"At least you'll never forget this. Forget me. Tattoos are permanent." She whispers the words, but they still rattle me inside.

I have a feeling every moment spent with Adalyn will be permanently engrained in my memory. Tattoo or no tattoo.

Swallowing past the lump in my throat, I unclasp my hands and move an arm over her, gently draping it over her back. She exhales a heavy breath and nuzzles further into my T-shirt.

I tear my eyes off her. "I won't need a tattoo to remember everything about you, Adalyn."

THREE DAYS LATER, I'm pulling Adalyn's luggage into the elevator at our hotel in Paris while she prepares to FaceTime her parents. Somehow, she's managed to hold them off for over a week, but they've become overly—and understandably—insistent.

The elevator doors have just shut us in when she says, "For the love of God, please don't wave at them when we get in the room. There's no way we could explain the tattoos if you did."

"No waving. Got it."

"My father is a living lie detector, so try not to lie either. Just wiggle around any questions you think will expose us," she adds, rambling now.

Instinctively, I stroke a hand down her rigid spine and huff a laugh when she jumps and then relaxes. "I know your parents. You can breathe. I won't give us away."

She nods. "It's not that I don't trust you. I do. This is just not something I've ever done before."

"You mean, you haven't drunkenly married anybody in Ireland before?"

Rolling her eyes, she lightly punches my arm. "You know what I mean. I've never lied to my parents about anything big like this before. They never gave me any reason to lie growing up, so I'm just feeling really guilty right now."

"I get that. I'm pretty sure I'm too old to be lying to my parents. But you know how my dad is. If he's really as desperate for me to get married as it seems, then this would send him over the edge. I'd never hear the end of this supposed fairy tale he would turn it into. That damn romantic."

He can keep his ooey-gooey feelings turned on his wife. The old man has always been a total suck, but I draw the line at him butting into my personal life with his ideas of happily ever after's. If mine comes along, then I'll accept it with open arms. But I don't want him involving himself, even if he swears I deserve it after doing that exact thing to his relationship when I was a child.

The difference between now and then is that I was just a

nosey kid, and he was a blind old man who needed the push when it came to Scarlett. My marriage is fake. A sham.

They're not the same.

"Adam and my dad are so similar it's a bit freaky when you think about it. They're two total simps for their wives. It's adorable, isn't it?"

The way she speaks about it, like she's giddy over the idea, pulls at my interest. Our previous conversation about her want to be in a serious relationship starts to make perfect sense.

"You want that, don't you?" I ask, adjusting the strap of her carry-on over my shoulder as the elevator doors open to our floor. We walk down the hallway side by side.

"I do. Who wouldn't want someone to be so utterly in love with them that they would do anything to see them happy? My dad was ready to throw everything away for my mom. His career, his future. The only thing that mattered was her. Of course I want to experience a love like that," she says softly, dragging her suitcase behind her.

I clear my throat. "I don't think it really hit me until Maddox and Braxton got married."

"What hit you?"

"How quickly life moves. How regret can fester in the deepest parts of yourself and wear you down. How jealous I am of what they have and how hard they fought for it, even after a decade of being apart. I was so young when my dad got married to SP, so while I knew what was going on between them, it wasn't the same as seeing it happen to my best friend years later," I admit, feeling a weight lift from my chest. "I might not know how to be a partner like that to someone, but I can't help but want to learn."

I only notice that we've stopped in front of our room when Addie steps toward me, and I look between us to see my feet planted on the carpet. It's quiet, so damn quiet, as we stand there, neither of us speaking. For the briefest moment, I wonder if maybe I shouldn't have unloaded all of that onto her. But the expression on her face tells me I was an idiot to think that she would judge me for even a second.

A soft kind of appreciation glitters in her eyes beneath the yellow hallway light. Like maybe she feels as seen as I do right now, in this moment. I smile down at her, my heartbeat picking up speed.

I catch the slow movement of her hand as she lifts it and softly cups the side of my face, warm palm flush to my jaw. I stop breathing entirely when her thumb strokes the side of my throat, lingering on my pulse.

"Whoever you give your real ring to someday is going to be the luckiest woman in the world. You're an amazing man, Cooper White. I feel so incredibly happy to consider you my husband, even if only for a brief moment of time," she murmurs.

Her words race through my head, leaving me frozen in the doorway. I don't move, even as she drops her hand and slips into our room, leaving me out here alone, wondering why on earth I want to pull her into my arms and keep her there for days.

14

Adalyn

"Oh my, I've missed you so much!" Mom gushes, holding the phone far too close to her face.

Tears swell in her eyes as she stares intensely at me, as if trying to commit me to memory. I blink profusely, refusing to cry at the image of her so worked up. *This damn woman.*

"Mom. I've barely been gone for two weeks," I mutter.

"I've been telling her that, but you know how she gets," Dad puts in, sticking his face into the camera. He casts an adoring look at Mom before kissing her cheek.

Taking the phone from her hands, he flops down beside her on the couch and holds it in front of them, not too close this time. My chest warms at the image of them all cuddled up.

"I just miss our only daughter, Oakley."

He chuckles softly. "I miss her too. But look at her. She's alive and smiling."

"I see that," Mom hums. "Are you enjoying yourself, sweetheart?"

"I am. Sometimes it can be a bit overwhelming, but I'm truly loving it. We met the cutest old man in Madrid, and I can confirm Irish beer is way better than it is anywhere else in the world."

"Becoming a beer connoisseur, are you?" Dad teases.

Cooper's cologne makes my nose tingle as he finally joins me in the room. His eyes sweep over me behind the phone, leaving a lingering warmth on my skin. My breath catches when our eyes meet and hold, and shit does my heart ever skip a beat at whatever lives in that stare of his.

"I wouldn't go quite that far. You should see her guzzle down a glass of red wine after walking around and exploring all day," he says, sitting beside me, thigh pressing right up against mine. I try not to look at him to see if he's noticed how close he is.

"That's my girl," Mom coos, grinning. "I hope you're keeping her good company, Cooper."

"Of course."

"I'm loosening him up a bit." I smirk.

Mom's eyes twinkle so bright I notice through the screen. "It sounds like you're having a great time. I'm happy to hear it. I was worrying a bit over here."

"A bit is an understatement. Thank you for calling us," Dad says.

Guilt churns my stomach, and my smile slips away. "I'm sorry I didn't call sooner. Time got away from me, I guess. I didn't mean to make you worry or anything."

A hand on my thigh tears my eyes from the screen, away from my parents and their apologetic expressions. I stare at a tattooed finger instead and the thumb that strokes my bare thigh only once, just below the hem of my shorts.

I bite the inside of my cheek to try as I try to fight a shiver. My swallow is thick when I glance back at the camera and refocus on the conversation.

"It's okay, Addie. We understand what it's like to be off doing your own thing. You're grabbing life by the horns and trying not to miss a second of it. Don't apologize for that.

We're here for you always, regardless if we're talking on the phone or not," Dad says softly.

I tug one side of my mouth into a partial smile. "Thank you. I love you guys."

"We love you t—"

"Is that my sister on the phone?" Maddox cuts Mom off before she can finish.

I roll my eyes as my oldest brother grabs the phone from our parents and holds it in front of himself. His playoff beard is gone, which means playoffs are over. Another jolt of guilt rolls through me, only this time, Cooper falls victim to it too. He hisses a breath between his teeth, and it takes everything in me not to look at him to see if he's okay.

"Your beard is gone" is what I choose to say. Not a "hello" or an "I miss you."

He notches a brow. "Thanks for stating the obvious."

"Did you guys win?" Cooper asks, the words tight.

I know we're both thinking the same thing. *How did we not know?* The answer is obvious, but that doesn't make it any easier to swallow. I haven't reached for my phone more than a handful of times since we arrived in Madrid. My social media notifications are muted, and the only messages from those important to me have caught my attention.

Nobody told me Maddox played his last playoff game of the season. Win or lose, I don't know. *We* don't know.

"Nah. Lost in game seven," my brother says as if it isn't a big deal.

"Why didn't anybody tell us?" I sound as offended as I feel. *God, I'm a hypocrite.*

Suddenly, my ring finger burns.

Maddox's eyes soften as he tells me, "Because it isn't a big deal. I'll be back next year to try again. You don't need to be over there feeling bad for me when you can be having fun."

"You should have told me, Dox. Doesn't matter where I am, I want to know what's going on in your life," Cooper says.

"Shit. I'm sorry. I didn't think it would be a big deal. Braxton was here to kiss me better afterward."

My features relax slightly at that, a smile toying with my mouth. Sensing Cooper's lingering discomfort, I change the subject. It's more than my brother's loss that's bugging him.

"Where is your better half? And your little man? I miss them."

My brother lights up the way he only does at the mention of his wife and son. Pure love seeps from his every pore. "Liam managed to wrangle her into sleeping with him for his nap. They're in my old room, so he refused to sleep alone. You know how he is with sleeping anywhere but his crib."

Memories of the late nights I've spent babysitting my nephew flood my mind. He's never liked to sleep much, but put him on your chest while watching a show and he'd be out like a light every damn time.

"Don't be picking on your son, Maddox Hutton. I remember you refusing to sleep worth a shit when you were a toddler," Mom half-heartedly scolds.

"Adalyn was the only one of you that slept well. She was our reward for all the trouble you and Noah caused us. Like the universe was issuing us an apology," Dad adds.

I stick my tongue out at Dox as he rolls his eyes at Dad. "Hear that, asshole? I think that was confirmation that I am indeed the favourite child."

"Dad didn't say that," he grunts.

"He didn't have to say it word for word. Read between the lines."

"Maybe you need to stop reading between so many lines. You're beginning to sound like a conspiracy theorist."

"You're so dramatic. I don't know how Braxton deals with you."

"My dazzling personality, obviously."

I snort loudly. "Now who sounds like a conspiracy theorist?"

"It's not fair to start arguments when you're too far away for me to toss you in the pool."

"Aw, are you scared I'll win if you don't cheat?"

He snorts. "I don't cheat."

"Yes you do!"

"Nope."

"What do you call shutting me up by dumping me in the pool or stealing my stuff, then? Tell him, Cooper. You know I'm right. Maddox is a dirty cheat."

The laugh that escapes the man at my side makes my toes curl, and I pull my feet as far into the couch as I can, hoping he can't see.

"I plead the fifth," he says.

I scowl at him. "You can't plead the fifth. This isn't a courtroom."

He meets my stare, curving a brow in answer. "Are you going to make me say otherwise?"

"Yes. I damn well will," I huff.

"How do you plan on doing that?"

An idea takes root in my head. A terrible one, really.

I straighten my shoulders and shift toward him, pressing the side of my body harder against his. Our knees knock as I bat my eyes at him, trying not to take a big sniff of his cologne.

"Is it time yet?" I ask him.

"Time for what?"

When his brows furrow in confusion, I make a show of accidentally dropping my phone on the cushion beside him. I flash a dimpled smile at him while reaching across his lap and covering the back of my phone with my hand.

His breath hitches at the feel of my body over his lap, but I think he may stop breathing entirely when I lean my cheek close to his chest and peek at him through my fluttering lashes.

"For me to beg," I whisper, the words only for him.

His delayed response almost makes it that much better. I'm

already pulling away, phone in hand, when I catch a quiet "Good Christ" slipping from his mouth. My grin is instant.

"Sorry, guys. The plane ride must have taken more out of me than I thought," I apologize to the waiting faces on the screen.

"That's okay, honey. We'll let you go before your brother steals the phone again to finish your argument. Call soon, okay?" Mom says.

From the corner of my eye, I catch Cooper pulling at the collar of his shirt and clearing his throat, fist to mouth. Pure satisfaction runs through me knowing he isn't as immune to my presence as he appears to be. I'm not completely alone in that regard.

"Of course. I'll call before we leave Paris."

They approve of the idea, and then we say our goodbyes. It isn't even a beat after I end the call that Cooper's up and off the couch. I stifle a giggle in my wrist and watch him stalk toward the bathroom.

My eyes snag on his ass in the pair of tight khaki joggers he put on for the plane ride this morning, unabashedly checking him out. In my defence, it is a really great ass.

He's about to shut the bathroom door behind him when I call out, "You never did answer me."

My stomach tightens with anticipation as he stares at me, the look in his eyes sending my mind reeling with a world of possibilities. Most of which I know for a fact I shouldn't be thinking.

"If I wanted you to beg, you'd know, Adalyn."

15

Cooper

We spend the next morning and afternoon at the Louvre before wandering back to the hotel to get ready for dinner. Adalyn listened to me gush about the art for hours without complaint. She nodded and awwed and asked more questions than I thought someone could possibly come up with on the spot.

Even if she did blurt out that the *Mona Lisa* was incredibly underwhelming and earned several dirty looks from passersby, I couldn't have asked for a better partner to share that experience with. She only spoke what I'm sure several others, especially those who don't care for art the way I do, were thinking.

To me, it was a moment I will never forget. To witness such beautiful, historical work in person, even just for a minute . . . it's life changing for someone like me.

I clear my throat and continue buttoning up my shirt. It's warm tonight, and for the first time since we've begun this trip, we're going to a nightclub. I've made a promise to myself to stay on a water-only diet tonight, and I intend to keep it. The last thing we need is to have a repeat of our night in Ireland. Although, I'm not sure what the alternative to getting married would be, and I don't want to find out.

I glance at myself in the mirror and smooth my hands down my shirt, the silky material of it cool beneath my palms. The air conditioner blows loudly in the room, drowning out the music playing in the bathroom as Adalyn gets ready. Every once in a while, I can hear her belt out an out-of-pitch lyric or two, and I find myself smiling, knowing that she's enjoying herself.

It's odd coming to terms with an unexpected friendship, but with every moment I spend with her, the more I'm becoming addicted to her presence. To the sudden bursts of energy and fits of flirtation that are starting to leave me buzzing in their wake. *Fuck, if Maddox could see me now.*

I shouldn't have been hurt that he didn't tell me about his playoff loss. Not when I'm hiding something from him that will undoubtedly change our friendship. But in the moment, I couldn't help it.

We've been best friends since we were in diapers. It feels like the ultimate betrayal to be standing here right now, ignoring the reality I'll have to face the moment we touch back down in Canada. I have no idea how things are going to go once we face the music, but I can only assume they'll be disastrous.

I adjust my watch and brush my finger over the inscription, making a mental note to check in with my mom tomorrow before she starts to worry.

"Ready?" Adalyn shouts over her music.

Moving away from the mirror, I knock on the bathroom door. The music quiets instantly before she peeks her head out.

She slowly rakes her eyes over me before whistling far too loudly. "I'm about to have the most handsome date in all of Paris."

My face goes hot. "You're a flirt."

"You love it," she sings before pulling open the door and twirling beneath the bathroom lights.

I don't reply. Not because I don't want to . . . but simply because I *can't*.

My head is void of anything but the image of her in front of me. The glossy pink lips spread in a shy, so *un*-Addie-like smile, bright blue eyes and matching silk dress that hugs her body *just* right. Short sleeves, a slit up the thigh. A swooping neckline and two bumps over where her nipples should be. I gulp past the stone in my throat, unable to turn away like I should.

Her shoes make us nearly the same height, and as I grip onto the edge of the countertop for support, I'm not sure if that's a good thing or a bad thing. She's so close, and I don't know if it was her who stepped forward or myself.

She smells so good, and I can't help but lean forward and breathe her in, filling my lungs with flowers and honey and something purely Adalyn. My fingers tingle, begging for me to touch her, so I do.

It's a cautious, nervous touch. Just a brush of my fingers to her waist. But then she shivers, and those glossy lips fall from that smile and part on an exhale. That brush turns into a steady hold before I realize it, my palm to the curve of her body, holding, waiting. Breathing is a task as the air thins, almost like it's being sucked out through the vents.

"Do you like it?" she asks, the words breathy and low.

Like it? There has to be something wrong with me because I nearly blurt out just how much I do before I say, "Yes. You look stunning."

For the very first time in my entire life, I watch her cheeks turn pink. It's a soft pink, a gentle caress of warmth, but damn it all to hell, I never want to forget it.

"Thank you," she says, blinking up at me with those wide doe eyes.

I nod as my fingers press deeper into the flesh of her hip, as if a soft touch isn't enough. Tension creeps up my spine as I wait for her to tell me to back off, knowing damn well it would only take a single word for me to retract my grip, but she doesn't. Instead, she curves slightly toward me, stare unflinching.

"We match."

"What?"

Slim fingers with pale pink, manicured nails run down the front of my shirt, pinching the silk. "Our clothes. We match."

I twirl my thumb over her hip bone. "Was that on purpose or a happy coincidence?" I ask, remembering how I found this shirt laid out on the bed for me earlier, just seconds before she disappeared into the bathroom.

"Take a guess."

"I don't think you believe in coincidences."

She smooths her hand over my chest. "No? Why not?"

"You're above coincidences. You make your own choices, forge your own path. Everything that happens, happens for a specific reason. Destiny be damned."

Her breath catches, eyes widening slightly. "It sounds like you've done your research."

"No." I lean in, bringing our faces closer together. *Too close.* "You just make it hard not to pay attention."

As she takes in my words, a terrifying look of determination flicking across her features, I drop my hand and take a step back.

I don't know what is running through her head right now, but that look screams danger. And when a tiny voice in my head screams at me to reach out and touch that uncontrolled flame at the risk of getting burnt, I realize I was too close to crossing a line I could never come back from. One that I don't think even a girl as fearless as Adalyn is ready to risk crossing.

The club is in the basement of a theatre. The ceiling is low, the air thick with cigarette smoke and sweat. Techno music shakes the ground beneath us, making my eardrums throb. A DJ controls the crowd like a conductor of an orchestra, moving them every which way with a sway of his hand.

Adalyn moves in front of me as we make our way inside. I lay my hand on her lower back, spotting the stamped pink star beneath my knuckles as I follow close behind. Bright lights twirl around the room, helping make out a route to the bar.

"This way!" she shouts at me.

The groups of people around the bar seem to part for her, and it nearly makes me laugh out of pure astonishment. I've started to notice how her presence affects people during our time together. Some might label it as ostentatious, but that would only prove how little they know her.

Adalyn doesn't strive for attention; she beckons it naturally. We're all simply moths to her beautiful flame.

And while I can sympathize with them for the way they watch her, it's hard not to want to spin them all around and keep her for myself. It's wrong—so damn wrong—but I can't find it in me to care.

She orders herself a cocktail and water for me before beginning to inch closer as we wait. Each second that passes has me tensed tighter and tighter. By the time the bartender slides two cups toward us, her back is to my front, my arms on either side of her. I clasp sweaty palms around the glasses and pray I don't drop them on the floor as we turn and head for an empty table near the front.

"It's not as loud over here," she says, forfeiting her side of the booth for the extra space on mine instead. I don't say a word about it.

With a tiny black straw in her mouth, she sips on her drink, eyes darting enthusiastically around the club, head bobbing to the music. I rest my arm across the back of the booth behind her and gulp my water.

"Are you sure you don't want anything a bit riskier than water to drink?" she asks after a beat.

"One of us has to keep a level head tonight."

"Oh, please. You just don't want to be hungover again."

I chuckle. "Maybe that too."

"I don't plan on being hungover either. I give you permission to cut me off after a few more, even if I complain."

"You got it."

"I mean it. Throw me over your shoulder and drag me out of here if you have to."

"You told me that you loved being tossed around from time to time. I don't want to give you a reward for misbehaving."

She tosses me a dimpled grin. "Of course not. That just means you'll have to punish me later to make up for it."

Thank fuck the DJ yells something in French that I can't quite pick out before the music shifts to something quicker. A perfectly timed distraction. I glance up at the ceiling and will my blood to keep from flooding south at the images trying to barrel through my head.

Adalyn splayed out on my bed, hands crossed above her head, rope keeping them together, even as she begs to touch me. My face between her legs as I pull away when she starts to writhe—

"I know guys your age don't usually like to go out on the town, but thank you for coming with me tonight," she teases, changing the subject.

I choke on a laugh. "That mouth of yours is going to get you in trouble one day."

"If I had a dollar for every time I've heard that, Sparrow, I would never have to work again."

"I'm glad you haven't let anyone change you," I admit, setting my empty water glass on the table, wishing I had another. "We might bug you for being so smart-mouthed, but that's who you are. It's what makes you Adalyn. I can't imagine you any other way."

She shifts to look at me, eyes bright, almost glowing, and it has nothing to do with the lights above us.

"See, I told you. Your heart *is* the size of a dinner plate," she teases.

I laugh, wrapping a silky strand of her hair around my finger. "Don't tell anyone."

"Your secret's safe with me. I'm honoured to be one of the few who know your little secret."

"Is it really that big of a secret?"

"No. But it's possible to be a nice person and just not care as much as you do. You've always been nice. I just didn't know how soft you were inside until this trip. I have a feeling not a lot of people do."

"I don't see the point in exposing everything about yourself to people who are just passing through."

Her throat moves with a swallow. "Is this your way of telling me I'm different?"

"I thought that much was obvious. You could never simply be like everybody else."

My heart stills in my chest when she replies, "Good. Because neither could you."

16

Adalyn

I GLANCE AWAY FROM COOPER, SUDDENLY TOO SHY TO KEEP eye contact. It's silly, but he makes me feel vulnerable. Not in a bad way, of course, but in a new, unexpected way. Like he's seeing me for all that I am and only grows more curious, not wary.

I've grown attached to him. I trust him in a way I don't trust a lot of people. That in and of itself is more than I bargained for this summer.

He's brave in a way that comes from age and maturity and life experiences. I've never had a problem with speaking my mind and telling everyone exactly what I feel, and I think that draws me to him. He might not be as outspoken as I am in that way, but he never makes anything feel one-sided. Even when I drive him a little crazy.

Maybe it's the boys I've dated in the past that make it hard for me to understand how he can be so open and honest about everything. My dating life is nothing to write home about. I've had a handful of boyfriends over the years, starting when I was sixteen and told the captain of my high school football team, Ben Levy, that I liked him and insisted he be my boyfriend. His yes was instant, but there was only ever one love in his life, and it was a brown leather ball. We broke up three months later.

There were a handful more boys after that, but nothing ever serious. I was just a timepiece for them. The model with a famous family. They weren't worth my time, and I never hesitated to cut them loose when I started to recognize that.

Plus, when a guy thinks your clit is somehow on your pussy lip and refuses your help to find its real location, is there really a reason to stay with him?

Cooper seems like he could find it with his eyes closed. In all honesty, I would put money down on his ability to make a woman come in two minutes flat if he really wanted to. My vibrator is the only thing that's ever been able to succeed with that.

Maybe I'm off base with that belief, but something tells me I'm not. *Not in the slightest.*

"Do you want to dance?" I blurt out, staring at the bodies drifting across the club.

"I'm not much of a dancer."

"I can teach you."

He blows out a soft laugh, and I can't help but look at him, catching his subtle smile. "Will that make you happy?"

"Very." Wings flap in my tummy.

"Alright," he says and then presses his hand to my spine, nodding for me to slip out of the booth. "I'm trusting you not to let me look like an idiot out there."

I flash him a toothy grin. "Never."

He stays close as I lead us to the dance floor, his front to my back, arms nearly wrapped around me in a protective embrace. I feel almost invincible in this crowd of people, like nobody could touch me with Cooper here.

I jerk backward when a tall man spins in front of me, eyes bulging when he notices me standing so close behind him. It doesn't take long for him to recover, and I paint on a smile when he doesn't immediately move out of the way.

"*Je ne veux pas être trop direct, mais tu es la plus belle chose que je n'ai jamais vue,*" he says, shouting over the music. I barely hear him, let alone understand him, but he doesn't seem to care.

I shake my head, about to tell him that I don't speak French when Cooper's voice rumbles at my back, making me pause.

"*Si tu parles encore une fois à ma femme, je vais te casser les dents.*"

A shiver travels down my spine, but I don't know if it's from the demanding, rough sound of the words or the fact Cooper speaks French fluently enough to say them. Fingertips press into my hip as a warm hand envelops my side. My toes curl into my shoes at the possessive gesture, a moan almost slipping out.

The man in front of us doesn't hide his surprise well and raises his hands apologetically before disappearing into the crowd. I give in to the urge and press back against the wall of muscle behind me, exhaling at the new feeling.

He leans over my shoulder, his lips so close to my ear that I feel his breath skitter across it. "Keep walking, Adalyn."

My nod is as shaky as my knees. I take a few more steps forward before stopping again, this time directly beneath the racks of glowing lights hanging from the ceiling. It's warm in the club, but it's almost unbearable amongst the throng of dancing people.

The bass pulses at my feet, and the energy around us is intoxicating. My blood zips through my veins, and I reach for Cooper before I can think twice about it, wanting him closer, the hand on my hip not enough. Grasping his wrist, I pull him flush to my back and rest my head against his shoulder, encouraging him to sway side to side with me.

His movements are jerky, making me swallow a giggle. Is he nervous or embarrassed?

"You're too tense," I tell him, eyes locked on the thick cords of his throat as he swallows.

Cautiously, he palms the opposite side of my waist with his

other hand. My eyes fall shut as his fingers splay over my hip and his thumb twirls circles over my dress. His touch is electric, burning my body, and I must be a masochist because I ache for more of the feeling.

"You're tense too," he mutters.

I almost laugh but turn my face into his chest instead, saying, "If you relax, I'll relax. We're supposed to be married, yet we couldn't look any further from it."

"I shouldn't be touching you like this at all. If your brother were here—"

"Shouldn't or don't want to?" I cut him off, twirling my hips in a cautious motion, not wanting to scare him off. He doesn't reply. Doesn't move away. "My brother isn't here right now. It's just us and a fuck ton of strangers. Whatever inner battle you're fighting right now, *please* let it go."

I move my hips again, this time pushing back against him. My breath catches, heart coming to a thudding stop when I feel the length of him against my ass. Heat slips over me, covering me from head to toe, arousal sparking from my every nerve ending. Like he's dropped a lit match on my gasoline-soaked insides, I burst into a giant flame of want. *For him.*

But then, as if suddenly noticing exactly what I'm feeling, he tries to pull back. I'm quick to cover his hands with mine, lacing our fingers.

"Cooper." It's a breathless plea, but the reality of what I want from him right now might push him away. It's completely out of bounds. Terrifying, even. But I can't help it, can't change how I'm feeling or the ideas flaring to life in my brain.

He squeezes my fingers and stops retreating, as if he can tell that I'm freaking out a little inside.

"Relax, Addie."

I take a deep breath and zone into the spread of his hands as they drift across my stomach, using the soft touch to ground me. I'm brave and strong and courageous. This is nothing. Asking him to do this is simple. Right?

Ripping off the Band-Aid, I lean up and say, "You owe me a favour, remember?"

He hums low in his throat. "I do, you wing bandit."

"I have a list! A list of all the dirty things I've never done and want to. Things I don't trust anyone enough to do with me!" I shout, loud enough that I wouldn't be surprised if my words carried over the music.

Seconds tick by with no response. My stomach curls into itself, rejection a knife to my pride. But just as I'm about to tell him I was just kidding and prepare to beg him to forget what I said, he draws his body from mine and quite literally drags me out of the club.

"Are you going to say anything?" I ask, unable to stand any more of this weird silence.

It's been twenty minutes since Cooper tore through the club with me in tow. He hailed a cab and didn't utter a single word the entire way back to the hotel. The elevator ride is beyond awkward as I stare at my reflection in the mirrors on the walls, annoyed by how damn frustrated I look.

I wonder if I should be embarrassed about what I said back there, but I'm not. If anything, it feels good to get that off my chest and tell someone for once.

I've wanted to experiment sexually for a couple of years now. There's something about pushing myself in that sense that makes my blood boil with intrigue. I've never had anyone to try the things I'm curious about with before. Nobody I've trusted enough. Until now, obviously.

I may only be twenty-one, but I'm damn old enough to know that I don't want boring vanilla sex with guys whose main concern is their pleasure and not so much mine for the rest of my life. It may scare the shit out of immature man-babies, but there's nothing wrong with a woman who knows what she wants, sexually or otherwise.

"If you're ignoring me because you're planning how to tell me that I shouldn't want to explore things or that I'm too young and don't know what I want, so help me, Cooper, I will rip your dick off and sho—"

"I wasn't going to say any of that."

I cross my arms and lean against the wall as the elevator climbs. "Great. So, what is it, then?"

"We're not having this conversation in an elevator, nor were we going to in a crowded club."

"I don't remember giving you permission to tell me what to do."

A deep, rough laugh escapes him as he crooks a brow at me. The air around us stills, the space growing tight. It's a struggle not to back down from his intense stare, but I hold my own.

"This is exactly why we're having this conversation in our room," he says.

"So, you can bully me into taking it back? Because that's not going to happen, Sparrow."

"You're fucking stubborn."

I flash my teeth. "And proud of it."

The elevator dings, and the doors open. I wait for Cooper to step out first, but he ushers me through the doors before following behind. Once we reach the room, he slips the key card into the door and swings it open. I drop my purse on a nearby bench seat and kick off my shoes.

"First of all," he starts, drawing my attention. I find him sitting on the edge of his bed, knees spread, fingers tugging at the buttons of his shirt. "A conversation like this doesn't happen in public. Especially not when you shout something like that for everyone to hear."

His fingers fall to the fourth button, exposing more of his chest, all while never taking his eyes off me. They're different tonight, and I'm a total fool for hoping it's me that sparked that change.

"I didn't shout it for everyone. Just you and whoever else managed to pick it up," I correct him.

"What did I tell you about that smart mouth?" he mutters.

Excitement buzzes through me. "I don't remember."

"Are you drunk?"

"Off one cocktail?" I snort. He doesn't so much as blink. "No, old man. I'm not drunk. Not in the slightest."

His stare darkens ever so slightly at the name, and I shiver beneath it. He undoes the final button on his shirt and then shrugs it off, carefully draping it over the back of the desk chair before saying, "Tell me what's on your list."

"My list . . ." I trail off, eyes wandering.

His chest is bare. So perfectly bare. It's not the first time I've seen him half-naked on this trip, but it must be the tension in the air tonight because holy fuck. He's sexy as hell.

While most of the guys I know have perfectly chiselled, hard-as-stone abs lining their stomachs, Cooper doesn't. He's just a wall of pure strength, no abs needed. Spackled with a dusting of dark hair, his torso is hard and wide. Shoulders thick, waist trim. I want to drag my hand up and down, side to side. Want to learn the feel of him and beg him to explore me in return.

I was wrong when I said I wasn't drunk. I am, but not on alcohol—on lust. *Good god, I'm lust drunk.*

17

Adalyn

"ADALYN. YOUR LIST. WHAT'S ON IT?"

I gulp, forcing my eyes up. He's watching me with a coy smile, and I pull one leg in front of the other, the throb between them becoming nearly unbearable. When his stare falls to watch me squeeze them together, I bite the inside of my cheek to keep a beg from slipping out. *He would love that too much.*

A muscle flutters in his jaw as his eyes caress my bare legs. My heart flutters at that look, at the pure approval dripping from it.

"Once I tell you, you can't pretend you don't know. The knowledge of what I want will be there forever," I tell him softly, carefully.

A heavy pause and then, "Go on."

Nerves make my skin warm, but I refuse to let it stop me now. Pulling my shoulders back, I take three confident steps toward him, leaving only an arm's length between us.

"The idea of sex in public turns me on, and I think I want to try it. I want someone to choke me hard enough I see stars, and . . ." I pause, my heart thumping hard and fast as I fight to keep eye contact. My next words are shaky. "Anal. I'm curious if I might like it, but I'm scared I won't."

Cooper's expression visibly shudders when I finish. The silence smothers us. Seconds pass, each one making my nerves multiply in my stomach.

"That's quite the list." His voice is strained, pulled tight.

I swallow, nodding.

He clears his throat. "You mentioned a favour. I'm assuming that this list is what you had in mind."

I nod again.

"I can't help you with this."

The blood drains from my face as I stand in front of him, feeling so damn vulnerable. My deepest wants and desires are on full display for him, and his dismissal—although the slightest bit excepted—cuts deep. But I refuse to feel embarrassed just as much as I refuse to ignore the desire I saw in his eyes just seconds ago.

"If this is because of my brother, I don't accept your refusal. We're already married, Cooper. *Married*! And until we sign either an annulment or a divorce, it's going to stay that way. What better way to learn how to appear intimate with each other than actually *being* intimate," I argue, my voice growing in strength with each sentence.

"It's more than just your brother. It's your entire family. I don't think when they told me to keep you safe on this trip that they meant for me to touch and fuck you in all the ways you're wanting. We may be married, but you're my friend first. And as your friend, I'm telling you that this isn't a smart move."

I must be too far gone in a fog of lust because my ears snag on the way he says fuck, like he's almost angry at the word, and keeps it on replay in my head.

"You say that as if they won't already be pissed at us for getting married. Plus, who's going to tell them about this? Me? You? *Nobody* is going to tell anyone." I can see the indecisiveness in his stare as I lift my chin and deliver my final blow, hoping it blasts apart the last of his stubborn refusal. "And as my friend, you would be the best person to help me. If it's not you, then I'll have to ask someone else, and I don't trust people easy, so who knows if I'll just eventually want to experiment so bad that I just go rogue? By the time I can't wait anymore, maybe I'll just take someone home from a club one night and—"

"Strip."

The world stills. "What?"

His eyes flash as he slips them over my body, interest snagging on my chest—on my nipples—for the briefest second.

"I told you that mouth of yours was going to get you into trouble. Now, take off your dress and sit on the bed. Then we'll discuss rules."

"So, you're saying yes?"

"That depends on how well you can take orders, which so far doesn't look promising."

"I'm not wearing a bra."

A brow quirks. "That's not new information."

Alright then. With a quick inhale, I pull my dress up and over my head and then lay it over his shirt on the chair. The change in temperature has my nipples tightening. I don't have to glance down to know they're hard and pointed directly at him.

"Sit," he orders, softer this time.

I move around him and do as he says, the bedding smooth and cool beneath my thighs. "Was this a test?"

He turns to face me and meets my stare, his eyes seemingly intent on not wandering. *I wish they would.*

"Yes. It's one thing to say you want something, and it's another to actually mean it. If we do this, there's no forgetting it ever happened. You'll remember this for the rest of your life, and I won't have you hating me or yourself for it."

"You think awful highly of yourself to believe I'll never

forget what we do together," I mutter before I can think better of it.

Those intense eyes flare with heat. "I don't just believe it, Adalyn. I can guarantee it."

"We'll see."

He hums low in his throat, eyes dipping to my chest. I can't help but arch beneath the weight of his stare. "When did you get your nipples pierced?"

"Two years ago."

It was a spur-of-the-moment decision I made while standing in front of my bathroom mirror, naked and wet from a shower, curious as to what my boobs would look like pierced. A few hours later, I had bars through both nipples, and six months after that, I became a nipple play whore.

"Are they sensitive?" he asks.

"Very."

"Show me."

My lips part on a silent gasp, my stomach dipping with both anticipation and a new kind of nervousness. He must take my silence as a refusal because before I can take my next breath, he's closed the distance between us and pinched my chin between two fingers, using the grip to tip my head back.

"I want you to play with your nipples while I tell you how this is going to work. If you're not comfortable enough to do that with me, then we're not continuing. I'm not going to force you into something you think you're ready for but really aren't. This isn't a simple transaction. We're not going to risk relationships with those we love over something you don't really want. I'm taking this risk because there's no possible way I'm letting you do these things with anyone you don't trust. Do you understand?"

I nod quickly, speaking a foreign concept.

His thumb travels the length of my bottom lip. "You are in control of this. This is your list, your fantasy. If you change your mind, it's done. We back away. We move on and continue this trip the way we were this morning. But if you're sure, you need to show me. If you decide afterward that this isn't what you want, we stop, but there won't be much forgetting once we start."

"I understand," I breathe.

Without hesitating any longer, I bring my hands to my breasts and brush my thumbs over my nipples before pinching them softly. The swell of pleasure between my legs is instant, and I bite my lip to stifle a whimper. Approval glows in his eyes, and it only intensifies the feeling.

"You're in charge of what we do, but I don't release control easily. I need some semblance of it. When I tell you to do something, I expect you to do it. We'll need a safe word so I know when you're uncomfortable and want to stop."

"Okay," I whisper.

He watches me tug at my nipples, the diamonds on the tips of the bars between them bumping against my fingers. The useless scrap of fabric between my legs is drenched, and as I squeeze my legs together, I feel my arousal slick on my inner thighs.

"Pick a word."

"Please." It escapes me without a second thought.

He laughs quietly. "A different word. That one will do the opposite of stop me. Especially when you say it like that."

It's hard to think about anything besides how badly I want this. With each tweak of my nipples, it's growing harder to keep quiet. I feel like I could burst, the stimulation almost too much.

"Skateboard," I rush out.

He nods. "Good. Now, stop touching yourself and place your hands in your lap."

With a frown, I reluctantly drop my hands, folding them over my tense thighs. It's easier to breathe now as my blood stops boiling, settling on a simmer instead.

"Is there anything else on your list that you haven't told me yet?" he asks.

"No."

"Okay." Nodding, he reaches for his belt and begins unbuckling it. He moves it slowly through each loop on his pants as if trying to tease me, but I only grow more excited than frustrated. "The first rule is no sex."

"What do you mean?" I sputter, eyes wide.

"I can show you everything on your list without having sex with you."

"Are you kidding? Is this your attempt at blue balling me? Because if so, you're a royal asshole."

His lips lift into a subtle smile. "No. I just want to keep the line clear. Sex will complicate things even more than they are now."

"I don't accept these terms."

He shrugs. "Then we don't continue."

My stomach sours. "Do you not want to? Am I not your type or something?"

He looks down his body, and I do the same, finding the thick ridge of him pressing against his slacks. My already shaky resolve threatens to disappear completely.

"It's not a matter of whether I want to. You're every man's type. Mine included. But we just can't," he says.

"You say that now. But you can always change your mind."

"I could. But it won't happen."

The messed-up part of my brain that turns everything into a dare flickers to life. He can say that he won't give in, but I think he's just afraid to admit to himself that he's wrong. I don't go down without a fight.

"Fine. Can we start now?"

"So impatient," he coos, smoothing a hand over his hair.

"You would be, too, if I had you stroking your dick for ten minutes only to tell you to stop before you got off."

Desire sparks in his stare. "Is that how good it feels for you when you play with your nipples? The equivalent of me stroking myself?"

I exhale shakily. "Yes. The piercings made them sensitive enough that I've almost come from just nipple play."

"Almost? You never have?"

Oh God. Would he— "No."

"That should have been on your list."

"Oops, my bad. It actually is. Let's not forget to cross it off." I smirk.

He rolls his eyes before stepping closer. I part my legs on instinct, and he moves between them. Holding still, I watch him wet his lips before cautiously bringing his hand up to cup my cheek. It's an innocent enough touch, but I'm too damn horny to think about it rationally. Instead, my body screams at me for release, and the words just tumble out.

"Make me come, Cooper. Fucking *please* just make me come before I lose my goddamn mind," I plead, attempting to shut my legs, knowing damn well I can't ease the throb between them with him in the way.

His smile is barely there, just big enough for me to catch a glimpse of it before it's gone. "See, I told you you'd know when to beg."

And then I'm falling backward, my body sinking into the mattress and Cooper's hands hot on my skin.

18

Cooper

Adalyn will be the death of me. She knows exactly where my buttons are and just how hard to press them to make me lose both my mind and control. I would never back away from this, knowing she was going to go out and find someone else to help her explore all of the things occupying her mind, and she damn well knows it.

I know that it should be wrong to feel as protective of her as I do. But even as I watch her splayed out before me, those long, toned legs beneath my fingertips, skin so damn soft, it feels the furthest thing from wrong.

"If you're even the slightest bit unsure about this, tell me to stop before everything changes," I murmur.

Trailing my fingers up her legs, I swallow a groan at the sight of the goosebumps that rise at my touch, as if I commanded them to the surface. She's so beautiful it's hard to believe it was me she asked for this.

"Don't stop. I might die if you do," she breathes, fingers spread tensely on the comforter like she's struggling not to reach out and touch me.

I slip my palms over her knees and her thighs, moving up,

up, up, before sliding outward to her hips. She wiggles in my hold, lips jutting out in a pout.

"Let's explore later," she huffs.

"Good things come to those who wait," I purr, dipping my head to brush my nose across her lower stomach. My tongue darts out as I lick above the band of the tiny panties she's wearing.

She gasps, hips pushing up. I press my hand over her belly button to hold her in place and look up at her through my lashes. "Tell me what you want from me," I order.

"You've got to be kidding," she huffs.

"Do you want me to stop?"

Her eyes spark with annoyance. "No."

"Then tell me."

She sucks in a slow, determined breath. "Put your mouth on me."

"Where?" I kiss the taut muscles of her abdomen, just below her rib cage. "Here?"

"Higher," she whimpers.

I move higher, to the underside of her right breast. "Here?"

"Higher."

Those tense fingers finally move from the sheets, threading through my hair and scratching my scalp. Her grip is tight but not painful, and I reward her for finally giving in to the moment by sucking just beneath her nipple.

The mewling sound she releases has me aching in my underwear. I want to reach down and pop the button of my slacks to relieve the pressure, but I don't. Not when this is about her.

She deserves all of my attention. Every last bit of it.

The moment I wrap my lips around her nipple and give it a gentle, cautious suck, her body quakes beneath me. A breathy moan fills the room as the taste of her fills my mouth.

I roll my tongue over the metal bar and the studs on either side before sucking again, harder this time.

"Holy fuck," she cries out, nails pressing into the back of my head. "More."

She begs so beautifully. Each plea is like a hand wrapped tight around my cock, stroking once before disappearing. I want more of it. Would go wild in my attempt to pull another one from her.

"You're getting the hang of it now," I rasp, pulling her nipple between my teeth and biting down softly.

Arching her neck, she pants out a curse, tightening her legs at my sides. I smooth a hand over her stomach and palm her other tit, squeezing it roughly. The piercing scrapes at my palm before I start to pinch her nipple between my fingers and tug.

"Cooper," she whines, a pair of deep blue, desire-drunk eyes meeting mine, snuffing out the air surrounding us with a single glance.

Fuck. This is a picture I'll never forget. She would be a beautiful painting. A prized portrait on a wall, hung above all the others. It would take hours, maybe even days, to get the exact colour of her eyes right. Not too blue but not grey. Not teal or navy. They deserve a name of their own, reserved only for her.

"Tell me how to get you there without touching your pussy," I groan into her wet skin.

She curls one leg behind mine, and I don't know if it's because she's trying to pull me closer or if she just wants more leverage. Either way, I reach back and hold behind her knee, keeping her steady.

"Pull on them. Bite them. Just a little more," she pants, eyes squeezing shut. "It's right there. This is where it stops."

Determination strokes down my spine as I bite the nipple in my mouth and twist the other at the same time. I should be tearing that scrap of fabric from between her legs and thrusting two fingers inside of her right now in my effort to get her off, but as much as it kills me to make her wait, I know this will be ten times more rewarding for both of us.

"Again." It's both a cry and a plea, and I don't hesitate before complying.

My heart thumps rapidly in my chest as I watch her fall apart beneath me. An expression I never dreamed of witnessing crosses her features, knocking the breath from my lungs as her sounds of pleasure bury themselves deep in my memories.

"So good," she mewls, heel digging into the inside of my thigh, nails biting the back of my neck. "So *fucking* good."

I can't look away from her, even after I settle back on my knees and steady my heart rate. Her cheeks are stained a deep red as dark as her lips. A primal feeling claws at me when I watch her lick those lips and whimper as the pleasure seeps away.

What would it have felt like to kiss her? Is she as impatient when she kisses as she is when she begs to come? It shouldn't matter, but for some reason I can't seem to shake, it does.

"Are you okay?" I ask after a moment of silence.

"Mmhmm. Very okay. Are you?"

"Yes."

"I am a bit tired, though." Her smile is soft, almost shy.

Blonde, blue, and pink hair covers the white duvet. She looks so tired as she watches me, blinking slowly. I don't know what time it is, just that it's late.

"You should sleep," I say, pushing off the bed.

Fingers wrapping around my wrist keep me from getting too far. I glance back at her as she says, "You haven't changed your mind now, have you?"

"Why would I do that?"

She rolls her lips. "You're just leaving quick. I wasn't expecting you to cuddle me or anything, but maybe sit with me for a while. I haven't even thanked you yet."

I frown. She thinks I'm running off? "You don't have to thank me. And I was just giving you some time to get ready for bed. You look like you're about to fall asleep."

"You should never tell a woman that she looks tired, Sparrow."

"Don't start with me. Go take your makeup off before you fall asleep with it on and then complain to me first thing in the morning when you have flakes of mascara in your eyes. I'll be here when you come back."

With a lighthearted huff, she crawls out of bed and rushes to the bathroom, swiping the T-shirt she wore earlier from the floor along the way.

"Fucking hell," I whisper to myself.

How is it that we can do something as intimate as what transpired a few minutes ago and then go back to normal like it never happened? I've never experienced a situation like this before.

I've been with a few women over the years, but it's never been as easy as this. Maybe I should have expected this. Adalyn may be my wife, but she was my friend first. She still is.

When the tap begins to run in the bathroom, I chuck off my slacks, exchanging them for some loose sleep pants. I debate tossing a shirt on but decide against it before adjusting Adalyn's pillows and pulling back the duvet so she can crawl straight into bed.

By the time she wanders out of the bathroom, I've managed to wish away my hard-on and prop myself on the bed with the TV on. Wearing nothing but an oversized graphic tee that reaches her mid-thigh, she looks toward the bed and grins when she spots me waiting.

She flops down beside me and pulls the covers up to her chin. "What are we watching?"

"What are you in the mood for?"

"Something scary."

I chuckle, opening the menu on the TV. "I should have known you like horror shows."

"Because I'm so terrifying?" She bares her teeth at me teasingly.

"That's definitely it."

Settling on a ghost-hunting show, we fall silent for a moment, both of us curious.

"No matter how fake these shows are, I can't help but love them," she says once the show fades to commercial. "They're hilarious."

"My mom loves these shows," I tell her, glancing down to find her watching me. She tilts her head, expression open and curious. "We watched them a lot when I was growing up. When she would come visit me at Dad's, we were either always watching old Disney cartoon movies or some sort of paranormal chasing show."

"I don't think I know much about your childhood. Only what I heard in passing."

I nod. "Up until I was a teenager, Mom only ever really saw me at Dad's house. We went out, too, but only if Dad were with us. You've probably heard how she was when I was a baby."

Mom's bipolar disorder is a topic we don't really discuss outside of our family. Adalyn's parents know everything, but there wasn't much reason to spread it around beyond our inner circle. There are still days when I realize Mom hasn't forgiven herself for keeping me a secret from Dad for those first couple of years, but if I had it my way, she would have let it go years ago.

She was brave enough to bring me to him when she knew she needed help, and we've been a family ever since.

When I was younger, it was hard to understand why she did the things she did, like handing over parental rights to Dad instead of sharing them. Of course, I assumed she did that because she didn't love me as much as I loved her, but I've long since understood her actions and have grown to respect them.

I've watched her take her life back and become the happiest version of herself.

"Your mom is a badass, Coop. And she makes amazing lemon bars," Adalyn says, grabbing my hand from atop the blankets and threading our fingers together.

I pull our hands to my lap. "I'll make sure to tell her that the next time I talk to her."

"Please do. I have a sinking feeling that she favours Maddox, and that just won't do."

Laughing, I run my thumb over her knuckles. "So, you plan on buying her favouritism with compliments?"

"Bribery at its finest."

"Something tells me that you don't need to bribe anyone to love you. They just can't help themselves."

Her eyes twinkle beneath the light of the TV. "Better tread carefully, then. Wouldn't want you to get bit by the Addiebug."

Something tells me to heed her warning.

19

Adalyn

"Your dad would run me over with a semi-truck if he knew what we were about to do," Cooper mutters.

"He definitely would. But it's a risk I'm willing to take."

He snorts a laugh. "Nice to know you're okay with the idea of your dad running me over."

"Don't be dramatic, Sparrow. He won't find out."

"Sometimes I think you forget who you are. The second one of your fans sees us out there, we're going to be all over social media."

"Don't tell me you're backing out now. We're already ready to go!"

"Consider it a lapse of judgment."

"Come on," I groan. "Step outside of the box with me. How many people can say they've been to a nude beach in France?"

"Not many sane people, I would assume."

She rolls her eyes. "Don't make me go by myself. Knock this off my bucket list with me."

"Who even has this on their bucket list?"

"People like me," I snap, a little offended.

He blows out a breath. "I didn't mean it like that. You're

just not like me. That's not a bad thing, just different. I'm trying to adjust here, and you want me to dive in blind."

"I hate to break it to you, but I'm pretty sure we already did that last night. It's too late to back out now, just like you said."

Memories from last night fill my head, making me swallow harshly. I half expected today to be awkward between us, but it's been the exact opposite. We're as normal as can be. Just two good friends spending their final day in Paris together as if they didn't just agree to embark on a weird sexual relationship the night before.

"We both know I wasn't referencing going to a nude beach," he says.

I chew on the inside of my lip, contemplating my next words. "I swear I won't look if that's what you're nervous about."

"It's not you looking that makes me nervous."

"Oh. You're shy?"

"I'm not shy. I just can't say I've ever had the urge to strip naked and show random people my soft dick."

From what I remember seeing last night, he doesn't have any reason to be shy about his dick. Even in a pair of slacks, he looked massive.

"You don't have to get completely naked where we would go. But even if you did, I guarantee some of them would enjoy the view."

"Them or you?"

I hold back a smirk. "I thought I wasn't looking."

"*Right.*"

"*Pretty* please come. I did a lot of research before I decided I wanted to visit this place. Being naked in public might seem like a sexual thing to you, but to most nudists, it's completely normal. There's nothing sexual about it."

I can't say what possessed me to want to visit a nude

beach, but there's no way I'm leaving without checking it off my list. I'm too close now.

It's not for everyone, and I would never force Cooper to come with me if he truly didn't want to. All he has to do is tell me no and I'll let it go. I'm sure he could find something to do while I'm there.

He rakes his fingers through his hair and looks at me with a no-bullshit expression. "I'll come. But if things get weird, I'm leaving."

"If things get weird, we'll *both* leave. 'Kay?"

"Okay."

"Thank you!" I grab his cheeks and pull him down to my level so I can kiss all over his face before stepping back. "I'll have the front desk call a cab for us."

He nods, standing frozen for a moment before clearing his throat and beginning to fuss with his suitcase. A buzz of excitement travels through me as I get our ride sorted.

An hour later, we're dropped off in a packed parking lot along the highway. Hills keep the beach hidden from the view of traffic. If it weren't for the sign in front of a break in the hills, you wouldn't be able to tell a beach was hidden here.

My beach bag swings off Cooper's shoulder as we stand together in silence. I want to run toward the beach, but he looks reluctant.

"We'll stay together, and if it's too much, we'll leave," I tell him, laying a hand on his arm.

"Yeah, alright. Come on." He leads me toward the beach with a reassuring, steady hand on my back. I press back into the touch, loving it more than I should.

The moment the beach comes into view, I gasp, jaw hanging loose. I've seen my fair share of boobs during photoshoots, but this is so far beyond that. I rub my eyes just to see if I somehow passed out in the cab and entered boob dreamland. *Nope.* Still here.

"Holy tits," I breathe, glancing at Cooper.

He's staring up at the sky, face so red it probably feels sunburnt. I giggle, pulling his attention.

"Are you laughing at me?"

I touch my pointer finger to my thumb, holding them between us and saying, "Maybe a little."

"You think it's funny now, but wait until you see a swinging dick."

"Nah, I prefer boobs. Much prettier to look at."

His eyes fall to my chest, so intense it seems as if he might be trying to undress me with his eyes. "That's something we can agree on."

I wet my lips and pull my shirt off before he has a chance to add anything else. The summer air caresses my bare skin, and I sigh out a relaxed breath.

"A warning next time, Adalyn," he tells me, voice much deeper now.

"It's not anything you haven't seen before," I tease.

"That's true, but this is a public place. Go easy on me."

An idea strikes me then, one that Cooper would most likely say no to. But then again, he did agree to help me with my list, didn't he?

I push that away for now as we search the beach for someplace to sit. It's a task not gawking at the people around, especially when this is such a new experience, but I do my best to be respectful.

We find a more secluded area on the beach, a bit away from the large crowds of people. Most of those around us are just topless, not fully nude. Maybe we found the nude beach newbie section.

Cooper is quick to spread our blanket over the sand and sit, staring out at the water. I shimmy out of my flowy skirt and join him in just my bikini bottoms, not feeling the least bit nervous about being half-naked. It's empowering being able to just not give a fuck about other people and free the nips.

Leaning against him, I pinch his T-shirt and wiggle my

eyebrows. "You're more dressed now than you would be at a normal beach."

Laughing softly, he reaches behind his head and pulls the shirt off before setting it beside him.

"Better?"

"Much." Desire pools low in my belly at the sight of him shirtless. It seems something snapped inside of me when it comes to him last night. I think I like whatever is going on here. "Would it be cliché of me to ask you to rub sunscreen on my back?"

He huffs a laugh. "Yes, but I'd do it anyway."

"Thank you." I grab the bottle from my bag and hand it to him.

Squirting some into his palm, he flicks his eyes to the blanket. "You're welcome. Are you going to lie down or just spin around?"

"Do you have a preference?" I ask. It comes out sounding far dirtier than I meant it to.

"I'd prefer you on your stomach, but I don't think all of these people want to see me straddling your back, so maybe just sit in front of me."

He scoots back on the blanket and then spreads his legs, making room for me between them. Once I'm settled in front of him, his knees bent at my sides, he starts to smear the lotion across my back. A moan slips free of its own accord as he digs his fingers into my shoulders and then spreads them outward, over to the back of my biceps.

"Would you prefer a massage?" he asks in a light, teasing tone.

"Are you offering?"

"Maybe later. I think you would scandalize the beach too much if I did that here."

My lips curl into a small smile. "Do you have magic fingers or something?"

His hands freeze on my back for the slightest moment

before moving again. "I don't know about magic, but I haven't had any complaints before."

"I don't know if I believe you."

His chest rumbles with a quiet laugh. "Are you trying to provoke me, Adalyn?"

My breathing speeds up. "That depends."

"On?"

"If it's working," I breathe.

His thumbs push up my back, pressing deep into the muscle on their way to my neck. The moment he starts to knead the skin below my hairline, I whimper.

I feel him move closer, his front so close to my back I can feel the heat radiating from him. A warm gush of air brushes the back of my ear.

"Don't make that noise here," he whispers, fingers trailing down toward the dip of my spine.

I curl my fingers into the blanket in front of me and glance at him over my shoulder. His eyes meet mine. They're dark, edged with something I want to dig my fingers into.

Last night changed something between us, broke some wall that kept us from allowing our minds to wander to this sexual place, and now I can't seem to go back. We've been here for all of five minutes, and I already want to push him onto his back and crawl up his body.

"Take me somewhere I can be noisy, then."

"Adalyn." It's a warning.

I blow right past the warning when I drop my head back against his shoulder and lean against him, ensuring our bodies are flush. The feel of him hard against my back is enough to sever the last of my willpower.

"What is happening right now?" I breathe. I'm hot beneath my skin, burning from the inside out.

His hands fall to my thighs as he holds them in place, not allowing me to spread them like I want to.

"It's the atmosphere," he rumbles.

I shake my head. "It's not." It's not sexual here. The people might be naked, but they don't matter. I haven't even looked at them since we've arrived. "This is all for you."

His fingers press harder into my skin. "What is?"

"Touch me and find out."

"Fuck," he grinds out.

"Yes."

"Adalyn." He says it again like it's both a curse and a blessing.

"You want me too. I can feel how badly you do."

"Then I won't bother pretending otherwise. But it isn't happening."

This time when I look at him, I find him searching the beach, jaw tense. I open my mouth to ask what he's looking for when he pushes to a sudden stand, bringing me with him.

He pulls me close to his body, keeping me blocked from the view of the majority of people behind us. His next words make my stomach drop with excitement the way it does when you fall from the top of a roller coaster.

"A nude beach isn't where I thought we would cross off your fantasy of public sex, but I guess we'll take what we can get."

20

Adalyn

Cooper finds an enclosed area a few feet down the beach. It's a small rock face separating the main beach from a deserted section, not too far from everyone else but far enough the odds of someone stumbling over here and finding us are slim.

A full-body shudder moves through me as the idea of someone stumbling upon us doing whatever it is Cooper has planned sends me spiralling. My bikini bottoms are so damp I want to tear them off and throw them away. I'm goddamn needy, desperate beyond belief.

My knees go weak as he pins me against a smooth rock, cushioning the back of my head with his hand. The desire in his eyes makes the world around us disappear. It's only him and me and the sexual tension between us that's grown so strong I don't stand a chance at fighting it. As if I would want to.

His breath is hot on my face as he moves even closer, naked chest against naked chest. "Do you want me to find somewhere else?"

"Fuck no. This is perfect."

"You can't be loud out here. You need to be quiet, or I'll have to stop."

At this point, I'm pretty sure I would agree to just about anything if it meant he would put me out of my misery and just touch me.

I grip his waist and pull, still not satisfied with how far apart we are. But maybe he isn't either because he grabs me beneath my thighs and lifts me, pressing me into the rocks. He settles between my legs, and the pressure of his cock against my centre has my eyes rolling back, shocks of ecstasy rippling through me.

"If you don't touch me, Cooper, I will be loud for an entirely different reason," I warn, wrapping my thighs tight around his waist.

His eyelids droop over those pretty brown eyes of his as he glances between us, his lips parting on a deep, growly noise. I nearly scream when he drops his hand and brushes his thumb over my core, the touch featherlight.

"More," I sigh, pushing my hips to try and get more pressure.

Slowly, he hooks his finger into the side of my bikini bottoms and moves them to the side, exposing me. I whimper, watching his finger move toward where I'm slick and ready for him.

He slides that finger over my slit a single time, groaning, "This is all for me?"

I nod furiously. "God yes. I told you it was."

Approval flashes across his features. "Can I taste you, Adalyn? Can you be quiet enough for me to do that?"

Jesus Christ. *Have mercy on me, please.*

"Yes."

My approval is all he needs to hear before he's pushing me up the rock wall and dropping to his knees. He sets my legs on his shoulders, and I thread my fingers through his hair, gripping it to hold myself steady.

"Holy fuck," I hiss when he cups my ass in his hands and squeezes, using his hold to pull me so close my pussy is just a breath away from his mouth.

"I won't fuck you, but there are so many other things I can do to you that don't involve my cock. All of which I plan on being very, very thorough with."

My fingers curl in his hair. "Then what are you waiting for?"

He grins up at me from between my legs before leaning forward and dragging his tongue up my wet flesh. I tear one hand out of his hair and slam it on the rock wall as I bury my teeth in my lip to stifle my scream.

My thighs quiver when he covers me with his mouth and slowly circles his tongue around my clit, drawing noises from me that I never knew existed. Waves upon waves of pleasure unravel me at the seams faster than I can keep myself together.

"Quiet," he orders, digging his fingertips into my ass cheek.

I bang my head back against the rock wall, but the small bite of pain does nothing to subdue the pure bliss. "That's easy for you to say. You try having to be quiet with your cock down my throat."

"I guarantee I could be quieter," he rasps before sucking my clit between his lips.

I squeeze my eyes shut, fire building in my belly. "Want to bet on that, old man?"

A finger slipping inside of me has my eyes flaring open. Cooper's brow is arched in a silent dare as he sinks that finger deep, stretching me.

"Say it again."

I heave a breath and slowly lick my lips. I drag my fingers to his mouth, pressing my thumb into his bottom lip.

"Say what again, old man?"

The next few seconds move quickly. Suddenly, my feet are

hitting the sand, and Cooper's standing in front of me, his hands firmly holding my shoulders. That playful gleam in his eyes is gone, replaced now by something heavy and daring. It's a look that demands respect.

"Get on your knees."

Excitement bubbles in my blood. "Yes, sir."

Falling to my knees before him, I let my hands wander over his legs and up over his hips and waist. He's so hard all over, so firm, like he must work out every single day, yet he hasn't been to the gym once since we've been together.

He towers over me like this, all that thick male energy and confidence raining down on me. My eyes are level with the bulge in his swim trunks, and I tug at the waistband, glancing up for permission.

A firm hand smooths the hair at the top of my head before looping it around a fist and pulling just enough to tilt my head back.

"You're going to suck my cock, Adalyn, and then you're going to swallow my cum and let it wash that fucking name out of your mouth. Do you understand?"

I don't bother with words.

With a stifled moan, I tear down his shorts and watch in awe as his cock comes into view. My mouth waters as I take in the hard length of him and then whisper a broken "Fuck" at the metal gleaming up the shaft.

The last person in the world I expected to have a dick piercing was Cooper. But it's right there. And there isn't just one. There are three. A Jacob's fucking ladder.

My heart skips too many beats as I reach out a cautious hand and wrap my fingers around him. He's too big for them to touch completely, but by the sharp intake of breath above me, he doesn't seem to mind. I stroke him a single time, my grip firm.

"If I knew all it would take to get you to stop arguing would be to drop my shorts, I would have done that days ago," he mutters, using his grip on my hair to guide me forward until my lips brush the drop of liquid on his tip.

I keep my eyes on his as I lick it off, making a show of moaning at the taste of him. "Will I hurt you? I've never done this with anyone with these piercings."

"Just keep your fangs to yourself," he murmurs, stroking his knuckles down the side of my face before pinching my chin and forcing my lips open. "Now, suck."

I lean forward and take him in my mouth. Slowly at first, just swirling my tongue over the head, lapping at the cum he can't seem to stop leaking. Knowing that he wants me as badly as I want him has my eyes trying to roll back in my head.

His grip on my hair tightens as he inches closer, forcing me to take more, until the first set of silver balls pass my lips. I breathe through my nose and push further, only stopping when he hits my throat.

"That's it. You can take more," he groans, breathing harshly.

I can, and I make damn sure that I do. Not for his pleasure—not entirely—but for mine. It took far too long to learn how to push past my gag reflex, and what good is that skill if I don't use it on a cock as nice as Cooper's?

Resting my hands on his hips, I look up and meet his dark stare as I push forward, taking him into my throat. I dig my fingers into the sides of his ass cheeks as I reach the final set of piercings and then move back, sucking on the tip of him before starting my descent again.

Complete, unabashed pleasure ricochets across his features, and it makes me preen, knowing I've made him feel so good. It's an addictive feeling, and I know immediately that I want to feel it again. Multiple times, if possible. The praise whore inside of me rears her head and bellows with pride.

"Fuck," he hisses when my nose bumps his pelvis, and I whimper, rubbing my thighs together.

I wouldn't be surprised if there was a puddle on the sand

beneath me. My breasts hang heavy, nipples hard, begging for his touch.

Pulling off his dick, I lick the tip and hum, letting the vibrations travel down his shaft. "You're not being very quiet, you know."

His face tightens, throat bobbing with a heavy swallow. "I wasn't expecting you to be able to deep-throat me like it brings you pleasure to do so."

"It does bring me pleasure, Cooper," I purr, cupping his balls, rolling them softly. "But do you know what I would love even more?"

"*Shit.* What?"

"For you to fill my mouth."

I move my hand from his balls to his shaft, gripping the base and stroking as I slip him back inside my mouth and reach between my legs to touch myself. I'm so slick my finger sinks inside instantly, heat flaring through me.

Moaning around him, I use my arousal to rub circles around my clit, already so close to reaching an orgasm that it won't take long to get there. A few more seconds—

"Get up and face the rocks," he orders gruffly, softly urging me to ease off his shaft.

I could cry as I reluctantly pull my hand from between my legs and stare at him, so keyed up my eyes blur with tears. "Please, Cooper."

"Please what?"

"Let me come. I can't take it anymore," I whisper. Sitting back on my heels, I set my hands in my lap and realize I'm shaking.

The hard persona he adapted when he demanded I get on my knees softens as he cups my face and drifts his thumbs beneath my eyes, where the skin is surprisingly dry.

"Just a little bit longer. You're doing so well. So good for me."

I nod, and he offers me his hand, guiding me to face the

rock wall. As he settles behind me, his fingers move down my back and over my hips before tucking beneath the band of my bikini bottoms. When the bottoms start descending down my legs and pool at my ankles, I press my palms to the rocks and heave a breath.

"If a man doesn't fall to his knees and thank you for sucking his cock by making you come on his tongue, please leave him, Adalyn. He doesn't deserve you."

I bury my face into my arm and scream when his mouth seals over my wet, swollen flesh, and two thick fingers slide inside. My head clears of all thought, my ears ringing. I'm barely aware of the distant sound of voices and how they start to grow louder, as if whoever is speaking is moving closer, but I can't think past my own pleasure.

The moment a third finger fills me and curls, my knees are shaking. Fuck, my everything is shaking.

"I'm going to come."

"That's a good girl. Give it to me. Everything, Adalyn. *Now.*"

My teeth sink into my arm when an orgasm more intense than any I've ever experienced slams into me, bringing something feral with it. My vision darkens as I curl against the rocks, arms too weak to support my body.

I sense Cooper move behind me, and the sound of his grunts mixed with a wet slapping noise only intensifies my release. Imagining what he's doing behind me . . . *fuck.* As if on instinct, I push myself to spin around and fall to the same position as just moments ago before shoving his hand from his cock and pulling it into my mouth instead.

Our eyes clash and hold as he grits his jaw and releases on my tongue and down my throat. I swallow it all, taking and taking and taking from him.

Blood pounding in my ears, I wait for him to finish and then pull away, licking my lips.

"That was . . ." I trail off, a tired smile tugging at the

corners of my mouth. Aftershocks have me unable to get up just yet.

Cooper scrapes a hand down his face and nods. Reaching for his shorts, he tugs them up and goes to take a step toward me but stops himself. He settles for glancing over my body, as if to make sure I'm not hurt.

"Are you okay?"

"Are you kidding? Of course I am. You're insane, Cooper. Like, in the *best* way."

Colour stains his cheeks. "Likewise."

Feeling bashful, I stand, pull up my bottoms, and close the distance between us to hug him tight. A blanket of contentment falls over me as the reality of what just happened sinks in, but it doesn't scare me. I press my cheek to his chest and sigh when he wraps those big arms around me and holds me tight.

"Your heart is beating fast," I say softly, nuzzling into him.

He laughs, the sound so genuine. "Yeah, it is."

21

Cooper

sparrow

I spend the rest of the day watching Addie swim in the ocean, making friends with damn near everyone she comes into contact with. And when she comes running to me with arms outstretched and the sun beginning to set on the horizon, asking me to join her in the water, I let her pull me along.

I'm pretty sure I would do anything if it meant seeing her smile at me afterward.

It happened out of nowhere, but I care about her deeply, in a different way than before. In a way that goes far beyond friendship and responsibility. I want her to be happy always, even if it means I have to turn my skin wrinkled from spending hours in the ocean with her to do it.

Things are changing so quickly between us, yet it feels so natural. Sure, our marriage and Adalyn's list might have pressed fast forward on it in some way, but it doesn't feel wrong. What happened between us on that beach felt too good to be anything but right.

The thought of flying home when this is all said and done and not having her beside me on a daily basis drops a rock in my gut. I feel possessive of her. Jealous of everyone who gets to share her time with me. Angry at anyone who's ever made her sad.

We still have time to plan for what comes next, but I'm beginning to wonder if an annulment is the right move. Is it bad to be curious about if this could actually work between us? Fuck. I'm in way over my head here. *I need to slow down.*

Subconsciously, I rub my ring finger and tuck those thoughts away to deal with later.

"Don't tell me you're not hungry after complaining about it the entire way here," Adalyn says, pointing her straw accusingly at me across the table.

The cheeseburger in front of me is untouched, with only a few fries missing from my plate. It's just a normal food choice, but after spending the past few weeks trying different types of food, I was craving something boring and familiar.

"I'm trying to savour it," I reply, deadpan.

She rolls those beautiful blue eyes and fights back a smile. "Savour a burger? Who are you?"

I stare pointedly at her plate, at the few bites missing. "Looks like you're doing the same."

"I'm trying to not shove my face full the way I want to with the table of girls watching us," she sighs. Glancing at the two teenagers a few tables away, she paints on a smile and waves. "We've done so good at not being recognized only for our streak to be ruined at a bistro in France. I'm sorry."

"Don't apologize. Do you want to say hi to them?"

"Is it rude of me to say no?"

I shake my head. "You don't owe them anything."

She eats a french fry. "I've enjoyed just being a normal person with you. I haven't been missing checking my social media a million times a day and posting photos that I don't really care about. I've just been Addie the person with you, not Adalyn Hutton the social figure. But I guess it couldn't last forever."

My chest tightens at the genuine sadness in her eyes as she

shrugs and takes a sip from her straw. Without thinking twice about it, I reach across the table and cover her hand with mine, rubbing her tattoo with my thumb.

"I hope you know that you are more than what you portray to others. If they had any idea how incredible you were . . ." I swallow. "You're always Addie the person. To me and everyone who deserves a spot in your life."

Something warm fills her stare as she nods slowly and flips our hands, intertwining our fingers.

"I can see now why everyone wants to be your friend."

"Why's that?"

"You always know what to say. And I feel safe with you, like I'm sure you'll always be here to protect me. Am I wrong?"

I can't look away from her as I reply, "No. You're not wrong."

"I might not be able to protect you to the same degree, but I'd try. Small but mighty are my middle names." She winks.

I chuckle. "I'll keep that in mind."

"How about you take a bite of your burger, and I'll take one of mine."

"Deal."

"On three?"

She grips her burger and brings it in front of her mouth. I do the same with mine.

"On three."

"One," she says.

"Two."

She grins so wide her dimple pops as we say together, "Three."

The familiar taste of beef and bread fills my mouth as I sink my teeth into the burger. I fight off a laugh, knowing it'll make me choke when she takes almost as big of a bite, ketchup squirting out the side and smearing across her cheek.

I set the burger down and chew, watching her clean the

ketchup with her tongue. She's adorable—so fucking cute it makes my chest ache.

There's no explanation for why I blurt out my next words other than her presence has worn down every single one of my walls, exposing me to her completely.

"I got the job at the university. I start in September."

Her burger falls from her fingers, splatting onto her plate. Genuine pride fills her expression as she smiles, reaching for me again. This time when she takes my hand, I decide I don't want her to let go of it again.

"Are you kidding me? This is amazing news! Oh my God, are you freaking out inside? This is your dream," she gushes.

"I've been freaking out inside since I got the call. I still can't believe it."

"How did I not hear about this sooner? This is incredible. You deserve this job more than anyone!"

"You're the only one I've told," I admit.

She pauses, searching my face for any hint of a lie. "Seriously? Why? It's not that I'm not flattered, but everyone will be so, so proud of you, Sparrow."

I flip our hands and stare at the tattoo on her finger, almost finding comfort in it.

"It doesn't matter now. I'm going to tell them as soon as we get back."

"For the record, I always knew it was going to happen."

I arch a brow. "Oh yeah?"

"Yeah. You're brilliant and incredibly talented. It would have absolutely been their loss to turn you away."

I pull our hands to my mouth and brush my lips across her knuckles. Her breath hitches, and I do it again, suddenly addicted to that sound.

"Thank you, love."

A gasp this time. "Did you just ca—"

"Are you Adalyn Hutton?" a nervous, non-accented voice asks.

Addie tightens her grip on my fingers as if her first instinct is to turn to me for help before she reluctantly pulls her hand away. I nearly snatch it again before thinking better of it.

She turns to face the two girls standing at our table, both of whom have their phones in their hands, the screens open and cameras on.

"Yeah. That's me." Her smile is fake, so un-Adalyn-like.

The tall redheaded girl standing beside the shorter brunette turns a deep shade of pink and giggles. "Would we be able to get a picture with you? We're huge fans."

I sit back quietly and watch the innocent enough interaction, noting the moment Adalyn becomes uncomfortable.

It's the brunette, the one with sharp green eyes and a weird sort of arrogance about her, that asks, "Actually, do you think you could give us the name of Noah's private Instagram? I know you said once that he doesn't have one, but I saw on Twitter that someone found it."

I look back at Adalyn and find her frowning at the girl, pushing a pink curl behind her ear. "I'm sorry, but Noah's private life isn't your business."

"That's your opinion. But as fans of him, I think we should know about these things," the girl replies, a hand on her hip.

The first girl elbows her friend, glaring. "Don't," she whisper hisses.

Addie's gaze turns sharp on the brunette, dangerously so. "What are your names?"

"Luna."

"Lily," the first girl says softly.

"Right. Well, Luna, respectfully, if Noah wanted you to know about his personal life, he wouldn't feel the need to have a separate personal account. So, no, I will not be giving it to you."

"So, you admit there is one."

It's me that says, "Yeah. There is. Now, please drop it."

Slowly, the girls look at me, surprised, as if having missed me entirely. I can't blame them for not noticing me when Adalyn is right there.

"Cooper White," Lily whispers to herself, quickly glancing away, face an even deeper shade of red. "Maddox's best friend."

Adalyn kicks me subtly beneath the table, rolling her eyes when I look at her. I wink before looking back at Lily.

"Do you want me to take a photo of you and Addie?" I ask.

Nodding erratically, she shoves the phone toward me. "Please."

As if we've all had the same collective thought, we don't give Luna any more attention. Clearly, she's not as nice of a person as her friend.

Adalyn stands and wraps her arm around the nicer of the two, and I quickly snap a few photos of them, knowing one would never suffice in girl world. Amelia taught me that.

"You're even more beautiful in person," Lily tells Addie once they break apart. "I just wanted to say that before we left. Sorry if that's weird."

I chuckle when Adalyn flushes a soft pink. "Thank you. You're gorgeous."

"Oh God. Thank you," Lily whispers, grinning. Slowly, her eyes land on me, her curiosity obvious. "Are you guys together?"

"Cooper's my husband," Adalyn says instantly. A beat later, her eyes go wide, as if realizing what she's just exposed. "I'm kidding!"

Lily blinks repeatedly, looking incredibly taken aback. I touch my tongue to the back of my teeth before stepping in.

"We're filming something for her page. A husband-and-wife prank."

Adalyn winces, a silent apology in her eyes. I shrug a shoulder, playing it off.

"Right. Well, I can't wait to see the video. Thank you so much for taking a photo with me," Lily says, clutching her phone tight to her chest. If she didn't buy my terrible attempt at a cover-up, she doesn't show it.

"You're welcome," Addie says.

"Come on, Luna."

I step to Adalyn's side, and we watch Lily grip Luna's arm and drag her away. The smirk on the second girl's face is enough to make my stomach curl.

"Why do I have the sinking feeling that we're going to wake up tomorrow to a thousand phone calls from our families?" Addie asks me.

I ghost a hand over her back, selfishly needing to touch her. "I do too. I suppose we need to get our story straight."

22

Cooper

My dad wastes no time in calling me the next morning. I step onto the balcony, softly brushing past Adalyn as she tries to calm a frantic Oakley over the phone. She looks beyond exhausted, and I know she barely slept last night, tossing and turning until well past 2:00 a.m. I was doing the same, an uneasy feeling churning my stomach until I thought I'd have to sleep on the bathroom floor.

The news broke early this morning. A viral tweet featuring a very zoomed-in, grainy photo of Adalyn and me, her hand in mine as I kiss her knuckles. The tweeter drew a circle around Adalyn's ring finger, over the tattoo we share.

I should have known our secret wouldn't last long. If it wasn't for that snobby teen last night, something else would have come along. I'm a bit relieved that it's out there now. There's something about hiding our relationship that doesn't sit well with me. Adalyn deserves more than that. Fake marriage or real one. And I'm beginning to accept that I might consider it a lot less fake than I did a week ago.

That's probably ridiculous. We've only been on this trip for two weeks. Yet, it feels like it's been months. I've gotten to know her so well in such a short time, and I suppose that's thanks to our close proximity.

Spending every single day, morning and night, with someone makes it impossible not to grow close at a faster-than-normal pace. We have no option but to share things about ourselves and become friends on a level that takes most people months to reach.

The circumstances are different with us, but I wouldn't expect anything less with her.

"Hey, Dad."

I stretch my neck and lean against the railing, looking out at the city. It's early, but the streets are packed, the shops already open. My stomach grumbles as the smell of fresh bread wafts up toward us.

"Hey, kid," he says.

"I'm too old for you to be calling me a kid."

"You'll never be too old in my eyes."

"Right. Well, get on with it, then. I'm assuming you've heard the news."

"You mean the news that my only son got married and I wasn't invited?" he asks, and for whatever reason, his voice is as calm as ever.

"It wasn't a real wedding. Not like that," I sigh.

"Try telling that to your mother. I spent an hour this morning trying to talk her down from buying a plane ticket to wherever the hell you are and beating you with a stick."

I wince. "She's upset?"

"Of course she is. You're her only child, and she just found out you got married without a word to her about it."

"Fuck."

He hums. "Fuck indeed. You know, I never expected that it would be Adalyn who would make me a grandpa, but I'm not one to complain about a good thing."

"Woah, slow down. Nobody is making you a grandpa anytime soon. This isn't like that."

"You know, you keep saying that, but I have yet to hear as to why it isn't 'like that.' Are you telling me that you married her for what? Some kind of joke?"

"No. It wasn't a joke."

"So, what, then?"

"It was an accident," I mutter, embarrassed.

There's silence on the other line. I rub a hand down my face and groan.

"You married Adalyn Hutton on accident?" he asks slowly.

"We were drunk."

Suddenly, he roars a laugh into the speaker. "You idiot. You goddamn idiot."

"It's frowned upon to call your children idiots, Dad. And to laugh at them at dire times like these."

"I'm at a loss for what else to do. The minute you touch down in Canada, Oakley and Maddox are going to destroy you. I don't know if I can protect you at this point. Maybe we'll need to say our goodbyes right now."

"You know, you're really not funny. At all."

"Agree to disagree."

"Did you call me to laugh at me? Because I was expecting you to tell me how disappointed you were in me."

"Disappointed? Is that what Oakley said to Adalyn?"

I glance over my shoulder at the open balcony door and the woman talking animatedly into the phone at her ear on the couch. Her eyes lack the shine they've had during this trip, and that alone is enough to make a wave of protectiveness wash over me.

"I don't know what he's said. They're talking right now."

"Well, depending on what you plan on doing with this new marriage, I don't think I'm disappointed in you. *Do* you know what you're going to do?"

"I emailed your lawyer the morning after it happened to try and find someone to help."

"So, you don't want to stay married?"

A tight feeling grows in my chest at his question, and my lack of immediate response is a terrible sign. *No* is the only plausible answer. But it feels like the wrong one.

"I don't think we should," I choose to say instead. "If I'm going to be married, it should be with someone I love."

"Usually, yes."

I scrunch my brows. "What do you mean usually? You don't marry a woman on a whim, let alone one who's ten years younger than you and your best friend's sister, without loving her."

"I agree, but you're already married. Accidentally, yes. But still married."

"I don't get your point. You know better than I do her family won't accept this. And she deserves better. A real husband and a real wedding."

"Who's to say that can't happen for her with you?"

I choke on a laugh. "Stop playing matchmaker for five minutes and actually think about what you're suggesting."

"You should have heard him on the phone with Ava this morning! I thought they were going to start house hunting for the two of you already," Scarlett yells in the background.

"Not true. We didn't know where you would want to live, so we decided to hold back on the hunting for now," Dad corrects her.

"Jesus Christ," I mumble, shaking my head.

"See? Not the entire Hutton family hates your guts. Ava couldn't be more thrilled with the news. Although, we're both obviously a little upset we weren't there."

"Dad, please. If you don't have actual advice for me, I'm going to hang up."

"I'm sorry. I'm just excited. It's not every day my son marries my best friend's daughter."

I hate that I can understand where he's coming from. I

can't be a people pleaser right now. "Well, enjoy it while it lasts."

"Have you thought about just letting things run their course? Like maybe seeing where it could go with her? This could be a blessing in disguise," he says, sounding far too hopeful.

"That's exactly what I've been doing the past week, and now every person who's ever heard the last name Hutton is well aware of what you consider a blessing. Everything is going to change now."

And I'm terrified. The blowback from this will be devastating. For both of us. It was fun playing pretend, but now we're back in the real world.

"Maybe you'll end up falling in love, and you'll have just saved a shit load of time by already being married. Yes, a lot will change now, but it doesn't have to be for the worst. The Hutton men will get over themselves and forgive you both. Ava will make sure of it."

"I'm not sure Ava can protect me from Maddox. Oakley, maybe, but Maddox is different. He won't forgive me."

"Have you talked to him yet?"

"We've only been up for an hour. You're the first person I've talked to."

"Maybe it's smart to let him cool off a little before talking to him, anyway. What's the plan for you newlyweds now? Has this ruined your trip?"

I look at Addie again and frown. She's no longer on the phone. It lies limp in her hand, her stare far away. Clearing my throat, I push away from the balcony.

"I'm not sure. I need to talk to her."

"Alright. I love you, even when you don't use that big brain of yours and do things you shouldn't."

I bite back a laugh. "I love you too. Thanks for not hating me."

"I couldn't even if I wanted to. Keep me updated."

"Will do."

We hang up, and I walk back inside. Addie glances up at me when I round the couch and sit on the empty seat beside her. As soon as I rest my arm on the couch back, she comes close and tucks herself beneath it. Something settles inside of me at her closeness, making it all too easy to lower my arm to her shoulder and pull her into my body.

"How's your dad?" she asks gently.

"As mischievous as ever. But not angry like I expected. How's yours?"

Her laugh sounds shaky, pained. "Mad, hurt, frustrated."

"We can't blame him. Even if that would make it easier."

"I knew there would be consequences for our actions. I guess I just expected them to come when I was ready for them to. If that time ever came. He's more hurt than mad, I think."

"When it comes to you, maybe. He probably wants to kill me."

It would be worth it, that annoying voice in my head sings before I shut it up.

"Oh, he does. Preferably after torturing you for a few hours first," she states.

"There's no beating around the bush with you, is there?"

She shifts her body, and those blue eyes blink up at me, giving me a look that says *you're joking, right?* "I don't see the point in giving you false comfort when it will be so short-lived."

I blow out a breath, tipping my head back to stare at the ceiling. "What do you want to do now?"

"I don't want to go home yet," she whispers, snuggling into my chest. She drapes her arm across my abdomen, squeezing tight, as if she's scared I'm going to get up and walk out if she doesn't hold on to me.

"Then we won't go home yet."

"But I think we have to. I couldn't pretend my family isn't

at home hurt and upset while I continue having the time of my life with you. That's not fair, is it?"

"No, it's not," I relent.

Disappointment is heavy in the air. What was supposed to be a two-month trip has been cut to two weeks. This was Addie's chance to branch out and explore the world, and I feel a bit responsible for it coming to such a quick end. It may take more than one person to get married, but I'm the older one. The one who was supposed to have his shit together enough not to allow something like this to happen.

I failed my only job.

"I'll pay for your new tickets and refund you the money you lost on your current ones. This was my trip, after all," she says.

"You're not doing either of those things. This is on me."

"It's on *us*, but you wouldn't have even come along if I hadn't convinced you to. So let me make it right."

"Not happening," I grunt.

"You're stubborn."

"So are you."

"Isn't my stubbornness one of your favourite qualities about me?"

"No. That would be your incredible wit."

"Oh, how you flatter me."

Fighting back a smile, I press a kiss to the side of her head, taking in a whiff of her perfume. "What do we do when we get back home?"

"You mean other than try to beg our families for forgiveness?"

"Yes. Like . . . with us. While we wait for the annulment, what exactly do you want to do?"

She stiffens briefly before slowly relaxing. "I don't want to go back to how things were before. How do I even do that?"

My lungs pinch at the thought of going back to only

seeing each other every few months. It's painfully obvious that it's not an option for me.

"You're my wife. As far as I'm concerned, nothing will be the same ever again. Let's just roll with it and see what happens."

Her breath hitches, and her stillness makes panic fill my blood. "What do you mean?"

"We haven't finished your list, and a deal is a deal. We keep doing what we're doing, even when we get back, and then go from there," I rush out.

"Right. Okay, we can do that," she breathes, nodding, her cheek rubbing my chest.

She sounds about as unsure as I do, but until I find another option that doesn't make me want to hurl, it's the only one we have.

23

Adalyn

Cooper tells the Uber driver to wait while he helps me haul my suitcases out of the trunk. I try not to show how devastated I feel being back in Vancouver already. He already feels responsible enough for this, regardless of how many times I tell him it's not his fault.

Returning home after being away always feels good. Like you're back where you belong. But this time, home is the last place I want to be. And as Cooper shrugs my carry-on over his shoulder and looks to me with a similar sad look in his eyes, I can't help but think that he feels the same way as me.

"I'll come up with you and make sure you're safe before I leave," he says, gently urging me up the sidewalk.

"You don't have to. I doubt anyone broke in and hung around while I was gone."

And having you inside my apartment will only make it harder to say goodbye.

"Just humour me."

I nod, and we walk inside the building. Sammy, the body-builder-looking security guard, gives me a smile as we pass him, and I muster up a weak one in return.

"See, Sammy wouldn't let anything happen to me. He's got my back." I try to sound teasing but fail miserably.

"I'm not letting my wife walk into her apartment alone after it's been empty for two weeks. Just let me do this."

Just like every single time he calls me his wife, I fight off shivers. It shouldn't sound so good, but hearing it come from Cooper's mouth is enough to send me into a horny spiral.

It's become abundantly clear to me that I've caught the Cooper bug. I'm not surprised. Actually, I am, but not at the fact I've grown feelings for him, but because it took me two weeks to realize it.

He's not who I would go for had the circumstances been different. And I think that's why I've grown to care about him so deeply. He's not like the other guys I've dated, and that's what makes him so special. Nobody has ever made me feel as important and listened to and cared for as he has. We can talk about anything, and I know he won't judge me. God, I didn't see this one coming. Talk about a forbidden crush.

"Fine. But only because you're so damn handsome."

From the corner of my eye, I see him blush, and that alone is enough to lighten my mood. Even just a little bit.

We take the elevator up to my floor and then walk inside the apartment. It smells like cleaning products and vanilla. Ivy's things are gone.

I dread being left alone.

"It's a nice place," Cooper notes, shutting the door behind us. "I expected more pink, to be honest."

I slip off my shoes and walk further inside. The apartment *is* nice. It's one big open floor plan with tall windows and grey wood floors. Modern, but not too modern. Two bedrooms and one bathroom.

"Ivy wasn't a big pink girl. I toned it down a little."

"That's a shame."

"Is your favourite colour secretly pink, Sparrow?"

He smirks, eyes darkening. "No. But some of my favourite things are pink."

My stomach begins to flutter as I look away, my skin suddenly feeling too hot. "Stop trying to get a rise out of me."

"I can't help it. It's become one of my favourite pastimes."

I change the subject before I overheat. "Are you going to do your scary-husband apartment check now? I'd like to take a shower with decent water pressure again."

"Right. Do you want me to put your bags in your room for you?" He pushes my suitcase in front of him.

"You can leave them there. I'll probably keep them unpacked for the next week, anyway."

He laughs softly. "Okay. I'll be back."

"Do you want a weapon, or are you planning to tell the imaginary killer hiding in my bathtub a bunch of lame jokes until he simply dies of boredom instead?" I ask before he gets too far.

"One thing you didn't mention being on your dirty list was spanking, but keep at it and I'm going to add it to the lesson plan anyway," he sings over his shoulder and then disappears into Ivy's old room.

My exhale is strained as dirty images fill my head. Suddenly, the thought of Cooper bending me over a table and spanking my ass seems like an all-too-appealing idea.

"I don't think an empty bedroom is a likely hiding spot," I call, following after him.

Popping my head into the room, I find him shutting the closet doors. The lack of furniture in Ivy's room is startling.

Thankfully, he doesn't linger after completing his look. We walk down the hall to the first of two bathrooms. Pausing outside the door, I nod to the shower curtain.

"Would you like a weapon? You could use the plunger," I suggest.

He narrows his eyes at me. "What am I going to do with a plunger? Suction it to his face?"

"How do you know the robber is a man?"

"I'm going to suction the plunger to your face if you don't leave me alone."

I throw my hands up in front of me. "Sorry. Do your thing, big boy."

"Big bo—you know what? Never mind." He stalks toward the shower curtain and rips it open. "All clear."

"Where to next, Captain?" I ask. He brushes past me and heads to the second bedroom. "Are you sure you can handle being alone in my room with me and all my girly unmentionables?"

"I'm not a teenage boy. You and your unmentionables don't scare me," he grunts.

"Oh, I'm well aware of that fact."

He throws a smirk over his shoulder. "Is that so?"

"Mmhmm. You're obviously far too old to be a teenage boy."

"If I'm so old, you probably shouldn't be letting me into your bedroom."

"Maybe I have a thing for older men." *For one older man, to be exact.*

He comes to an abrupt stop in front of me, just inches from my bedroom door. I collide into his back, my hands gripping his arms to steady myself.

"Scared after all?" I ask, giving him a shove.

"You have absolutely no filter." The words are deep, rasped.

"Is that why you froze? I promise I don't actually seek out old men." I wince.

He shakes his head and steps inside the room. "No, I know you don't do that."

"So, did your knees lock up or something?"

"I don't suppose you'll just let this go."

"Is that what you want me to do?"

"Preferably."

Heading straight for my closet, he pulls open the doors and looks inside before closing them again. There are not many hiding spots in my bedroom, and after another minute of looking around, he appears to deem it safe.

I sit on the edge of my bed and ask, "Spill."

His eyes bounce around the room, looking at everything from my makeup vanity to the collection of skateboards I have hung on the wall beside my beanbag chair. I push further onto the mattress and cross my legs in front of me.

When he finally moves that lazy gaze to rest on me, I inwardly swoon. If a look from someone could be a compliment, the way Cooper's staring at me would be the most flattering one.

"I don't like the thought of you with other men."

It's a brutally honest answer. And one that threatens to undo me.

"Ever? Or just right now?"

His throat bobs with a swallow. "My Uber driver is still waiting for me. I don't want to have to call another one."

"Come on, Cooper. Don't be that guy."

"What guy?"

I roll my eyes, straightening my back. "The one who can't be honest about what he's thinking and how he's feeling. Don't play games with me."

"I'm not playing games. I'm keeping the line drawn."

"Fuck the line. I've never been a fan of being told where I can and can't go."

"Please, just let it go. We can talk about this when we're not on a time crunch," he begs.

Fatigue is the only explanation for why I wave him off, letting him get away with pussyfooting around what he's really feeling. I push to my feet and walk right past him, toward the front door. He's close behind me, but I don't face him until I've grabbed hold of the doorknob.

"Thank you for checking my apartment for me," I tell him, the words stiff with frustration.

Maybe I shouldn't be annoyed with him, but I am. Of all the things we've shared with one another—all the things we've *done* together—this is where he draws the line? No, that doesn't work for me.

"Adalyn."

When he gets close enough, I pull open the door. "If your Uber is gone, I'll call you another one."

Stepping closer, he reaches for my hand. My body betrays me by not snatching it from his grasp. I nearly fold when he rubs my ring finger, directly over the tattooed wedding band.

"I'm sorry."

I nod once. "Get home safe."

Slowly, he drops my hand and slips his shoes back on. My grip on the doorknob becomes sweaty fast, but I tighten my fingers, refusing to let go. I don't know what I would try to grab onto if I did.

"I'll text you." He says it so surely that I have no doubt he really will.

"Alright."

"Goodbye, Adalyn."

"Bye."

And then he's gone, leaving me all alone in this big empty apartment.

By the time I crawl into bed that night, I'm completely over being alone. I emptied my suitcase, did all of my laundry, and ate half of a freezer-burnt, frozen pizza for dinner.

I even called my publicist back after ignoring her calls for the past two days. She insists there's a way we can fix this, but in my mind, there's nothing to fix. So what if everyone knows

I got married to an amazing man? As long as they never learn that it isn't real, there's nothing to worry about.

It's safe to say she didn't agree, but that isn't my problem. Cooper isn't anyone to be ashamed of. I sure as hell don't feel that away about him.

True to his word, my darling husband texted me a few hours ago. I wasn't expecting a message so soon, but even after our last conversation, I couldn't make myself ignore him.

Turning away from the TV on my dresser across the room, I unlock my phone and scroll through our messages.

Cooper: Is it acceptable to go to the store and buy gelato for dinner?

Me: Depends on what kind you get.

Cooper: Raspberry?

Me: Only because that's my favourite kind.

Cooper: Do you want some?

It takes me ten minutes to reply to him. I deleted and rewrote what I wanted to say a million times before finally hitting Send.

Me: Another time

Cooper: It's a date.

I never replied. That was four hours ago, and now I'm wishing I had taken him up on that offer and spent the night eating gelato with him in my living room instead of alone, doing everything I didn't want to do yet.

Jet leg has me so far past exhaustion I should have been asleep already. But no matter how many times I attempt it, I just can't.

Tapping at my phone screen, I stare at his contact before

pressing the photo I chose for him, expanding it. It's one I took of us in the pub in Dublin after we'd started drinking but before we got hitched.

My eyes are wild, full of excitement and adventure, but Cooper's eyes are on me, impossible to read. His grin is lazy and happy, matching mine. I run my finger over it before exiting the photo and groaning.

"Get a grip," I mutter.

I'm about to toss my phone to my nightstand when it buzzes in my hand. The message makes my heart slam against my ribs.

Cooper: Are you awake?

Me: Is this your attempt at a "u up" text?

Cooper: No.

I pull my lip between my teeth and gently bite down as I text back.

Me: What's up?

Cooper: I can't sleep. I'm too used to having you in the same room.

Is that what it is for me too? *Fuck.* I'm not surprised.

Me: I can't either. It's too quiet without your snoring

Cooper: I don't snore

Cooper: Can I come over?

Me: That's not a good idea.

I delete the message before sending it and hover my fingers over the screen.

Me: Bring the gelato or I won't let you in

Cooper: Be there in fifteen.

24

Adalyn

With leaden muscles, I open the door and let Cooper inside. Dark bags heavy beneath his eyes, he looks as tired as I feel.

He steps inside and lifts a container of gelato between us. "As requested."

"Thank you."

I take it from him and grab two spoons from the kitchen while he takes his shoes off. We reconvene on the couch, and I flop down on the cushion beside him. I hand him his spoon before digging mine into the red gelato and slipping it into my mouth. The cold does little to wake me up.

"I'm surprised you could keep your eyes open long enough to drive here," I mumble.

"Me too." He scoops up some gelato. "It was worth it."

"Was it? To sit in silence on my couch at three in the morning?"

He clinks his teeth on the spoon before resting his hands in his lap. "If it means I get to be with you, then yes, it was."

"Don't start with all of this sweet talk. I refuse to be teased by it again."

"I didn't mean to tease you last time."

I jab my spoon into the gelato and leave it there. Setting the container on the coffee table, I shift to face him.

"If I overstepped, you should have told me. I'm not some sensitive little lamb that can't handle the truth. I want to know when I've pushed too hard so I don't do it again."

His eyes soften, his body heat wrapping around me in a warm hug. I want to lean into it, embrace it, but as stubborn as I am, I refuse to just yet.

"You didn't overstep. And I don't view you that way. You're the thing that eats lambs for breakfast, Adalyn."

My heart soars at the compliment. It's the kind of compliment only someone who knows the real me would say.

"Okay, so why wouldn't you just answer my question, then?" I frown at how hurt my words sound.

"Come here," he murmurs, lifting his arm for me to tuck myself beneath it.

Fuck, I'm so weak. I wrap myself around him, tossing my legs over his lap and pressing my hand to the centre of his chest. He settles back against the couch and drapes one arm over my back while the opposite comes across his front, holding me beneath my thighs and pulling me up closer. A thumb stroking my bare skin makes my eyes flutter shut.

"If I tell you how I feel, then we become more than best friends. And something tells me that I'll wind up too obsessed with you to let you go when we're done."

I bury my face in his chest, unable to fight off a smile. Something close to euphoria zips through me.

"I don't think that would be a bad thing," I whisper.

"It wouldn't be. Not to me. But it isn't just about the two of us."

"If you're worried about my family, they can be as pissed as they want, and it won't change anything for me."

That thumb keeps moving up and down my thigh in a soothing motion. His chest rises and falls softly beneath my cheek. Combined, the two things make one hell of a lullaby. Sleep turns my brain foggy.

"I know. You're one of a kind, love. Now, sleep."

I breathe in the smell of him and nod, fingers curling into his shirt. He feathers a kiss across my crown, exhaling heavily.

"Please stay," I slur.

"There's nowhere I would rather be."

His words linger long after I've finally drifted off.

"OH CRAP. Don't let him in here, babe."

"Mom, don't make me move you."

"You wouldn't dare."

The cacophony of voices jolts me awake. I peel my eyes open and rub my hand across them as the couch shifts beneath my face. With furrowed brows, I push myself into a sitting position and stare at the lap I was apparently using as a pillow last night.

"What's going on?" Cooper asks, voice growly with sleep.

I shrug and blink to clear my vision. "Is someone here?"

"Maddox Hutton! Get back here!" Mom shouts.

Suddenly, I'm on high alert. Fear has me scrambling off the couch and whipping my head around to find my brother rushing toward us, fury in his eyes.

"Take it down a notch, Dox," I warn as he comes closer. He doesn't listen to me.

"You and I will be talking about this later. Right now, I need to have a conversation with your husband." He spits the word *husband* as if it disgusts him. My stomach sinks.

I sense Cooper behind me before I feel his hand touch my arm. Gulping, I try to block him with my body, but he's one step ahead of me, moving me aside a beat before Maddox reaches us.

It happens so quickly. One second, my brother has Cooper by the neck of his shirt, and then the next, he's punching him in the face. Cooper doesn't even attempt to protect himself. He just lets my brother hit him.

Anger boils my blood. As Cooper bends at the waist, cupping his bleeding nose, I shove my brother's chest, drawing his attention again.

"You had no right to hit him!"

"No reason? He married you. He just had his hands all over you! That's more than one good reason," he sneers.

"All over me? I'm pretty sure we were *just* sleeping. And it takes more than one person to get married, you hotheaded ass!"

"Guys," Mom says gently, and I spot her beside Dad, a few feet away.

"What is he even doing here? Didn't you have enough fun together these past two weeks?" Maddox asks.

"Don't speak to her that way."

I shut my eyes as Maddox turns on his best friend again. He looks like a bull with a red flag waving in his face. Cooper doesn't back down. I wish he would.

"I don't want to hear your voice right now," Maddox tells him.

"And I didn't want to get punched in the face first thing in the morning, but here we are. If you want to be mad at someone, be mad at me. But don't take that tone with Adalyn."

"I agree with Cooper," Mom joins in.

All I want to do is rush toward her and hug her after being away for these past two weeks, but now is not the time. Dad's beside her, but he still has yet to look at me. Hurt pinches my stomach, our last conversation replaying in my mind.

He might not have told me outright, but he's deeply upset with me and my actions. I don't remember the last time I upset him this much.

"Why are you all here?" I ask.

"I wanted to see you, sweetheart. I didn't know Cooper was here," Mom says sheepishly.

Maddox scoffs, glaring at me. "What a surprise it was to walk in and have our mother try to shove me back out when she found you cuddled up in my best friend's lap."

"What can I say? He has a very comfortable lap," I reply.

Cooper must not care much for his life because he grabs my hand and interlocks our fingers, squeezing tightly. "I wouldn't have come if I knew you would be making a surprise visit."

"You shouldn't have come at all," Maddox grunts.

"Can we all sit down and talk before someone ends up with more than a bloodied nose? Adalyn, you should help Cooper clean himself up," Dad suggests, finally stepping in. "Maddox, clean up the blood from the floor and then go make some coffee for everyone."

"You're not suddenly alright with this?" Maddox asks him, sounding bewildered.

"No. But throwing punches isn't going to change anything."

"I like my coffee with an eighty-twenty creamer-to-coffee ratio, Maddox. The opposite for Cooper. We'll be back," I say before pulling Cooper right past my brother and toward the bathroom.

Once I lock us inside the small room, he sits on the toilet lid, and I grab a washcloth from beneath the sink. I gasp when I get a good look at his face.

"He got you good, huh?" I crouch in front of him and hold his head in my hands, turning it side to side as I examine the damage.

"It's not broken. Just hurts like a bitch."

"Maybe I should go back out there and punch *him* in the face."

"Don't break your hand defending my honour. I deserved the punch. Hell, I was expecting it one day or another."

"That doesn't make it any better. He's being dramatic."

"He's hurt."

I wet a washcloth with warm water and begin to dab at the blood on his chin and upper lip. "Well, now you're even."

"Not quite, but it's a step closer."

"You didn't do this to spite him. He has to see that."

"He will. Sooner or later," he sighs.

With a soft kiss on his nose, I stand and start to put everything away. I hang my head, breathing quickening when he steps behind me and drops his hands to my hips, spinning me around.

"Thank you," he says, voice gravel.

I tip my head back and meet his stare, the deep brown colour of his eyes so damn beautiful, even in the terrible bathroom lighting. He wets his lips, and I can't help but be drawn to the motion, unable to look away. My chest moves rapidly with nerves.

Is he going to kiss me?

"You're welcome," I breathe.

My lungs struggle to expand on a full breath when he brushes my hair out of my face and drifts his knuckles across my jaw.

"What I said last night . . . I meant it. But I also think it might be too late to—"

A fist thumps against the door, surprising us both. Cooper curses under his breath, a war waging in his intense stare. He drops his hand from my face but doesn't remove the one gripping my waist. If anything, he holds me tighter. Almost possessively.

"Time's up. Get out here so we can have a family meeting," Maddox snaps.

"Cooper isn't family. Does that mean he gets to leave?" I call, voice sounding as shaky as I feel.

"As long as you're married, he's family. We're waiting for you, so hurry up."

I swallow. "I'm sorry in advance. If I didn't think you would fall to your death, I would help you jump out the bathroom window. But we're far too high up."

His laugh brushes my lips as he leans forward and presses our foreheads together. "You'd have to push me out before I let you deal with this yourself. I got you."

"You got me," I repeat, letting the confirmation settle some anxious part of me.

I freeze when warm, soft lips touch the corner of my mouth. It's only a brief touch, a ghost of one, really, but it sends me spinning.

Even as he backs up and stares at me with eyes heavy with emotion, I remain frozen until there's another bang on the door. This time, Cooper yanks it open and glares at Maddox.

"We're coming."

"Seemed like it," Maddox replies, glaring at us as if he knows exactly what was happening behind that door.

"Back up, Maddox. How are we supposed to get out with you blocking the way?" I sass, curving a brow.

"Smart-ass," he retorts but steps aside.

It takes everything in me not to check to see if Cooper is following as I leave the room, heading straight for probably the most uncomfortable conversation of my life.

25

Cooper

sparrow

A ROUGH HAND GRABS MY SHOULDER AND JERKS ME TO THE side before I can get away from Maddox. One look at him has me swallowing my frustration at being grabbed as Adalyn heads toward her parents.

"I need to talk to you alone first," he grits out.

"Have at it."

"Don't look so guilty. It's pissing me off."

I just shrug, unsure how he wants me to reply to that.

"You could at least try to appear confident in your actions. Not like you *know* you fucked up. My sister isn't anyone's fuck-up."

"I'm well aware of that. But I can't help feeling guilty for hurting you. There isn't anything you can say to me that I haven't already said to myself."

He looks me over, eyes harsh, betrayal burning bright. My chest pangs.

"I need you to answer one of my questions right now, away from everyone else. No bullshit, only the fucking truth. Got it?"

"Got it."

"Did you plan on this? Was there anything going on between the two of you before you left?"

My throat threatens to close at the hurt in his words. I did that, and I'm not sure how long it will take to fix the damage I've done, but I'll keep at it until I have.

"No. You should know that already. Everything that happened between us . . . it's new. *Really* new," I answer on a long exhale.

He nods once, stiffly. "I just had to ask. Braxton told me I was an idiot to think otherwise, but it's hard not to go there."

"Where is she, anyway?"

A flicker of warmth in that cold stare. "At the house. Liam caught a bit of a bug recently."

They always come back to their second home in Vancouver for a few weeks after hockey season ends, needing to be around family again instead of staying in Ontario the entire postseason. I'm grateful for it. I miss them when they're gone.

"Does she want to punch me too?"

"No. The minute she hears about what I did to you, she's going to kick me to the couch for a week."

"I'll tell her to go easy on you," I offer.

He scowls, mentally shoving a wall between us. "Don't. I don't want to owe you anything right now."

"You wouldn't owe me anything. Fuck's sake, Maddox. You're my best friend."

"Apparently, that doesn't mean much when it comes to sneaking around behind my back with my sister."

I pinch the skin between my brows, struggling with how to go about this. He doesn't—and *won't*—know what has completely happened between Adalyn and me, but it seems he's already come to his own conclusions. Until we sit down together, there are going to be a thousand unanswered questions and assumptions.

"Can we just go hash this out with everyone right now?

There's no point in trying to work it all out in private like this," I suggest.

"Lead the way."

"Great," I mutter.

We reach the dining table at the same time there's a knock on the front door. Confused, I look at Adalyn, finding her already watching me. Her smile is sympathetic.

"It's open!" Ava calls.

A tired groan escapes me when my dad walks in, waving casually at us. "Who invited him?" I ask the table.

It's Ava who says, "Me. He should be a part of this conversation."

"You just want to even the scale, sweetheart," Oakley mutters.

She tries and fails to hide a smirk. "Me?"

Her husband shakes his head but strokes her hand where it rests on the table.

"There's my boy!" Dad shouts, pulling me in for a tight hug.

"Hey, Dad."

"You look tan. Did you spend a lot of time outside?" he asks, taking a seat at the head of the table, across from Ava at the other end. I follow suit, a bit annoyed when Maddox purposefully takes the spot next to Adalyn, leaving me beside Oakley.

"We did, actually! I had no idea Cooper was such a water bug until I had to drag him out of the ocean in Paris," Addie jumps in, eyes on me, suddenly so full of mischief.

It's her attempt at bringing some ease to the heavy conversation and calm my anxiety, but when memories of what else we did so close to that ocean fill my head, I become the furthest thing from calm. I cough into my fist and focus on the angry man sitting beside me.

Oakley has never been anything but supportive and kind to me, but as his glare burns into the side of my head, I know he would throw me in a snake pit without a second thought.

Dad smacks my shoulder and grins at Addie. "You must bring out that side of him. I haven't seen him go into the ocean since the last time I brought him to the beach as a kid."

"You know what, I think you're right. I don't remember the last time he joined us on any beach trips," she replies.

"I wasn't aware you had been paying attention to whether Cooper joined us anywhere when you were younger," Maddox butts in.

She turns narrowed eyes on him. "I wasn't. And you damn well know that. But it wasn't hard to tell when he didn't come with you somewhere. You would pout and grumble every time. It was almost as bad as if Braxton didn't come."

"I think it's fair to close down all thoughts of Adalyn and Cooper having been interested in one another before this trip. Right?" Ava asks the table.

"Yes," I state over an array of accepting hums.

Oakley leans forward, clearing his throat. "I want Cooper to explain to me how this happened."

"I'm not a fan of how this feels like we're being asked to explain ourselves after being caught sneaking out as teenagers. We're not children, Dad. We're adults," Adalyn tries but is quickly shut down.

"You will always be my little girl, Adalyn. That will never change. I won't accept this as it stands right now. This is not how you were supposed to get married. Honey, you don't even have a real ring. This isn't right for you. You deserve better," he breathes, wringing his hands on the table.

Ava sighs, and I grimace, the realization of what Oakley's feeling striking deep. He's not angry. He's hurt and worried and blaming me for not giving his daughter what she deserves.

"I love you, Dad, but you don't get to decide what I deserve or what's right for me," she tells him. He goes to reply, but she shakes her head, addressing the entire table this time.

"As you all know, we didn't plan on getting married. It was a drunken idea that we ended up turning into a reality. But that's just it. It was an *idea* on *both* parts. It's not fair to put the blame on Cooper because he's older. I'm a twenty-one-year-old woman. I had just as good of a shot to say no as he did. So please, stop painting me as the victim here. And I love the ring I have, by the way."

"You have options, right? Can you get a divorce?" Maddox asks, his voice slightly calmer than just minutes ago.

"An annulment would be faster. But they have to be approved for one," Oakley says.

Adalyn's eyes meet mine across the table, and the softness I find there makes my lungs squeeze and lock. It's impossible to pretend I'm not already obsessed with her. Every pastel, sparky, extroverted part of her. I'm grateful I'm sitting because my legs go weak when she tugs her lips into a discreet smile. One just for me.

The words just burst out of me, and for the first time in my life, I don't care how they make anyone but her feel.

"We're trying for an annulment, but that doesn't mean there isn't anything real between us. Because there is. I want to explore it, and I think she does too. Whether we have your support or not."

Ava sucks in a sharp breath, and Dad laughs softly. I don't look at her brother or father to see their reactions. Not when Adalyn grins that dimpled smile at me.

"You *would* tell me this in front of everyone," she says.

I wink. "You're nothing if not a grand-gesture type of woman."

"Fuck my life," Maddox mutters.

"I think I would have preferred if you had brought your better half with you today," Addie tells him.

He flips her the finger. "I'm sure you'll tattle on me to her soon enough."

"Already done, bro. Let me know how the doghouse treats you tonight. I think we're expecting rain."

"Don't think I've forgiven either of you yet. I just need some time to recover from the torture of having to watch you give googly eyes at each other for the past ten minutes."

"I don't need your forgiveness. We're family. You don't have a choice but to love me. Give it a few days and you'll be inviting me over to babysit Liam again."

"Don't hold your breath. I only have one sister."

"Will there ever be a time when you two don't bicker?" Ava asks, shaking her head. But I don't miss the small smile she tries to hide.

"Probably not." Maddox snorts.

"It seems you didn't need me here after all, Ava," Dad says.

Addie's mom shrugs. "I'll never pass up a chance to see you."

"Group dinners are going to be a lot different now," Oakley notes gruffly.

Now, there's something we can agree on.

EVERYONE LINGERS for a bit longer before leaving, my dad with an offer for Addie and me to come for dinner this week, and Oakley with an invitation to meet alone with him tomorrow afternoon under the pretext of grabbing lunch.

I know he really wants to talk with nobody butting in and standing up for me. And after everything that's happened, I owe him as much. That doesn't make it any less nerve-racking, though.

"I'm sorry about my family," Addie says, pushing the dining chairs beneath the table.

"Don't apologize. They just care about you."

"That's not a good enough excuse for being rude. Or for hitting you."

"I'm just grateful it was Maddox and not Oakley that hit me. I have a feeling your dad would have broken my nose."

She laughs softly. "You're probably right."

Once the chairs are pushed in, she sighs, pressing her back to one of them. Crossing her arms, she tilts her head, watching me.

"You don't have to meet my dad tomorrow if you don't want to. I can't begin to imagine how awkward that's going to be. I'm sure you have other plans, anyway."

"Why do you think I have plans? We've only been back for a couple of days."

"But we've been gone for weeks. I actually don't know much about your real everyday life when we're not off travelling the world."

She looks upset by that, and I make a promise to myself to tell her absolutely everything as long as that look goes away.

"I don't have plans that don't include you."

"Oh," she whispers.

"Do you have plans already, Adalyn?"

She shakes her head. "I haven't really talked to anyone yet."

"So, you're all mine, then? For a few days, at least." I like the sound of that. *A lot.*

"I'd say so. You surprised me back there, you know," she says.

"I know."

"You meant it, then? Everything you said?"

I quirk my mouth and take slow steps toward her. Thick lashes flutter as I close the space between us. Those plump, pink lips part when I press our fronts together and slip my hand around the back of her hand, fingers curling in her hair.

"Every damn word," I breathe, and then finally, I kiss her.

26

Adalyn

You know the feeling when you first sink into a bubble bath after a long day? When your toes go beneath the hot water and you slowly lower your aching body beneath the suds? That feeling of pleasure and satisfaction that washes over you once you're fully submerged?

That's what kissing Cooper White feels like.

Pure. Fucking. Bliss.

His lips meet mine cautiously, almost like he's testing whether I'll back away. He should know better because that's the last thing I want to do. When I push up on my toes and kiss him harder, his lips part on a throaty groan that makes my head spin.

As if we haven't already begun to learn one another's bodies these past few days, our hands start to wander—exploring in a different way than we were allowed to before. His hands are hot on my skin, burning into me as he pushes them beneath my shirt and holds my bare waist. With a kick of his foot, the chair behind me goes flying, and I'm being set on the table. He steps between my legs, eating the space between us as he settles there.

There's a part of me that doesn't really believe this is

happening. That this man isn't really kissing me like he's desperate for more. Like he can't get enough of me. But he is, and I'm behaving the same way, taking and taking until there shouldn't be anything left, yet somehow there is.

"I've wanted to kiss you so many times," he rasps, dragging his mouth along my jaw and beneath it, sucking on the sensitive skin there.

"Why didn't you?"

Teeth nip at my throat before he licks away the sting. "Wasn't the right time."

I release a strangled moan when he palms my breast and softly pinches my hard nipple. Squeezing my thighs around him, I try to pull him in closer, desperate for something to soothe the ache between my legs.

"You make the prettiest sounds, Adalyn. I could become addicted to them."

"I could make more."

He cradles the back of my head, tilting it back until our eyes meet as he slowly and carefully twists my nipple. My cry is wanton, so fucking needy I would be embarrassed had I not been so far out of my head already.

"Say please," he whispers.

"Please," I gasp, arching into his hand.

His eyes flash with dark approval as he presses his cock against me, giving me some momentary relief before pulling away all too quickly. I whimper at the loss before he takes my mouth in another hard, lip-bruising kiss.

"Go to your bedroom, take these goddamn clothes off, and wait for me on the bed. On your knees, facing the headboard," he commands, voice so deliciously firm.

Oh my God. My panties are destroyed. There's no saving the soiled things after this. A subtle flutter of nerves fills my stomach as I nod, hands still travelling over his body. Over the hard expanse of his torso and muscled arms, even the perfect trim of his waist. I can't get enough.

So, when he covers my hands with his, stopping their exploration, I can't help but pout. It feels unfair not being able to get my fill of him right now.

I swallow as he pushes his thumb into my bottom lip. "Don't pout. You'll have time to touch me, I promise. Now, go. Your list isn't going to cross itself out."

My eyes widen slightly at the subtle hint of what's to come. I quickly slip off the table, and with one final squeeze of his waist, I do as I'm told.

Shedding my clothes as I go, I'm naked by the time I reach the edge of my bed. I force my lungs to expand on a full breath as I set my hands on the mattress and dare a look over my shoulder, finding myself still alone.

Is this actually happening? Is he finally going to quit teasing and give us both what we really want? The thought alone is enough to curl my toes, pleasure heavy in my bones.

This goes beyond wanting to finish my list. Sure, I still want to cross each of my fantasies off it, but this is about so much more than that. I want Cooper. All of him. The sweet, the caring, the controlling. And not under the pretence of experimenting.

He could give me vanilla, and it would still be the best fucking vanilla known to man.

The sound of his footsteps has me grappling every last ounce of my courage and crawling up the bed, stopping when my fingers brush the edge of my pillow. The position feels incredibly submissive, but it doesn't bother me. If anything, it makes me wetter.

"*Fuck.*"

I hang my head, unable to keep it up as the guttural sound of his groan causes my limbs to shake. Need pools between my legs, and it takes everything not to shove my ass in the air and beg him to fuck me already.

"I like that plan," I say.

Footsteps, and then the ghost of a touch across my ass. I

bite my lip, quieting my whimper. The bed dips as he moves closer, but I don't risk looking back. I don't trust that I won't come on the spot if I see even a hint of desire on his face.

The moment hot breath caresses me between my legs and his mouth closes over my slit, it doesn't matter if I look at him. I'm nearly there anyway, pushing back into his face like I might die if he stops. Fingers curling into the bedding, I hiss out a breath and try to slow down, but it's a lost cause when his tongue strokes my throbbing clit.

Fire flicks down my spine as I moan so loudly I'm sure my neighbours can hear. I've never felt so good so quickly. Somehow, each time with Cooper tops the last, taking me to new heights I fear ever falling down from.

An unrecognizable noise escapes me when he grips my ass cheeks and spreads them while continuing to feast on me. I squeeze my eyes shut, mouth falling open when he drags his tongue back, back, back—

"Cooper!"

He freezes, mistaking my gasp of surprise for a plea for him to stop. Closing my gaping mouth, I push back just a little toward him, chasing his mouth with a wiggle of my hips.

"I didn't say skateboard," I whisper. "It's just new. You surprised me."

Pressing a kiss to the inside of my thigh, he says, "I should have asked you first."

"You would have stopped if I told you I didn't want to do it. That's all that matters. *Don't* stop, please. I want to come."

"You want to come," he echoes, licking and biting the curve of my ass. "Where?"

My tone turns mischievous. "Ooh, I get to choose?"

His teeth sink into my flesh, harder this time, as he sinks two fingers inside my soaked pussy. "Answer me."

"Your cock, Cooper. I want to come on your cock," I mewl.

He hisses a curse. "No."

I swallow a frustrated noise. "Your mouth, then. Please, just make me come. I can't take any more of this."

He curves his fingers deep, and I cry out, seeing stars behind my eyes. A wet tongue finds my ass hole, and my entire body quivers at the surprising pleasure that sparks. The feeling is new, almost forbidden, but fuck if those aren't also the two best words to describe our relationship.

Did I just relate our relationship to getting my ass eaten for the first time?

Holding my cheeks apart with his fingers, he swirls his tongue around me, increasing the pressure. It's hard to focus as he continues burying his fingers in my pussy and rimming my ass, and once he adds a third finger, stretching me for him, I go off like a rocket.

"*Yes* . . . yes, Cooper! Fuck," I moan, my ears ringing as an orgasm tears through me.

Still shaking, I fall to my forearms and try to collect my bearings. The air is cold behind me when he shifts off the bed and disappears into the bathroom. He's only gone for a brief moment before coming back.

Not surprisingly, one orgasm wasn't enough to satisfy me. Not when it comes to Cooper. I turn my head and rest my cheek on the bed as I stare at him. He's so close yet too far. His shirt is off, and his jeans from last night are unbuckled, baggy on his hips. One shove and they would be on the ground, out of the way.

"I hope you're not done with me," I tease, mouth quirking in a coy smile.

"With you bent over for me like this, your pretty pussy dripping and aching to be filled, it would be a waste to stop now," he says, the words sound so damn dirty coming from him.

"I didn't expect you to have such a filthy mouth."

"Does it bother you?"

"No. It makes me crazy," I admit.

His eyes flash, and then he's on the bed, his back against the headboard as he reaches for me, pulling me onto his lap. I shake my head and hold myself above his thighs as I push at the waistband of his jeans. With my help, he discards them quickly, leaving his briefs the only thing keeping me from sinking down onto that huge, pierced dick of his.

I slowly lower myself over him, rubbing my slick, naked flesh along the covered length of him. The metal balls along his shaft press into me as I slide over it, so goddamn desperate for him that I'm willing to take whatever I can get.

"You're soaked. So wet for me, hmm? Is there something else you want?" he asks on a groan.

I nod, lip between my teeth. One of his piercings slips beneath me, right under my clit as I grind down. "*Please.*"

"Take me out," he orders, hands smoothing down my arms.

My hands shake from anticipation as I shove down his underwear and watch his cock spring free. Sighing in awe, I take him in my hand and scoot down his thighs until I can slip him into my mouth. I lick away the bead of precum and moan at the taste, loving the way his chest rumbles in response.

"Deeper. That's it. Right to the back of your throat," he grits out, fisting my hair.

The tip hits the back of my throat and then slides further before he's pulling me back and using his grip on my hair to bring me back up his body. Mint fills my nose before our mouths collide. He tastes like toothpaste, and suddenly, his disappearance to the bathroom makes more sense.

It's a battle of lips and teeth and tongues as I press us together, both of us bare for the first time. The warm feel of his cock slipping across my core is enough to do me in. I drop my eyes to watch as I rest my hands on his shoulders and drag myself over him, coating him in my arousal.

Fuck, it feels good. The bars beneath the skin of his shaft

press against me with each pass of my hips, winding me up and up and up.

"Do you have a condom?" I ask. I'm so riled up that I don't even recognize my voice.

A sharp nod as he reaches toward my nightstand and grabs a foil packet that wasn't there earlier. He tears it open and covers himself with the condom.

"There's no going back after this," he warns, but it sounds weak.

I wrap my hand around him and hover myself over his lap before lining us up and holding us there. With our eyes locked, I rub the tip over my entrance. His jaw is so tight it looks like it could snap.

"Good. I don't want to go back." And then I sink down onto him.

My lips part in awe as I take him inch by inch, my arousal helping with the sheer size of him. I claw his shoulder and drop my head back, unintelligible words falling between us.

"You're so big," I whimper.

His piercings rub along my inner walls, adding to the intense pleasure as he stretches me. My eyes are unable to focus as I let my head fall forward so I can try to see how much more of him I have to take. I'm already so full.

"You can take it. I know you can."

Gripping my hips, he rocks me forward, and somehow, I do. As I bottom out, I hiss, feeling him damn near in my chest.

"Perfect," he breathes, rocking me forward again, dragging my clit across his pelvis. "So proud of you. "

The praise is like a twist of my nipple. I feel it everywhere.

I circle my hips once and then settle on my knees, letting him slip halfway out of me before slowly taking him back in. The movement has my eyes rolling back, my hands gripping his shoulders as hard as I can.

"You feel so good. So tight and wet," he groans.

I nod quickly, starting to ride him properly, the promise of release driving me, making me wild. His eyes are so dark they're nearly black as he watches where we join, and when he settles a hand between us and begins to play with my clit, a deep noise of appreciation escapes him.

"Get there, Adalyn. Come like you're so desperate to."

"Cooper," I breathe, feeling the world dim, my spine tensing.

"My Adalyn," he rasps.

Thrusting his hips, he slides so deep I go soaring, release taking me to a different place. I cry out, collapsing on top of him, every nerve in my body sizzling with pleasure.

"*That's it.* Give it to me." Cooper pushes my hair from my sticky forehead and cups my face while thrusting into me, desire burning in his eyes, in his entire expression.

Desire for me.

Aftershocks make me squeeze around him as he moves his hand from my cheek to my throat and squeezes my thumping pulse. His grip is testing, and when my eyes roll back in approval of the new sensation, it tightens. He drops his face into my neck and grunts his release into my skin. His grip on my throat is so tight my vision blurs before he releases me, cupping my cheek so softly it's merely a ghost of a touch.

It's impossible to fight off a smile as I press my bare cheek to his, the reality of what just happened crashing down on me. Unsurprisingly, I don't feel a flicker of regret. Only a deep-rooted happiness and satisfaction that lights me up inside.

"You okay?" I ask softly, kissing his cheek and jaw.

"More than."

His lips brush over my throat as he kisses me there before doing the same to my cheek and, finally, my lips. My chest grows warm as he kisses me lazily, like he's in no rush. As if he's perfectly content sitting here, kissing me like this for hours.

If that's what he wanted to do, I wouldn't have a single

complaint. I've never felt calmer than I do right now. More at peace. That has to mean something, right?

Something I don't think the both of us are ready to acknowledge quite yet. Even if we're growing closer to that point with each day we spend together.

27

Cooper

sparrow

Waking up in bed with Adalyn wrapped around me for the first time is everything I expected it to be. Happiness in its purest form.

I assumed I was missing out on something great every time I chose my bed instead of hers, but we needed that boundary to keep things from escalating between us. However, now, I'm thrilled we demolished that damn line I drew in the sand. It was only a matter of time before Adalyn dragged her foot through it, anyway.

Her breath fans my chest as I press my face into her hair and kiss her crown. She smells like her shampoo—the stuff she bought in Paris. Her roots are darker now than they were weeks ago, and some of the pastel colours have begun to wash away. I wonder what colour she'll dye it this time or whether she'll leave it for a while.

Running my fingers through the strands, I hear her sigh, cheek nuzzling my pec. Fingernails drift over my abdomen when she stretches out, waking up.

"Have you just been lying here smelling my hair?" she asks, voice heavy with sleep.

"Yes."

A soft laugh escapes her. "Smell away, Sparrow."

I take a loud sniff, wanting to hear that laugh again. When I do, I feel it slide into my memory.

"Are you really going to see my dad today?"

"I doubt he would appreciate me backing out now. It will be fine. He just has questions he wants me to answer."

"And threats he's dying to make. You know, the whole 'hurt my daughter and face my wrath' thing. I love my dad, but he's been scaring boys away from the time I was a little girl."

"It's a good thing I'm a man, then, isn't it?"

She huffs, moving away from my chest to prop herself up on her pillow. I frown at the loss of contact.

"I'm not kidding here. He's going to tell you to break it off with me before things get serious."

Is that her way of saying what we have isn't serious? If so, that's an incredible attempt at downplaying our relationship.

"Is marriage not serious enough?"

"Of course it is. What I mean is, other than what you said at the table yesterday, they don't know that we're . . ."

"In like with each other?" I fill in her blanks.

"Is that what this is? Do we *like* like each other?" She waggles her brows, eyes bright and clear.

I lean close and flick the space between her brows. "Yes, we do. I'm too old to beat around the bush when it comes to what I feel. What we're doing is risky, but I think what we have is worth it, and I want to explore what it could look like in the real world."

"Even if it means you wind up roadkill beneath my dad's truck tires?"

I move in to kiss her but stop just before our lips meet to whisper, "Yes, love. Even then."

A FEW HOURS LATER, I'm waiting in the booth of Lucy's Diner for Oakley when my phone rings. I glance at the name on the screen before answering right away.

"Hey, Braxton."

"Why hello, Cooperoni. I'm glad to hear you're still alive. Papa Bear must not be there yet," says one of my best friends and Maddox's wife.

"I am. But you knew he wasn't here yet, or you wouldn't have called."

"Glad to know that college-educated brain is still working at tip-top capacity after my husband gave it a rattle. I'm sorry about that, by the way. I've since properly punished him."

I blow out a laugh. "Thank you, but that wasn't necessary. I deserved it. And he held back, or I would have had to make a trip to the ER."

"Men." She scoffs. "You did not deserve it. He's just protective of those he loves."

"You don't have to explain his behaviour to me. I'm not upset with him."

"Fine. But for what it's worth, I so saw this coming."

"Saw what coming? Me getting punches or a drunk marriage?"

"Don't play coy. You know exactly what I'm talking about."

"Feel free to elaborate, because I don't think we're on the same page."

"Oh, come on. You and my darling sister-in-law? After she caught the bouquet at my wedding, I just knew something was going to happen. She has always *loved* to pick on you, and I just thought, how funny would it be if they somehow ended up together someday? God, it's so adorable that you two managed to wind up married only a few years later."

"It's not a real marriage," I remind her, but the clarification is beginning to sound pointless, even to me.

"Oh, don't be such a stick in the mud. I only have a few more minutes to myself before Liam wakes up from his nap, and I don't want to spend them listening to you try to convince yourself of something we both know isn't true. I might not have been at the family meeting yesterday, but I heard all about what you said."

I smile appreciatively at the waitress when she sets another iced tea on the table and takes my empty one. She leaves a second later.

"I like her. I want a relationship with her. But things were different when we were travelling, spending every moment awake with one another. Everything was so free, and we were always happy. There was no real life to get in the way of anything. Things could change now that we're back."

And that terrifies me. I've let her into my life so quickly that having her leave now will undoubtedly hurt. My feelings are already so strong. In my heart, there's no chance we wouldn't work out. But in my head, there are a million reasons why we wouldn't.

Our careers are so different. She's a social presence, and I'm a homebody. Then there's our ages, our friends, and our families. The cards are stacked against us.

"They could," she agrees. "I don't think anyone wouldn't worry about those things before jumping headfirst into a new relationship. That's normal. Especially when you did grow feelings under such close proximity."

"We need this time to learn more about each other without being in those circumstances."

"I'm proud of you for going after what you want, Coop. Do right by her, okay? She might be the toughest woman I know, but something tells me you could hurt her worse than most could."

"I will. Promise." The diner bell rings, and I look up as

Oakley steps inside. I gulp when his hard stare finds me instantly, pinning me in place. "Oakley's here. Any quick words of advice for me?"

"Be honest. Brutally so. He appreciates that. Don't beat around the bush," she says.

"Got it."

"Text me after you leave so I know you haven't gotten yourself killed. Love you."

"Okay. Love you too. Bye."

Hanging up, I set my phone face down on the table and smile at Oakley. He doesn't return the smile, but he does wave while darting around a quick-moving waitress. Even if he weren't an absolute brute of a man—never seeming to have lost his hockey player physique over the years—I'm positive I would still be on the brink of throwing up.

The idea of asking a father's permission to marry his daughter seems a bit prehistoric to me, especially when Adalyn wouldn't care less if he gave it or not, but he still didn't deserve to be blindsided.

"Hey," he says, sliding into the empty booth across from me. "Thanks for meeting me."

"Hey. Yeah, of course."

"Have you ordered yet?"

Nerves have me the furthest thing from hungry. "No. I actually had a late breakfast."

"Adalyn's doing, I assume?"

I don't bother asking whether he knew I stayed at her place last night or if he's just fishing. Either way, Braxton's advice has me saying, "Yes."

He nods, stretching his arm along the back of the booth. "She's always been a breakfast girl. Never skipped that meal, no matter how little time she had to eat in the morning."

"Sounds about right. She wouldn't let us leave the hotel in the morning until we had eaten something."

The hint of a smile twists his lips. "How was the trip for you, really? Excluding that night."

He sounds genuine in his question, and my nerves settle the slightest bit. Maybe he doesn't want me dead after all. Just wounded.

"It was great. I never thought I'd get a chance to witness the kind of culture and art that lives in Europe. I've clogged my phone with a million photos. It's hard to believe we actually went, thinking back on it now."

"You enjoyed yourselves, then."

"We did."

The waitress stops by then, and we order our food. It's a welcome break in the tense, almost awkward conversation. I've never had a hard time talking to Oakley about anything, but I have a case of dry mouth right now.

Once we're alone again, he clears his throat and says, "I planned on coming today and dragging your ass across hot coals. But my wife seems to think I overreacted yesterday."

"I think you acted like any father would."

"I appreciate that, but neither you nor my daughter are incapable of making your own decisions. While I was blindsided by the news, I shouldn't have put the blame on you the way I did. I'm sorry for that."

I bury my surprise, not wanting it to show on my face. "I appreciate that. Neither of us set out to upset anyone."

"We know that. Well, most of us. You and my eldest son need to have a conversation, but that's on you two. Maddox can be a stubborn hothead, which I'm sure you're well aware of."

"You could say that." I laugh lightly. "I'm giving him time to cool down before reaching out."

"Probably a smart choice."

"For what it's worth, I tried to keep my distance. But Adalyn is . . ."

"Special," he finishes for me.

I blow out a long breath. "For starters."

"Of course, I would have preferred you two not already be legally tied to one another while starting a relationship, but I could think of worse partners for her."

"Is that a compliment?"

"The closest to one you're going to get from me anytime soon."

"Then thank you."

He snorts. "You're welcome."

The mood lifts after that, although I wouldn't go as far as to call it relaxed. Once our food arrives, we chat while we eat, and when the waitress brings our bills, we part on a better note.

As I slide into my car and watch Oakley drive off, I pull out my phone and grin. Addie's text is accompanied by a photo of her at the skate park. She's crouched, her arm extended above her as she smiles so damn wide at the camera, those blue eyes beaming beneath the summer sun. The custom pink-and-blue skateboard beneath her sneakers brings me more joy than I imagined it could.

Wifey: Do you still remember how to skate?

I type a quick reply, suddenly antsy to go to her.

Me: I'm a bit rusty.

My heart rate picks up when I see she's typing back already.

Wifey: Lucky for you I'm a pro. Meet me here?

Me: What skatepark are you at?

She sends me a photo of the sign near the entrance.

Me: Be there in ten.

And then I put the car in drive.

28

Adalyn

Cooper wasn't kidding when he said he was a bit rusty. He's gripping my shoulders tight as he stands on the borrowed board, his helmet clunking my forehead when he stares down at his feet.

"Just try rocking back and forth a bit. Test how much sway this board has," I say, stifling a laugh.

He glares at me but begins to softly rock. After a while, I take a step back, forcing his hands to fall from my shoulders as he sets his right foot on the ground and gives himself a push. His footing is awkward, but for someone who hasn't skateboarded in a while and who just moments ago couldn't sway without grabbing me, it's a win.

The pink elbow and kneepads I forced him to wear make his concentrated expression all that much more adorable.

"You've got it now," I praise when he picks up his stride.

Letting my board fall to the pavement from where I hold it upright with the toe of my sneaker, I push up beside him, matching his pace.

"You're praising me like a child who just learned how to walk," he mutters before switching his feet so his lead foot is in the back. "I just needed to get warmed up, is all."

"Okay, I believe you."

"No, you don't."

"You're right. You'll have to prove it to me."

I blow him a kiss and push off my board harder, taking off past him. The wind ruffles the loose hairs hanging out of my ponytail as I whip my head around and wiggle my fingers at his shrinking figure.

Making sure he's watching, I crouch and pop my board off the ground before kicking it into a spin and landing back down.

"You're a show-off!" he shouts.

He's picking up speed now, so I slow down enough to close the gap. "Don't be jealous, old man."

"There are too many people here for me to put you over my knee, Adalyn," he says when our boards fit side by side.

"People have never stopped us before," I tease.

Leaning his body over the gap between us, he cups my face and waist and brings me in for a quick kiss. My heart stills in my chest before taking off again. It's such a silly cheese-fest of a move, but it doesn't matter.

Voices carry over from where the other people at the skate park are watching, most likely taking photos to post online. *Let them.*

Let them take their pictures and talk about how lame it is to kiss in public. I'll make sure to leave a comment thanking them after stealing the photos for myself.

"How much longer do you want to stay?" he asks a breath later. We've nearly stopped gliding, so we push off at the same time.

"We can leave now. I wasn't expecting you to skate with me today, but thank you."

"I'll come here with you whenever you want me to," he says.

My grin is instant. "You mean that?"

"Yes. Now, think you can show me how to do a kick flip before we leave?"

He doesn't have to ask twice.

AFTER ANOTHER HOUR at the park and a stop through a drive-through for dinner, Cooper walks me up to my apartment.

My cheeks are sore from smiling so much, and my abs ache from laughing. Goddamn, I love being around him. I want to do it every day. Would he like that too?

I straighten my spine and tell myself that he would. He wouldn't have met me today if he didn't want to see me so soon after this morning.

His hand is steady on my back as we reach my door. He shifts behind me when I slip my key in and unlock it, his body a protective wall around me.

Pushing open the door, I turn to face him. "Are you coming in?"

He tips my chin with his knuckle and shakes his head. "Not this time. If I come in now, I won't be leaving until tomorrow, and I have a mountain of responsibilities waiting for me at home that I can't put off any longer."

"Does it make me selfish to want to ignore everything and just spend time together?"

"If it does, then I'm selfish too."

I blow out a soft laugh and step into his body, wrapping my arms around his waist. "Let me know how your adulting goes, okay?"

"I will. There's also something I wanted to give you before I leave."

Curiosity has me leaning back just enough to meet his stare. "I love a good surprise."

"Try not to lose it, okay?"

"Okay . . ."

Reaching into his pocket, he pulls out a silver key before offering it to me. My eyes go double their size as I carefully take it from him.

"It's a house key. I know you're a little sleuth and know where to find my spare, but this is yours. If you don't want it, I'll take it back, but the thought of you here alone in this big apartment doesn't sit well with me. At least think about coming to stay with me until you can find a new roommate or whatever."

I fist the key and press my knuckles into his chest. "Hold up. Are you asking me to move in with you?"

His cheeks fill with colour. "It would be weird for my wife not to live with me, right?"

"Depends who you ask."

"Then yes, I'm asking you to move in with me."

"Because you don't want me to be alone?"

His eyes slowly trace my features, as if trying to commit them to memory. "That, and it would mean we would never have to worry about spending nights alone."

Heaven. "In that case, I'll need a couple days to pack some of my stuff. I *am* allowed to bring my things, right?"

"No, you can only have what's already there," he says, deadpan.

I pinch his side, muttering, "Sarcastic ass."

His laugh fills the hallway. "Of course you can bring your things. Fill my house with all the pink you desire if it'll make you happy."

"Don't tease me. You know how I feel about that by now."

"I'm not teasing. Paint the walls Barbie pink if you want to. It's just a house."

"Were you this sweet with your past girlfriends? Because I'm having trouble processing how they would have accepted the ending of your relationship if you were," I blurt out.

Does he have an ick I have yet to see that they did? I doubt it, considering how much time we've spent together already, but you never know. In all honesty, it's hard to think of anything that could be bad enough to outweigh the good.

Crinkles appear at the corners of his eyes when he laughs. "You say it as if there's a choice when it comes to accepting a breakup."

I shrug. "I'm just saying, I won't give you up unless you give me a good enough reason for us not to be together. You're stuck with me now. Married or not."

I'm surprised when he looks genuinely content with that. "I'll hold you to it, love. Now, go inside before I lose my ability to leave again. We can continue the past relationship talk another time."

"Fine. But I want details. All the nitty-gritty ones that you haven't shared with anyone else," I say, hugging him again.

He wraps me up in his arms. "Alright, but I'll want the same in return."

"I'm already an open book."

We stand there for a little while longer, neither one of us wanting to let go. It takes everything in me to pull back when my next-door neighbour gets home, their keys rattling loudly as they fiddle with their door. I smile up at Cooper, pretending we're still alone.

"I'll talk to you soon," I say.

After kissing me one last time, he steps away, a pained look on his face. "Soon."

"Bye, Sparrow."

"Bye, Adalyn."

The sound of him saying my name lingers as I head inside and shut the door behind me. Silence welcomes me, and I sigh, turning the TV on.

I've never been a rational person, but even I know that my dependence on Cooper might be borderline obsession. So, instead of moping around doing nothing, I head to my room, grab my camera and laptop, and put my ass to work.

It takes hours to catch up on emails, plan out my posting schedule, confirm upcoming photoshoots, and upload the first of many travel photos, but by the time I'm done, I feel much calmer. I never complain about my job because I know how lucky I am to be able to do what I do, but it can be overwhelming at times. Especially when I let things accumulate the way I do far too often.

It helps that I have such an amazing publicist who takes care of the things that used to drag me down, but maybe I should find an assistant. Even Noah has an assistant, and he doesn't do anything besides record music in his bedroom that he won't let anyone listen to and perform covers at gross bars. It was Tiny's idea, but surely, he would have told her to fire his assistant if he didn't even slightly enjoy having one.

I remember when my brand was simply me going out and having fun. Somehow along the way, it's strayed from that. Is it possible to get back there someday? Or is this a forever thing?

The questions float away when one of those secret Noah songs plays from my laptop speakers. It's the one I stole back in tenth grade, before he moved out of the house and would stupidly leave his laptop lying out on the kitchen table.

The song is one of my favourites, one of the gentler ones I've heard from him. His voice is as deep and hard as it always is but somehow happier, if that's even possible. The only time I hear him sound this way is when he's singing or when a certain brunette is around.

He would kill me if he knew I had this in my possession. For some reason, he's insanely protective over his music. It's a shame because if this were to get out there . . . my brother's life would change. I know that without a doubt.

I want that for him so badly. He deserves to be recognized by the world as the pure talent he is. But as much as I wish I could help with that, there's no way he would ever forgive me for betraying his trust in order to ensure that happened.

Pausing the song, I shut my laptop and toss it to the side. For now, I'll just sit and wait for the chance he takes the shot for himself.

Hopefully, we'll all live to see that day.

29

Cooper

sparrow

Two days later, I walk inside my dad's house with Adalyn at my side. She's a ball of excitement, all wide-eyed and bushy-tailed as she looks around as if this is the first time she's ever been here. In reality, the entire Hutton family has been here a million times, but tonight is undoubtedly different.

This time, Addie is here *with* me. As my wife.

She stole my breath when I picked her up and found her wearing a ruffled, mid-thigh-length white dress. The sight of her in a white dress with those muscled, tan legs of hers on display short-circuited my brain. Even twenty minutes later, I'm still trying to reboot myself.

Scarlett is the first one to greet us, and despite the rough exterior she shows to those she doesn't know well, she pulls me in for a tight hug.

"I missed you," she says.

"Missed you too, SP."

After separating, Scar brushes me off for Adalyn. "And hello to you, Mrs. White."

A jolt of unexpected satisfaction brushes over me. Addie flushes, panicked eyes darting to mine for the briefest second.

"It's still Hutton, actually. You'll have to talk to

Cooper about that one. I don't think changing my name would be a great idea since we won't be staying married," she rambles, more flustered than I think I've ever seen her.

Scarlett just stares at her, grinning. "I'm just teasing, sweetheart. Come in and shake it off."

"Right. I knew that."

I tuck Addie beneath my arm before Scarlett can scoop her up. "Dad's finally tainted you with his terrible teasing habits, SP."

"I've done no such thing. She's always been this way beneath all that cool exterior," Dad interjects, winking at his wife. Smile lines appear when he looks at Addie and me. "If it isn't my favourite couple. Here at last."

I roll my eyes. "We haven't even been back a full week yet. And you saw us the other day."

"It's not a crime for a father to want to see his son often." He palms his chest, frowning dramatically.

"The older I get, the easier it is to realize why you and my mom are such good friends," Addie adds.

I let my fingers tangle in her hair as we stand there. Touching her has become far too addicting.

"The greats have to stick together, Adalyn," he replies.

I snort a laugh. "Not sure that's what she meant."

Dad scowls at me. "It's what I'm pretending she said. Come in and eat before the food gets cold. Your mom is running a bit late, but she said not to wait."

As he starts to herd us toward the dining room, I ask, "Where is she? And Amelia?"

"Your sister is in her room pouting because I told her she couldn't go out with her friends tonight, and your mom just got caught up."

The smell of all the different foods wafting from the dining room makes my stomach growl. Once the spread on the table comes into view, I nearly moan. It looks like they were planning on feeding a small army, which means we'll be going home with a million leftovers.

"This looks amazing," Addie says.

I pull a chair away from the table and wait for her to sit before pushing it in. The smile she tosses me over her shoulder is a goddamn gift.

Taking the seat beside her, I sit and glance around the table. "Dad's taken to cooking the past couple of months. I think he's preparing for the retirement he refuses to have."

Dad pours Scarlett a glass of wine before doing the same for himself. "I can't leave WIT in the hands of just anyone. Unless you suddenly want it, I have to work until I find someone else worthy of our legacy." He starts placing serving utensils in the bowls of food. "I'm also still young. There's no rush."

"There will be depending on how long it takes you to deem someone worthy."

Besides his children and wife, the White Ice Training centre is my dad's everything. He started the hockey facility back before I was brought to live with him and over the past thirty years has turned it into the new White family legacy. I've always understood his want to leave it in good hands when the time comes for him to retire, but it's turning out to be a lot harder to do that than any of us thought. He never pressured me into taking over for him, and I don't think I've ever told him how much I appreciated that.

I just want him to relax after all this time. He's worked harder than anyone I know, and he deserves to just . . . slow down. To travel and spend more time with his family and whatever else his heart desires.

"It's not a process I can rush, Coop."

Adalyn sets her hand on my thigh and looks at Dad. "I don't think it's a bad thing to want to wait. My father was so bored after he retired. I thought he was going to end up starting a beer league team just to get himself out of the house."

"See?" Dad asks me, his sly grin making me frown.

I reach beneath the table and softly pinch the outside of Adalyn's thigh, smirking when she sucks in a quick, surprised breath. Resting my hand over hers, I turn back to Dad.

"Oakley's retirement is different. He didn't have a choice, and there's a big difference between retiring at thirty and retiring at fifty."

"We can argue about this for days, but it won't change my mind."

"Can we all talk less and start eating before we're left with cold pasta?" Scarlett asks, waving a hand over the food.

Addie giggles while reaching for the bowl of fettuccine and plating some. My throat clogs when she digs in a second time but drops the noodles on my plate instead. I feel my father watching me when she moves to the bowl of sauce and scoops up some of it, purposefully avoiding the chunks of mushroom floating around inside. As she spreads the sauce over the noodles on my plate, Dad clears his throat.

"Since when do you not like mushrooms?"

My wife freezes, eyes flying to mine. I smile softly, reassuringly, and drape my arm over the back of her chair.

"Since always. But you love them, so I never said anything," I tell him, heat crawling up my neck.

Adalyn winces, leaning toward me. "I'm sorry. I noticed you avoided them when we were gone, so I just assumed," she whispers.

"You should have said something. Shit, I've been putting mushrooms in everything since you were a boy," Dad says.

"It's really not that big of a deal."

He exhales heavily. "What's next—do you not really like cheesecake either?"

"He does."

"I do."

Adalyn and I speak at the same time, and her following grin makes my stomach go wild with flutters.

The sound of footsteps travelling toward the dining room has the conversation coming to a thankful end. A beat later, Mom appears in the doorway, her happiness filling the room.

"I'm so sorry I'm late, everyone," she rushes out.

I laugh when she comes up behind my chair and wraps her arms around me, kissing my cheek twice. "Hi, Mom."

"Hi, honey. Gosh, it feels like you were gone for months." With another kiss, this time to the top of my head, Mom moves on to Adalyn, pausing as she stares at her with wide eyes. Curiosity blossoms inside of me when her eyes begin to water. "Look at their fingers, Adam. Oh, my God."

Silence, and then Dad roars a laugh, his wife joining in a second later. "Christ, you've been here two minutes, Beth. What happened to 'I promise I won't cry right away'?"

Mom throws her hands in the air. "You should have known better. I wasn't as well prepared as I thought I was. You never told me they had matching tattoos!"

"I didn't think it was important at the time!" he defends himself.

Adalyn leans forward and glances at me, looking just as confused as I'm sure I do. I choke out a laugh and shrug.

"Well, what else do I not know? Is someone about to tell me that they're not bothering with an annulment after all? Because I don't think I can take it."

Dad winks at me across the table before gesturing to the empty chair left for Mom. "Sit and eat. You're going to scare Adalyn away."

"I don't scare easy. Promise," Adalyn chips in, reaching for Mom's hand before she can get too far. "It's nice to see you again, Beth."

The first of what I assume will be many tears tonight trails down Mom's cheek as she squeezes Addie's hand back, bringing it to her chest.

"Likewise, sweetheart. We'll have to talk later and catch up."

Adalyn nods, smiling sincerely. "Absolutely."

Scarlett says something to Beth then, and the two of them begin to laugh together. I'm not sure what's so funny, and I don't care. I can't look away from my wife.

I underestimated what seeing her around my family like this would do to me. She's utterly destroyed me. Put me under a spell that I would pay to keep from breaking.

If I wasn't already positive I was falling in love with her, I would undoubtedly know it now.

30

Adalyn

After dinner, we're all chatting in the living room when Adam asks Cooper to help him with something outside. With a lingering kiss to the top of my head, Cooper gets up from the couch and follows his dad out to the backyard. Scarlett and I watch them leave, but Beth is quick to snag our attention again. I'm sure we look like sad, lost puppies without them, but they knew damn well what they were doing leaving us here.

It was a ploy to give Beth and Scarlett a chance to talk to me alone.

"I hope Cooper prepared you for the grilling I'm about to give you, Addie," she says.

I tear my eyes from the patio door, straightening my spine as I look at her with an excited smile. "He did. Take your best shot."

There wasn't much preparation needed on the drive over besides a quick mention that his mom might have some questions for me. Truthfully, I don't mind answering questions about myself, especially not in a situation like this.

Scarlett throws her feet up on the cushioned ottoman.

"What do you have to grill her about? You've known her for damn near her entire life."

Beth waves her off, keeping her attention on me. "Don't listen to her. She's just jealous because she doesn't have any good questions for you."

"Not true. I just already know all I need to right now," Scarlett sings.

"There's no rush. I'm not planning on going anywhere. You can ask me anything whenever you want," I say, lifting one shoulder in a shrug.

By the way my words make Beth's eyes glow with approval, I know I said the right thing.

"You don't know how happy I am to hear that. I think I speak for us all when I say we've never seen Cooper this way with a woman before. I know that's the most cliché thing ever, but it's true. Right, Scar?"

The second most important woman in Cooper's life nods, smiling softly. "She's right. You two complement each other very well."

Her recognition of something I've begun to realize myself makes my stomach swoop.

"He's the calm to my storm," I tell them.

Beth's eyes gloss over before she blinks a few times. "From what you got him to do with you in Europe, I think it's obvious that you bring out a side of him that I haven't seen in years. You bring him out of his shell a bit."

The shock on everyone's faces when we told them we had gone to a nude beach is forever ingrained in my memory. I thought Cooper's face was going to turn a permanent shade of red.

"I wasn't expecting him to let loose so easily, but he was a really good sport about most things."

"How is living together going to work? You've only been moved in for a day so far?" Scarlett asks.

I nod. "We brought some of my stuff over yesterday. Just the essentials. I don't know how it's going to work, honestly. I'm going to start looking for a new roommate for my apartment, but until then, I guess it'll be just like it was when we were travelling."

Only a lot scarier.

Suddenly, Beth blows out a shaky breath, wringing her hands in her lap. "Do you love him?"

"You can't ask her that yet, Beth," Scar says lightly.

I wet my lips and breathe in a steadying inhale. "It's okay. Honestly, it's only been a few weeks, but with him, time hasn't seemed to matter. I don't know if it's love yet, but it has to be close."

When it comes to recognizing what is love and what isn't, I wish I was older and more experienced. I've never been in love with anyone before, but I'm smart enough to be able to tell that what I feel for Cooper is much more than a simple crush. The things I feel for him are intense. So intense that the thought of being without him for even the shortest amount of time hurts worse than any physical injury I've ever had.

I didn't think twice about accepting his offer to move in with him, nor do I wish for even one second that we hadn't drunkenly found ourselves married. It seems so silly, but there's this part of me that wants to tell him to call off the annulment and to forget about a divorce if that's what it came to.

Is being in love with someone wondering how you'd survive in a world without them by your side? Because if it is, then maybe I am in love with him already.

"That's the look, sweetheart," Scarlett says. When I glance across the room at her, the sure way she's smiling at me confirms my suspicions.

"My mom is going to be so pissed she missed out on this gossip session," I blurt out.

Beth releases a watery laugh. "As long as you go home and give her a recap, I'm sure she'll forgive us."

She would simply because her little matchmaker heart would be too happy for her to stay annoyed with me.

"My dad, on the other hand, can never hear about this conversation." I wince.

"Our lips are sealed." Beth pulls an imaginary zipper across her mouth.

The patio door slides open, and Cooper slips through, Adam close behind. Summer heat and the smell of chlorine from the backyard pool seep in with them.

The moment Cooper finds me, his lips part on a grin that steals my breath. It's a smile that's just for me, and I accept it with open arms.

"Ready to go?" he asks, hands in his pockets.

With one long glance at Beth and Scarlett, I nod, feeling content. "Ready."

The next few minutes are a blur of tight hugs and kisses on cheeks. By the time Cooper helps me into his car, I'm buzzing, filled to the brim with love. I can't help but stare at him when he slips into the car and starts the engine.

His jaw is cleanly shaven and so damn sharp that it should be criminal. He's put his glasses on sometime in the night, and fuck my life, I've never met someone who could look so hot in a pair of glasses before.

Buckling my seat belt, I say, "You look like a porn star in those glasses."

His laugh fills the room, the sound choked. "I still haven't gotten used to your lack of filter."

"My own personal dirty professor," I tease. "When are your office hours, sir?"

"If you want to play, love, at least wait until we get home."

Squeezing my thighs together, I push aside the sudden throb of arousal between them and say, "Have I ever told you how much I love it when you call me that? For a while there, I was scared I was never going to get a pet name like everyone else."

His throat moves with a swallow. "Why would you want to be like everyone else? You're beyond a simple pet name, but I can't seem to help myself anymore."

The honesty renders me speechless as we pull away from his dad's house. I'm not a big book reader, but Ivy is, and I'm pretty sure Cooper is what she would consider a man written by a woman. He turns me into a puddle of mush without even trying. One honest, sweet statement and I'm ready to crawl across the centre console and beg him to take me in the middle of the road.

"Was that the wrong thing to say?" he asks after another few beats of silence.

"No. God, no. You said everything right. That's the problem."

He glances at me. "I'm confused."

"You're not supposed to say things like that to me after such an incredible night, when I'm already on cloud nine, and expect me not to want to tell you to pull over and fuck me in the back seat," I huff.

The car swerves as he curses and then quickly pulls us back into the proper lane. I push my hair behind my ears and bite back a laugh.

"You okay over there?" I ask.

His grip tightens on the steering wheel, but when he looks at me again, it's not anger or frustration I see in his eyes. It's desire.

"I had plans for you tonight, but apparently, we're going to change them," he mutters. I watch as he reaches toward the touch screen on the dash and turns the stereo volume down, confusion sparking in my mind. "Pull your dress up, take your panties off, and then hand them to me."

The lust dripping from his words brings goosebumps to my skin. Like he's reached inside my head and taken control of my actions, I lift the hem of my dress above my hips and shimmy out of my panties. I don't have to look at them to know they're wet when I hand them to him.

Cool air hits the wet flesh between my legs. Arousal fills my blood as I sit and wait for his next instruction.

"Touch yourself and show me how wet you are." He drops my panties over the bulge in his slacks. "These are mine now."

Spreading my legs, I move my hand between my legs, finding myself so slick my fingers become wet with a single touch. With my heart thumping in my ears, I lift my fingers in his direction.

I let loose a moan when he takes my wrist, uses it to pull my hand closer toward him, and then slips my fingers into his mouth. It's dirty in the best way, and I feel it all the way to my toes. They curl into my sandals.

"As soon as we get home, you're going to sit on my face so I can have a proper taste of you," he groans, letting my fingers fall back to my lap. "We're only a couple of minutes away. I want you to fuck your fingers until we get there."

"I'm going to leave a wet spot on your seat."

"I don't care."

The moment I bring my hand back to my pussy, I find myself not only soaked but swollen and sensitive. I brush my clit and bite my lip to stifle a whimper before slowly dipping a finger inside of me.

"Don't keep yourself quiet, Adalyn. Nobody is here with us, and I want to hear how good it feels."

"It would feel better if you were touching me," I breathe.

"I know. I'll give you everything you want when we get home," he promises.

My head falls back against the seat when I slide another finger inside, my walls tight around them. As I start moving them in and out at a quicker pace, the wet sound that fills the car makes everything feel more intense.

That intensity, combined with the excitement of what's to come once we walk inside the house, makes it hard to keep control of my movements. I have no doubt that if I come in this car, Cooper will spend the rest of the night punishing me for it. I clench my fingers, the idea sounding more appealing than it does threatening.

"Touch your clit, Addie. I want you on the edge by the time we pull up."

I bite down on my tongue and do as he says, circling it with soft pressure. The burn of his eyes on my skin comes every few seconds, bringing me that much closer to release.

"Tell me how it feels," he orders, voice strained.

"*So good*," I whine, hips pushing off the seat.

"Be a good girl for me and don't come."

A good girl. Right. But what if . . . No. *Good girls don't purposefully disobey orders*, *Adalyn*. Fuck. I listen to that annoying voice in my head and yank my hand away. My entire body feels like it's on fire, but I keep my hand in the air, sucking in lungfuls of air.

The car comes to a sharp stop in front of the house. Heavy approval burns in his stare as he drags it over me. It snags on my fingers. The ones I just had knuckle deep inside myself.

"Inside."

I don't have to be told twice. My adrenaline spikes as I all but dive out of the car and hurry up the sidewalk. Cooper's close behind, and as I stand in front of the door, a bundle of hypersensitive horniness, he hurries to unlock it and usher us inside.

After kicking off my shoes, I move in the direction of our bedroom, only to stop when his voice comes from behind me.

"We're not going to the bedroom."

Turning around, I find him standing in front of the doorway that I know leads to his basement studio. My heart skips.

"Are you going to paint me, Cooper?" I ask softly.

His next words ruin me. "Yes. Among other things."

31

Adalyn

The studio is clean and organized and smells like paint. I shouldn't have expected it any other way. There's a wall of easels, a blank white canvas hung on the wall, a couch, and shelves upon shelves of paint and pencils and brushes. I stare at it all in a state of wonder.

"It's a lot," he says behind me.

"It's amazing. You use all of this stuff?"

He brushes against my back, setting his hands on my shoulders before moving them down my arms and back up again. I press into him, letting my muscles go loose.

"Yes."

"And clearly, painting is your favourite form of art."

"It is. It's like carving out a bit of my soul and leaving it on a canvas. My mind expands in a different way when I pick up a brush, like there's no real end to it. It goes on forever."

"That sounds special."

His breath fans my neck as he kisses my thumping pulse. "Painting is my adrenaline rush. My free fall from an airplane."

"Your sex on the beach," I murmur.

"My days with you."

My chest grows tight, emotion racing through me. "Cooper."

Shaking his head, he leaves a lingering kiss on my throat and, too slowly, brings his hand to the front of my dress. He presses his palm between my breasts. "I know. I feel it too."

I close my eyes, fighting against the burn behind them. There's too much going on inside of me. An explosion of emotions that turn me inside out. But there's one that burns brighter than the others. A month ago, I wouldn't have believed that I would experience this feeling for the first time in my brother's best friend's paint studio. But there's no denying it now. No second-guessing.

I love this man. Husband or not, he's mine. Simple as that.

"Your heart is pounding."

A choked laugh. "It feels like it's going to explode."

I feel his smile on my skin. "Mine too."

"You're just nervous because I'm expecting to be painted tonight."

"I've never been calmer when it comes to painting someone, love. I could paint you from memory."

"What's making your heart pound, then?"

"Not yet" is all he says before grabbing my hand and leading me toward the couch. I sit and wait for him to join me, only to watch him lower himself to his knees instead. He touches my thighs and slowly spreads them apart. "Can I taste you, Adalyn?"

I try to get past how seeing him on his knees for me makes it hard to breathe and say, "Yes. Please do that."

He leans forward, lips brushing my inner thigh as he drags them up, pushing the hem of my dress along the way. Once it rests on my hips, exposing me, he blows out a harsh breath.

"I could spend hours right here," he rasps, parting my wet flesh with his tongue. Wet velvet strokes me from bottom to top before circling my entrance.

There's no need to tease anymore. The ride home was enough foreplay.

My mind goes blank when he sinks a finger deep inside my walls, curling it just right. I whimper, shifting my hips, trying to get him even deeper. Sensing my desperation, he adds a second finger, fluttering his tongue over my clit.

I've never had a man go down on me with such enthusiasm before. Like he's doing it because he loves to, not because he knows I do. That in and of itself has my orgasm gathering strength, lightning zipping through my veins.

"I can feel you gripping me, baby. So desperate to come, aren't you?"

My tongue feels swollen in my mouth. I tangle my fingers in his hair and pull, needing to feel some sort of control as he picks up tempo. He releases a growled noise against my core and drives his fingers into me harder.

An explosion of pleasure turns me boneless, wave upon waves

of it seeping deep into my muscles. Blood rushes through my ears, showing no sign of slowing.

I let his hair slip from my fingers when he pushes up and cups my face, kissing me like he fears he'll never get the chance again. His jaw is smooth beneath my hands as I touch him, keeping him close.

"You need to get naked," I mumble between kisses.

With hasty movements, I pop the bottom two buttons on his shirt and undo the leather belt holding his butt-accentuating dress pants up.

His laugh is hot on my mouth. "By all means, strip me, love."

I tug on his bottom lip and hold his dark stare. One sharp push and I get his pants down to his thighs. He steps out of them, then gets rid of his shirt next.

He curves a brow, standing in front of me in all his naked

glory. "Am I going to have to tear that dress off of you, or are you going to take it off yourself?"

"Wanna flip a coin?"

"Next time. Now, take it off."

"Yes, sir," I say, smirking.

Slowly, he takes a step toward me. "You say it like a joke, but I think I like hearing you call me that a bit more than I should."

"Hearing what? Sir?" I lean forward and pull my dress over my head, letting it drop to the floor.

He groans, long and hard, and then I'm tossed like a rag doll onto my back, body spread along the cushions. The dip of the couch as he moves between my legs makes excitement spark inside of me. His face is hard, muscles tense, but his eyes are burning, so fucking hot I can feel their touch on my body.

Tension ripples in the air as he grips me beneath my knees and lifts my legs, resting the backs of them along his chest. With a kiss on my ankle, I feel him drag the head of his cock through my pussy, parting me. Each tease against my entrance sends me into a tailspin. My lip burns from biting down on it.

"Please. *Please* put it in," I beg, reaching for the hand cupping my knee.

His eyes fall between my legs, watching us together. I'm jealous, the position blocking my view.

"Condom," he bites out, stilling.

I swallow my frustration when he pulls back. "Fuck a condom. I got the implant when I was eighteen. Haven't been with anyone in at least six months."

"Longer for me. A year, maybe." The muscles in his throat strain with a swallow. "Are you sure?"

I nod furiously. "Yes. Completely sure. I trust you." *I love you.* A garbled cry escapes me when he slides the tip in before pulling back. "*Cooper*," I whine.

"My love," he whispers.

This time when he slides in, he goes far enough for me to

feel the first piercing on his shaft. It's a tight fit on its own, let alone with my legs up like this.

I wiggle my hips. "Deeper."

A line forms between his brow when he pushes in, another set of metal balls dragging inside of me, and then another, until I'm so full of him I can't think straight. I grip the couch back and whimper, the pleasure almost too much.

"You take my cock like it was made for you, baby," he says, voice tight and raw.

He looks up from between my legs, and his breath catches when our eyes meet. Whatever he finds in mine has his entire expression shuddering.

Fuck me.

What did he find? The truth, most likely. I've always been shit at hiding my emotions.

"Maybe it *was* made for me," I rasp.

"Fuck," he groans, and then he's pulling that long cock all the way out before shoving it back in again, no hesitation.

The force of his thrusts rocks me back on the couch and rattles all thoughts from my mind. I'm already so close, my orgasm approaching at too quick a pace to prepare myself to hold back and wait. A low moan slips from my mouth when he brushes my G-spot, and his hips falter for the briefest second, fire dancing in his eyes.

Each drag of him inside of me is pure ecstasy. I'm on a cloud, floating so high I don't expect his next move. I swipe my hand out and grab hold of his bicep when he pushes my knees up toward my chest, still fully seated inside of me, and circles his thumb around where we meet to get it slick with my arousal. Stars burst behind my eyes the moment he carefully presses that wet thumb into my ass, eyes snaring mine.

"*Oh,*" I moan, the touch foreign but still good. *Really* good. Even as his thumb slowly stretches me, a slight burn following its movements.

"That okay?"

Words fail me. I nod, tightening my grip on his bicep.

He swallows, pushing his thumb further while twisting his hips and grinding against my clit. The combination of sensations is enough to shove me off the cliff. I go flying, losing all sense of time and place. Everything but Cooper.

"I'm coming," I choke, nails digging into his skin. He groans, pistoning his hips, even as I clench around him, trying to keep him deep. "Holy *fuck*."

As I start to recover, he removes his thumb and slows to an easy, lazy rhythm, watching me so intently it's like he's trying to memorize the way I look right now. The moment seems to go on forever before he moves again, a switch flicked in his head as he drives into me hard and fast. I meet his movements, giving just as good as I'm getting.

"I want to watch you come," I whisper, fingers relaxed, caressing his arm.

He grits his teeth and grips my hip, thrusting harder and harder until the studio fills with a guttural groan. The sounds of his pleasure are an aphrodisiac. Fuck, it's hot when men are loud in bed.

"Adalyn," he growls, burying himself deep and staying there as he starts to come.

My name has never sounded better.

After a few moments, he pulls out and helps my legs hug his hips before collapsing over me, his cheek on my breast. I wrap my arms around him and sigh, feeling simply . . . *beyond*.

The heavy, quick beating of my heart thumps against his, and the world around us disappears. It's just us. The way I like it.

"It's never been like this before," I whisper, brushing damp brown curls from his forehead.

He kisses the swell of my breast, ghosting his fingernails over my side. "For me either."

I believe him. I know I do. But fuck if after sex insecurities don't try to bury me alive in what should be a loving haze. I've worked hard over the years on training myself not to give a shit about those annoying voices in my head, but somehow, falling for Cooper has let some of them weasel their way into my subconscious. Maybe it's because I don't want to mess anything up with him, or maybe I've just gotten too comfortable. Either way, I decide to let those voices out, even for just a moment.

For right now, I let myself be vulnerable.

32

Adalyn

"You're not just saying that, are you?" I ask.

"No. Everything with you is different. Sex included."

There's no hesitation. As if his honesty has popped a balloon inside of me, I feel those insecurities woosh away.

"Can you tell me about your past girlfriends?"

He blows a rough laugh over my chest. "Now?"

It is a weird time to ask, but I've held my past relationship questioning off for as long as possible. I'm in love with him, and I think I owe it to myself to get the past out of the way.

"Why not? You're not going to tell me anything that's going to have me wishing I hadn't just let you rail me into tomorrow, are you?"

His teeth find the underside of my breast. "Never. I just want to stay in this after-sex haze with you for a while. Then, I was hoping to paint you. If that's okay."

I keep stroking his head, quickly drying curls slipping between my fingers, nails gently scratching his scalp. "I might get a bit jealous hearing about the other women who got to see this side of you, but I'll keep the claws in. And I've been waiting to see you paint, Sparrow. All you gotta do is tell me how to pose."

He kisses my sternum, staring up at me. "I didn't date in high school and only got my first semi-serious girlfriend during my fifth year of university. Her name was Regan, and she wanted to move faster than I was ready to back then. I didn't start taking dating seriously until I graduated, but nothing really stuck."

"Why did nothing stick? Just wasn't the right person?"

"You could say that. I think there was always also this prick in the back of my mind reminding me to be careful of who I let into my life. My parents are on great terms now, but there was a time when they weren't, and it was hard on everyone. I wasn't old enough to witness it, but I've learned about it all over the years. I'm not sure if your parents ever told you about their past with my mom?"

"Briefly," I murmur. From what I remember, it wasn't great. Nobody speaks of the past much, though.

"My mom and dad had a fling back in university. Your mom and mine never got along back then, so nobody really understood why Dad was with her. It surprised everyone to see them together, but their fling didn't last long before Mom up and left without a word. Three years later, Dad found out she was pregnant with me when she disappeared and, shortly after I was born, was diagnosed with bipolar disorder.

"When I was two, she brought me to him and asked him to take care of me. My dad, being the man he is, took me in without hesitation, and then she was gone again. She booked herself into a psychiatric hospital, and by the time she came back, I was old enough to begin wondering where my mom was and why she didn't want me anymore."

He clears his throat, grip on me tightening. "Once she left the hospital, she gave sole custody of me to my dad and worked to get back on her feet. My mom is incredibly resilient and worked hard to put her life back together before coming back for me. It was challenging having her pop back into my life, especially because I was so young and held such resentment toward her leaving in the first place, but we all learned how to make it work together, and she's been here ever since."

The strain in his voice makes me pull him tighter against me, wishing we were in a bed instead of on the couch. "I hope you don't think you're responsible for her illness."

His sigh is heavy. "I try not to, but how am I supposed to ignore that I'm the reason she struggled so badly? If she hadn't gotten pregnant, things could have been so different for her. We'll never know now."

"What were you supposed to do? You weren't asked to come into the world. That responsibility does not fall on you."

"I know. Mom's told me that more times than I can count. I've just always had a hard time not feeling responsible for things like that. I want everyone to be happy all the time. Especially those I care about."

"And we love that about you. But we want you to be happy too. Putting your feelings aside in order to please everyone else isn't fair to yourself."

Shifting, he scoops me into his arms and turns us on our sides. The couch is far from comfortable beneath me, but I can't find it in me to care right now. Not as he buries his face in my hair and exhales a long breath that sends shivers down my spine.

"I'll work on it. I'm already happier. You help with that."

"Maybe you need me to start pinching your ass whenever you try to be a people pleaser."

"Considering your obsession with my ass, I think you'd like that a little too much."

I gasp dramatically. "How do you know about that?"

"I'm not blind."

I scoff. "Well, it's not my fault you're so hot."

"I like that you like how I look, Addie. Stare at my ass as much as you want," he says, smoothing his hand over my stomach. "Now, enough about me. Tell me about all of the guys that came before me."

A laugh bubbles up my throat, but I swallow it down. "There's not much to tell. I'm far from a virgin, but I haven't been in a relationship serious enough to matter. Most of the guys I've been with I've met either through work or Ivy, and they weren't interested in more than a booty call here or there."

"I should tell you that I'm sorry you've had such bad luck, but I'm grateful for the lack of competition. I haven't thrown a punch in years."

This time, I let my laugh spill out. "I can't imagine you punching anyone. My brother was always the one doing that."

"I've never hit anyone before. It was a punching bag," he admits, almost sheepishly.

"I can't imagine you doing that either. Let me guess, Maddox talked you into it?"

He hums in confirmation. "I never took to it. He still trains with a bag sometimes, I think."

"I'm sure he printed off a picture of your face and taped it on one after he found out about us."

"Without a doubt. At least until Braxton found it and tore it off."

"And she would do exactly that. She loves me too much to let him destroy your pretty face. Picture or the real thing."

"We'll have to thank her the next time we're together."

"If we do, it will absolutely go to her head," I state.

My sister-in-law, while so incredibly humble, would make a huge deal out of knowing we were thanking her for protecting us from her big scary husband. She would never let Maddox live it down.

"Let it. I owe her for talking Dox off the ledge before he took you and stowed you away in a tower somewhere." He shifts his hand higher, resting it between my breasts. "There wouldn't be any fixing our friendship after I stole you back from him."

"I would have helped you by letting down my hair so you could use it to climb up to get me. Don't worry."

"So generous of you," he murmurs.

"I try my best."

A happy, content sigh warms my cheek as he leans over and kisses it, fingers tipping my chin toward him. He slides his lips to mine, so softly I barely feel them as my eyes slide shut.

We kiss like that until my neck gets sore, and I pull away, eyes growing heavy. "What time is it?"

"I'm not sure. Probably late."

I nod. "Will you tell me how to pose for you? I refuse to be teased when it comes to watching you paint."

There's already a canvas set up on one of the wooden easels across the room.

"We don't have to do that tonight. I can do it any other day. As you know, my schedule is pretty clear for the next few weeks still."

"No, I want to do it tonight. Please?"

Another kiss to the back of my head. "Alright. You can just lie here while I get everything ready, okay?"

"Okay." I'm not interested in moving right now, anyway.

As he slips out from behind me, I shiver at the cool air against my naked back. There doesn't seem to be much heat down here, but the cold didn't bother me when he was keeping me warm.

Noticing my shiver, he looks around the couch before grabbing a small blanket from the floor. It must have fallen off earlier.

"Here." He drapes the blanket over me and tucks it beneath my bare toes. "Better?"

I smile. "Much."

Content with my answer, he tugs his underwear and shirt on, then drifts across the room, collecting handfuls of things and disposing of them on the table near the canvas and easel I noticed earlier. He glances back at me a few times, catching me staring at him before smiling and looking away again. For the next few minutes, he works in silence, alternating between squeezing paint on a white palette and looking at me between mixes.

My eyes are drooping when he sets the palette down and moves the easel to the centre of the room. I blink, but it's a long one.

There's a soft touch on my cheek and then his voice. "Do you want me to carry you to bed, baby?"

I curl my fingers in the soft blanket and tuck it beneath my chin. "No."

"Okay. I'll take you up when I'm done, then."

"Yes."

Warm pressure on my forehead. "I'll be across the room if you need me."

"I always need you," I whisper.

He runs a hand over my head. "Sleep well, my love."

And I do, only waking what feels like hours later when I'm lifted off the couch and settled against a warm, hard chest. We sway, footsteps clapping on creaky stairs, and then the air becomes warmer.

The smell of home helps clear the lingering paint scent from my nostrils. We walk for a minute more, and then I'm being set down on cool silk sheets. I sigh at the feel of them and rub my cheek on my pillow.

"Did you finish?" I ask, voice heavy with sleep.

"I finished. I'll show you tomorrow morning," he whispers.

I frown. "I want to see it now."

A soft smile ghosts his mouth. He strokes a finger across my forehead. "It's downstairs."

"Bring it up. Please."

"Okay," he whispers.

After leaving a light kiss on my lips, he leaves the room. The minute it takes him to grab it feels like a lifetime. Between my excitement, exhaustion, and just blatant happiness, I'm a total mess of emotions as I wait.

Then, as soon as he steps back into view, I gasp. Staring at the canvas in his hands, it's like looking in the mirror. If the mirror was capable of turning every colour more vibrant and somehow, every inch of my face more lifelike. I've never seen myself this way. From the view of someone else, and that's exactly what this is. No photo could capture something so real.

From my closed eyes and the exact curl of my lashes to the chipped polish on the nail of the finger I have tucked beneath my chin, just peeking out ever so slightly. He's even perfected the small part of my lips as I breathed heavily in my sleep. Details I've never noticed about myself. The beauty marks I've never paid attention to and wisps of hair I've probably tried to yank out once or twice.

Cooper's talent is staggering. His precision and expertise. *His passion.* And the fact he chose to use that talent to paint me . . . fuck. Tears build and slip down my cheeks before I can stop them.

The canvas rests on the floor a moment before Cooper's kneeling in front of me, my face in his hands. I shake my head and roll my lips, swallowing back a whimper.

"It's beautiful," I manage to say. "Thank you."

"You're beautiful. I painted you, Adalyn. I just hope I did you justice."

My laugh is watery. "I don't think I've ever looked better."

"Doubtful, my love. But I appreciate the compliment." Wiping my tears away, he presses a soft kiss to my cheek. "We should sleep now. It's late."

The comforter falls over me as I nod, letting my eyes fall shut. "I need to brush my teeth. And take my makeup off."

When I hear him move away, I peek one eye open. He disappears into the ensuite. Drawers slide open, and the tap turns on before he's coming back with full hands.

"I'm surprised you could find everything. It's a mess. I'm sorry."

I haven't had a chance to put all of my stuff away yet. I've created an Adalyn explosion in his bathroom, and for someone who keeps everything as organized as he does, I'm surprised he hasn't told me to clean up after myself already.

"It's fine. I need to build a shelf or something in there for you. There isn't enough room."

My eyes widen when he lifts my toothbrush toward my mouth. There's a perfect line of toothpaste on the bristles.

"Are you going to brush my teeth?"

His mouth quirks. "Yes."

"I can get up and do it myself."

"Just let me take care of you," he urges gently.

I part my lips and let him. Mint explodes on my tongue as he brushes my teeth, eyes crinkling at the corners from how focused he is.

"Spit." There's a cup in front of me now, and I spit into it.

My stomach is a fluttering mess as he moves from brushing my teeth to taking my makeup off with a pack of wipes he found. I've never been taken care of this way before by someone who wasn't my mom or dad back when I was a child. It doesn't feel real. *He* doesn't feel real.

"There," he says before pushing up and taking everything back to the bathroom. Flicking the light off a minute later, he sheds his clothes and climbs into bed with me.

It takes no time at all to fall back asleep once he comes close and pulls me against his chest. With his fingers stroking my stomach, I let the world float away.

33

Adalyn

Ivy squeals the moment she sees me on the beach. I grin back, jogging through the sand toward her. It's been too long since we've seen each other. This shoot couldn't have come at a better time.

"My sweet love!" she calls.

"My Ivy girl!" I call back.

She's already been dressed in one of the new suits we're shooting campaigns for today. It's a neon green one-piece with a high cut in the front and a slit across her belly button. Her makeup is minimal, fitting the beachy vibe we're trying to capture today.

We've both been signed with Champagne Swimwear for over a year now. They're luxury swimwear at its finest.

"Is that a real tan?" she asks when we get close enough to hug.

I squeeze her tight. "For the first time in my life, this glow is all natural, baby."

"Oh, Cara is going to love that."

"She better. She gave me so much shit the last time I came with spray tan hands."

Our makeup artist is a total sweetheart, but she's beyond picky.

We break apart, and she holds me by my arms before gripping my left hand and bringing it in front of her face. She pulls a sharp breath between her teeth and rubs her thumb over my ring finger.

"Even after you sent me pics, I was expecting it to be marker."

"Your lack of trust in me is appalling."

"Oh, I trust you. If I didn't, I would be asking you what the *hell* you were thinking getting married without telling a damn soul."

I wince. "So, you're mad?"

"Not mad, no. But surprised and a bit concerned? Yes."

"You don't need to be concerned. Cooper is a good man," I state.

She narrows her eyes suspiciously. "Before you left, you were too nervous to even ask said man to join you."

"That was before. Things changed quickly."

"You're telling me," she mutters. Resignation trickles across her features. "I promised myself I wasn't going to chastise you today, so I'm going to stop. But we will be talking about this after the shoot. Actually, now that we're already on the topic of your husband, is he okay with you being here today?"

I pinch my brows. "Why wouldn't he be? This is my job."

The only thing he said to me this morning was to have a good day and that he'd see me after work. I didn't hide what I was going to be spending the day doing. He knows I'm shooting for a swimsuit launch today while he visits Maddox, hopefully coming home in one piece.

Ivy shrugs. "Some guys can't handle it."

"I like to think Cooper knows I'm not about to be told what I can and can't do by a man. Not that he would ever try. He's not that type of guy."

I'm almost positive that if I asked him to come with me today, he would have stood off to the side and watched me work with a grin of encouragement the entire time.

"Good, babe. I'm really glad to hear that."

We link arms and start toward the crowd further down the beach, closer to the water. Two white tents—one for hair, makeup, and wardrobe and another for the models to relax in between their shots—stand just far enough from the shoreline to avoid being hit by waves. This type of set-up used to intimidate me, but it's all second nature now.

"How's your new place?" I ask over the pop music that's growing in volume.

"It's amazing. *Really* amazing. The view is unbeatable. I'm still not used to the silence either. There are, like, no noisy neighbours."

I smile. "Good. Any problems with that ass-sucker landlord of yours?"

She laughs, shaking her head. "Not so far. I actually haven't seen him since I moved in. He doesn't seem to be around much."

"Lucky you."

"You sound bitter," she teases.

I roll my eyes. "That's because I am."

We reach the tents, and Sebastian, the lead photographer and one of my good friends, waves at me from the beach. He's in his typical floral button-up, tight shorts that stop way too high on his thighs, and a floppy sunhat. Seeing his style always makes me giggle. It matches his personality to a T. Outgoing, carefree, vibrant. We're pretty similar in a lot of ways.

Ivy peels open the flap on the first tent, and we head inside. There's only one other model scheduled to be here with us today, and she's sitting on one of the inflatable pink couches they have set up. Already looking like she's gotten ready, she spreads her glossy lips into a smile and glances up at us.

"Hey, Lola," I greet her, wiggling my fingers in a wave.

"Hi, sweet cheeks. You're a sight for sore eyes."

"Likewise. It's been a while since we've worked together. I was starting to wonder if you've been hiding from me."

She crinkles her adorable button nose. "Never. I think Seb is just getting too old to deal with our shenanigans, so he's been keeping us apart."

Speaking of the devil, the tent flap opens as he asks, "Did you just call me old?"

I smirk. "You have been doing this for a long time."

He scowls, but his eyes are light and warm. "I'm not much older than that new husband of yours, Adalyn."

Ivy and Lola make low *ooh* noises while I say, "Valid point."

"Question for you, Seb. If a man got a wedding ring tattooed on his finger for you, would you say he's crazy or just insanely in love?" Ivy asks, a wicked smile spreading her lips.

"Both." He laughs.

"That's real? I thought the tattoos were fake when I saw them online," Lola admits.

Lifting my hand, I scrub at my finger to show her that it is indeed real. "This baby is here forever."

"Or until you get it lasered off," Sebastian says.

I frown, a bit offended. "Why would I get it removed?"

"Your marriage is fairly new. Anything could happen," Ivy says as if to justify their lack of faith.

Their opinions don't mean much to me when it comes to changing my viewpoint on my marriage, but they do frustrate me. I try to remind myself it's only because they've never seen the two of us together. How are they supposed to know more than what the media and I tell them?

"There will be no lasering of this ring. For either of us. I love him, and until you have the chance to see us together for real outside of a social media post, you should keep your opinions neutral," I tell them, voice strong.

Sebastian raises his hands in surrender. "You're right. Consider me judgment-free."

"I'm with Seb. If you're happy, babe, that's all that matters," Lola says.

I look to Ivy, expecting her to say the same thing, but there's still doubt in her eyes. She's the only one here besides me who knows that my marriage was accidental, but it still hurts to see that she can't look past that, even now as I tell them how happy I am. To Seb and Lola, it just looks like my best friend doesn't approve of my sudden marriage, and I wonder what they're thinking about it.

"Listen, Vee, you know me. Which means you know that I'm not going to waste my time trying to convince someone of something that doesn't involve them. I know it was sudden, but I don't regret it. Not in the slightest. I'm happy. Really fucking happy."

She's quiet for a few moments, running her fingers through her hair repeatedly as if doing so might help her come to grips with what I'm saying quicker. Finally, she sighs, nodding.

"Okay. You're right. It's not my place for judgment. All I want is for you to be happy, and I believe that you are."

I smile softly at her, thanking her silently.

"Well, now that that's sorted. We have work to do, ladies. Hair and makeup is waiting for you, Addie," Seb says.

Excitement sparks in my chest. With one final look at the girls, I follow him out of the tent and into the next.

Cooper

Maddox finishes shaking his protein shake and sits beside me at his kitchen island. There's a candle burning on the granite countertop, the smell of apple a bit overwhelming. Sippy cups and snack containers fill the dish rack beside the sink.

"Are you sure you don't want anything? I know you don't like protein shakes, but I can get you something else," he says before taking a swig of the thick brown drink. My stomach rolls.

"I'm good."

He chuckles, shrugging. "Suit yourself."

"Where's Brax? I was hoping to see her too."

"Got called in for surgery. Golden Lab got hit on a country road."

"Shit." I wince, and my eyes find Hades as he lazes on the floor by Maddox's feet. The rescue bulldog is the couple's first baby. I don't know what they would do if anything ever happened to him.

"Yeah, these days are always hard on her." He frowns, glancing at the baby monitor.

"How long until I get to see my favourite godson?"

Maddox snorts. "He's your only godson."

"So? Still my favourite."

"He should be up soon."

I nod. "What are you guys going to do today?"

"Can we not do the awkward conversation bullshit? We're not new friends on a coffee date. You're my best friend of over twenty-five years," he mutters, setting his shake down.

I scrape a hand down my face, a sigh stuck in my throat. "I don't know how to act now. Are you still upset with me for being with Adalyn? Do you still want to beat my face in? What do I say here to fix what I broke?"

"You didn't break anything, Cooper. We'll always be best friends, even when I want to kill you. It's taking some getting used to, but as long as my sister is happy, I guess we're good."

"I feel guilty for hurting you. For hurting everyone. It's the last thing I wanted to do, and I wish I could say that I would take it back, but I wouldn't. I'm just . . . I'm in love with her, Dox. And it really sucks not having you to talk to about this with. I'm in so far over my head that I don't know which way is up when I'm around her. I know you don't agree with her moving in with me, but it feels so right. Like I've been living my life wrong because I haven't had her with me every day." It all comes out in rough, vulnerable rambles, but fuck it.

"I'm sorry," he says.

Not expecting to hear that, I ask, "You're sorry? For what?"

"I should have been here for you. Yeah, I was allowed to be pissed for a little while, but it's taken me too long to try and fix this with you. You were there for Braxton and me whenever we needed you, no questions asked, and I should have returned the favour."

"Braxton wasn't my sister, Maddox. It's not really the same."

"Not your sister in the real sense, but she was your best friend too. And now that I think about it, I don't think either of us has ever asked you how you felt about our relationship. We just assumed it was okay with you. Shit, I'm sorry for that too."

I can't help but laugh. This isn't at all how I expected this visit to go today. When he asked me to come over, I assumed it was to tell me off one last time, and then maybe, *maybe*, we could move on. I couldn't have dreamed this conversation up.

"I knew you and Braxton would end up together since the moment you introduced her to me. Yeah, we all became best friends, but in my eyes, you two were just blind idiots who couldn't see what was right in front of you. I've never had a problem with the thought of you two together, and I'm thrilled for you both. Maybe if you would have tossed me aside when you got together, I would think differently, but that never happened."

He swallows, appreciation heavy in his eyes. Relief too.

"I never thought about doing that a single damn time. You're my brother," he says.

I squeeze his shoulder. "And you're mine."

"We're actual family now, huh? Brother-in-law and all that?"

Choking on a laugh, I admit, "Never in a million years did I think I'd hear you say that."

He blows a breath hard enough his cheeks puff up. "Hell no. It's nice, though."

Yeah, it is.

34

Cooper

Liam squeals when I push him on his backyard swing set. His giggle is by far one of the cutest things I've ever heard. I would bottle it up and save it for a rainy day if I could.

Amelia's laugh was the same. So happy and bright and good for the soul. I used to think it meant she liked me best when I could get her to giggle as easily as I did when she was a toddler. It got to the point I convinced Dad to get me a joke book so that I had more material to use to get her to laugh with me. The age difference between us was hard sometimes—even now—but making her smile was never difficult because of that. It made me feel like a good big brother.

Maddox comes up beside me, shoulder to shoulder. Liam swings back, and I push him again.

"Do you still want kids, Coop?"

"Yes."

"So does Addie. But not yet."

"I don't think kids are on our radar right now," I reply, back rigid. This isn't a conversation I ever imagined having with Maddox, but it's just as uncomfortable as I would have expected it to be.

"Well, are you okay with waiting until they are? She might

not want to have kids for another five, ten years. That doesn't bother you?"

"I'm not fifty. I can wait until we're both ready. I'm not in a rush."

He nods, apparently pleased with that answer. Liam shrieks when his dad pushes him higher than I was. "Good. I had to ask. Big-brother duties and all."

"I know."

"Gotta be honest here, man. I fully expected you to die an ink virgin. Seeing you with a tattoo is tripping me out a bit."

I look down at my hand. "It's so small you can barely see it unless you're looking."

"Doesn't matter. Not only did Adalyn steal my best friend but also your tattoo cherry. I'm pretty jealous of my sister right now."

I roll my eyes. "She didn't steal me. Don't you know how to share by now?"

"I do, but I've never been good at sharing my favourite toys." He bumps my shoulder, wiggling his eyebrows when I look at him.

"I'm flattered," I say, deadpan.

"Momma!" Liam yells, drawing our attention toward the patio door as it slides open. "Momma! Momma!"

Braxton steps outside and waves, a tired smile twisting her mouth. "Hey, baby!"

"Is she talking to me or the actual baby?" Maddox asks.

I laugh. "I'm going to say the actual baby."

"Now I'm jealous of my son too."

Braxton grabs Liam's baby swing and stops his movement before laying a loud kiss on his forehead. "Have you been good for Daddy?"

"Swing!" he says.

Maddox wastes no time before wrapping his arms around his wife, kissing the side of her head as she relaxes in his embrace.

"Missed you," he whispers.

"Missed you more."

"I missed you too, by the way," I butt in after giving Liam another couple of pushes.

Braxton shoves out of her husband's arms, as if suddenly remembering that I'm here too. She rushes toward me and squeezes me so tight my next exhale is strained.

I open my mouth to tell her to relax a bit when she says, "Don't complain about how tight I'm squeezing you. I'm tired and just want to hug you, okay?"

I press my lips together and nod, rubbing her back. Maddox stares at her from the spot she left him, affection gleaming in his eyes.

A few moments later, we pull apart, and Braxton scoops Liam up out of the swing, giving him a hug before plopping him down on the grass. He takes off instantly, headed for the sandbox.

"If he sticks sand down his diaper again, you're cleaning him up this time," she tells Maddox.

"How about we rock, paper, scissors for sand duty?" he counters.

Braxton replies, but the sound of my phone ringing distracts me from paying attention. My stomach fills with dread when I read the name on my screen.

I step away from them and answer the call, forcing a greeting up my throat. "Hey, Jackson."

"Cooper, how are you?"

Jackson is the divorce lawyer my father put me in contact with. He's a long-time friend of my father's lawyer and supposedly one of the best in Vancouver. If anything, that knowledge only makes me feel sicker.

"I'm doing fine," I reply.

"Great. Is now a good time to talk, or should I call back later?"

"Now is fine." *Or never.*

"Alright. Well, first, I want to apologize for how long it's taken me to get back to you. I was away on business in London and only got back yesterday."

Small world. "That's fine. No worries."

There are shuffling noises in the background and then tapping, like he's typing on a keyboard. "Alright. Well, I wanted to ask you more about the logistics of your marriage. You said it happened in Ireland?"

"Yes. Dublin."

"And you followed all of the laws there beforehand?"

Ice water slooshes through my veins, chilling me to the bone. "What laws?"

A long pause. More typing. "It's a bit different to elope in other countries than it would be to elope in, let's say, Vegas, for example. There are different rules we have to play by in those cases. In Ireland, you have to notify the registry three months prior of an intended wedding. It's not much of an elopement, really, but for those who just want to get married somewhere foreign by themselves, it works well enough. I only ask because I'm having trouble accessing a marriage license."

Panic threatens to close my throat, my breath thinning. I cough in an attempt to open it back up, but it only draws the attention of Maddox and Braxton instead. Dox's eyes grow wide as he stares at me, most likely taking in how terrified I must look. My grip on the phone grows weak as my palms begin to sweat.

"I have a photo of a marriage certificate on my phone. I found it the morning after," I wheeze.

"Okay, would you mind sending it to me?"

"We didn't notify anyone three months prior. We got married after getting drunk off Irish beer," I rush out.

Or I thought we did. Fuck. *Fuck*. More typing fills my ears as I tip my head back and try to suck in a deep breath. It doesn't work. Bending at the waist, I grip one of my knees and squeeze my eyes shut.

"Coop?" I hear Braxton ask, suddenly right beside me. Her hand ghosts over my back in a comforting motion.

"Send it to me anyway, and I can at least try to find who scammed you both. This must be good news, though, right? No marriage means no annulment, and no divorce if that was the route we had to take. You're saving yourself thousands of dollars and a lot of stress," Jackson says. Every word he says makes my stomach churn faster and faster until I taste the bile trying to climb up my throat.

"Cooper? Jesus, you look like you're going to puke all over my lawn." It's Maddox standing in front of me now, his hands gripping my shoulders.

My tongue is heavy as I say, "Right. Thank you. I'll send the photo."

"We'll touch base in a couple of days, but congratulations on being marriage-free! Enjoy it—I can't tell you how many couples would be so grateful to have had their elopement turn out to be a farce. Talk later."

I wince. "Thank you."

The line goes dead as I slowly lower my phone.

"You're freaking me out. Who was that?" Braxton asks softly.

"The marriage lawyer." The words are hollow.

Maddox helps move me into a standing position. "Was it about the annulment? Is it done?"

Gritting my teeth, I shake my head. Saying it out loud with make it all that much more real. A nightmare that no longer lives only in my dreams.

"It's okay if you can't get the annulment, Coop. Maybe you don't have to go through with a divorce. If you two love each other, then what's the harm in just staying married?" Braxton asks.

Everything she's saying is everything that I've already thought of. Everything that I've decided I wanted to do if Adalyn had agreed to it. I didn't want a divorce anyway. Not anymore, after falling in love with her so damn hard. There's no way I could have gone back to how my life was before her. Not a chance in hell.

"There is no annulment or divorce because we're not married. Not legally. Whoever took us in under the pretence of an elopement was messing with us. I'm sure two drunk tourists were perfect targets for a quick payday." I blow an angry breath between my teeth. "We didn't have a physical copy of anything. Fuck, I'm an idiot for not realizing how weird that was."

"You're not an idiot, Cooper. How is anyone supposed to know how things like this work in other countries? Let alone under the influence of alcohol," Braxton says.

Maddox runs a hand over his head, tugging at the too-long pieces of hair. "Back up to the beginning. You're telling me you're not actually married?"

"We're not."

"And that's not a good thing, I take it?"

I pull at the back of my shirt, growing agitated in a way I'm not used to. "I was content with how we were. Happy with it. I didn't want anything to change, even though I knew I should. Who stays married to someone they weren't even dating in the first place? I should be happy right now. I know that. But I'm devastated. I feel like I could puke."

Adalyn is my wife in every way that counts. I know that with everything in me. But does she feel the same? Now that there isn't anything tying her to me . . . will she run?

"I can't do this," I choke out. My emotions are all over the place, and for the first time in my life, I don't have a grasp on them.

Braxton grabs my hand, keeping me from taking off. "You need to breathe. Talk this out with us."

My shoulders sag as I ask, "What if she leaves me? Adalyn is so far out of my league. I don't know if this marriage was all that was keeping her with me."

Vulnerability ripples through me. I feel so out of my head. So tangled up inside. I'm probably overreacting, but I can't seem to get that through my head long enough to relax.

Maddox frowns, disbelief etched on his features. "You're not serious. My sister might be an amazing woman, but you're a great fucking guy, and I've seen you two together. There's no way she was only with you because of your marriage."

"You have to tell her about this, Coop. She'll set you straight. I don't have a single doubt about it," Braxton murmurs.

Well, that makes one of us.

35

Adalyn

Paint roller in hand, I blow loose pieces of hair out of my eyes. My shoulders burn, and my lower back hurts like a bitch, but I continue painting the wall in front of me. With a shimmy of my hips to the beat of the music playing from my phone, I press the roller into the paint, soaking it again.

"Addie?" I hear Cooper call through the house.

"Back here!" Nerves begin to swell in my belly.

It wasn't my intention to paint Cooper's house, but Ivy is a dangerous influence, and when we went to look at paint swatches for her new place after the shoot, I couldn't say no. I did choose to stick to his spare room for now. Just in case he wasn't actually serious about me painting his walls.

How awkward.

I drop to a squat and rest the paint roller on the edge of the can before wiping my hands off on my sweatpants and pausing the music. The sound of footsteps moving down the hallway has me popping back up and spinning around, moving to block the entrance to the spare room.

"Hey, good-looking," I blurt out, my eyes clashing with Cooper's. He looks exhausted. Sad, even. I don't like it at all. "Are you okay?"

"Hi, love," he says, the words sounding weak. "How was your day?"

"It was good. I'm tired, though. Too much sun. How was yours? Did you get any Liam cuddles?"

I go to take a step closer to him, wanting to hug him after being apart all day, but he stiffens, making me pause. Fear swells in my stomach as I stay where I am.

"Is it the paint smell that's bothering you?" I ask.

He slowly slips past me into the room and stares at the pastel pink wall I've nearly finished painting. His throat bobs with a swallow while a broken expression twists his features. Regret throttles me.

My cheeks burn with embarrassment as I ramble my next words. "I can paint over it. I should have asked you if I could do this, but you told me I could decorate how I wanted, even if that meant painting. I figured I could just keep all of my stuff in this room because it was pretty empty, and then it wouldn't look like a pink fairy threw up in your house, but I don't know what I was thinking with the painting. I'm sorry."

He doesn't say anything, and I could smack myself upside the head at how silly this entire idea was. I've been here for all of a week and have already destroyed his spare room.

I swallow past the rock in my throat and shove my hands in my pockets, rocking on my heels. "How about we just shut this door, and I'll run out and buy some different paint? Is beige okay? I'll have to repaint the whole room so that it matches the old colour, or I can just try to match it to the other walls as best I can. Your choice."

Still silent, he looks across the room, focusing on the boxes of things I have pushed up against the opposite wall. They're mostly filled with random décor items like vases, lamp shades, and a couple of fuzzy throw blankets that I couldn't get myself to set out around the house.

"How much pink paint did you buy?" he asks, finally breaking his silence.

My brows pinch as I point to the can in the corner of the room. "Just that one."

He stares at it with something that looks a lot like astonishment before glancing back at me. The emotion I find in his eyes makes my pulse speed up. Shit, I don't know what I did to deserve being looked at like that. Like he would burn down the entire world for me if I asked him to.

"When I told you to decorate my house, I meant it. The pillows, the blankets, the fringe lamp shades, the goddamn painted walls. It should be out there, not in here, trapped away. You're not keeping any part of yourself hidden from me. Now, come with me so we can properly make this your home."

He doesn't wait for me to reply before gripping the paint roller in one hand and the handle of the paint can in the other and stalking off. My feet are glued to the floor as I watch him carry it all out of the spare room and disappear down the hall.

"Where are you taking that?" I shout.

"Come and find out."

Forcing myself to move, I take a long look at the pink wall and then scurry out of the room. I find Cooper in the master bedroom. He's begun pulling the bed from against the wall, determination written all over him.

"What are you doing?" I squeak.

He huffs a laugh. "If you want to paint the walls pink, start here. In our room. Not a spare room that has never seen anyone besides me and now you."

"I'm not painting your room pink, Cooper."

His eyes narrow on me. "*Our* room, Adalyn."

Ignoring the flutters his specification awakens in my belly, I wave a hand in the air. "I'm not painting *our* room pink. I'm truly okay with having the spare room as my dedicated space to decorate."

"You're so stubborn," he grumbles.

"I know."

My next inhale gets lodged in my throat when he grips the paint roller from where he set it on the can and drags it over the wall, his eyes holding mine the entire time. The hint of a smile tugs at his mouth as I watch him use the leftover paint to leave a pink line down the wall.

"Oops. Would you look at that," he says.

"If you're doing this because you think you have to, I need you to drop the roller."

His gaze grows more intense as he grips the roller tighter. "I'm doing this because it will make you happy, and when you're happy, so am I."

"Even if it means pink walls?"

"Fucking hell, Addie. I would paint myself pink if it made you smile," he states.

My brows jump, and then I smirk. "Really?"

"Really."

He watches me intently as I start walking toward him. I hold my breath, waiting for him to stiffen like he did earlier, but he stays relaxed. Breathing out in relief, I stop moving when the paint can is directly between us.

"Prove it," I mutter before dipping my hand in the can and spraying him with a palmful of paint. It hits his face with a splat as he recoils. I laugh loudly, eyes crinkling at the corners as I stare at him. "What was it you said? Oops?"

He shuts his eyes as he uses his thumb to wipe a splatter from his cupid's bow. When he opens them again, they're wild, bright with both excitement and the promise of revenge.

Oh, fuck.

I spin on my heels and take off. My blood thumps in my ears, even as I laugh and run through the house, unsure where to hide. The psychopath is whistling as he follows me, and that only makes me laugh harder.

"Come on, love. You want to play with paint? Why don't you let me have a turn?" he taunts me.

"No way!" I squeal, turning into the laundry room.

Stopping just past the doorway, I come to the sudden realization that there's nowhere to hide here. Footsteps sound down the hall, and I make a ballsy decision to try my luck somewhere else.

"I'll do a good job. I promise," he says.

I bite my tongue and peek my head out the doorway. *All clear.* Moving into the hall, I take soft, quiet steps toward the kitchen. A proud grin starts to tug at my mouth when a pair of arms wrap around me from behind and pull. My scream dies in my throat when warm lips brush the tip of my ear.

Looking down at the hands gripping my front, I find them stained pink. "You did not!" I gasp.

Those pink hands begin to move. They drift over my chest, and then one slides up the column on my throat before they both squeeze.

"I did. You are my world, Adalyn. I need you to get that through this beautiful head of yours."

The backs of my eyes begin to burn. Not because of the feel of his hand on my throat, the soft pressure cutting off some of my oxygen, but because of how that declaration affects me and how badly I needed to hear it without truly knowing I did.

He doesn't stop there, though. God help me, he continues to flay me open.

"You are my home, and this house should be yours. This isn't temporary for me. Not you and me, and not you living here."

I cover the hand he has on my throat with mine, drifting my fingers over his knuckles. "You're my home too," I whisper.

There's a question right there on my tongue, but I can't get myself to speak it out loud. *Why won't you tell me you love me?* I see it in everything he does and the words he speaks. Or at least, I think I do. Would he say it back if I said it first?

A flick of his thumb over my pulse as he asks, "Will you help me get our room ready now?"

"I guess," I whisper.

His lips kiss beneath my jaw, and I tip my head to give him better access. My eyes flutter shut, a sound of appreciation escaping me as I arch into him.

"You guess?"

"I haven't exactly finished what I was doing before."

Adrenaline bursts inside of me just seconds before I tear myself from his arms and run toward the bedroom. His laugh is loud and free and happy as it follows me, embedding itself in the walls. My grin is so wide I know my dimple is out, and when I reach the bedroom and crouch in front of the paint can, Cooper is already there, in the doorway, with a matching dimple.

"You've painted me," I begin, drawing a circle in the paint with my finger. "Now it's my turn."

His deep brown eyes snare mine as he reaches behind his head and pulls his shirt off. It falls to the floor.

"You've already marked me up inside. It's only fair that you do the same to the outside, I suppose," he says.

I stare down at the paint, watching as it ripples with every swirl of my finger. When I lift my eyes, I instantly zone in on his hand and the black ink on his finger. My chest warms, love burning me up from the inside.

"Can you sit on the floor? I don't want to get paint on the bed," I say, voice soft.

He doesn't hesitate. Sitting in front of me, he brings his knees up and spreads them just enough I can settle between them. My heart crawls up my throat, making it hard to breathe as I move the can closer and slowly lift my finger from the paint.

"Do your worst, love."

His stare is so warm, so soft that it becomes nearly impossible to fight the urge to just say the words I'm thinking. With my pink-tipped finger, I write them across his chest instead. Each swoop across his skin draws more of his attention, until he's palming my waist and watching my finger with such intensity it sucks the air from around us.

I roll my lips and let my hand linger on his stomach when I'm finished. He's breathing hard, each exhale warming my face. It's not until after he tugs on the hem of my shirt and I quickly take it off that I notice he's dipping a finger of his own into the paint.

A shiver rolls through me when he presses his finger to the swell of my right breast and starts to write on my skin. He's watching his movements intently, but I'm staring at him. I don't have to look at my chest to know what he's writing. His eyes say everything he hasn't said out loud.

Bliss as I've never felt awakens inside of me when he finishes with a brush of his thumb over my collarbone and glances at me.

I smile softly, bringing my forehead to his. He bumps my nose, and by the time I finally look down at my chest, I'm not surprised to find the three words written there.

They've already been etched beneath my skin for weeks.

I love you.

36

Cooper

sparrow

Paint fumes. That's the only explanation I have for my inability to tell Adalyn the truth. I was going to. I planned my entire speech on the way home. Every broken-hearted detail that I wanted to pretend wasn't real, I was going to tell her.

But then I saw her in the spare room, painting that damn wall with hope so apparent on her features that the thought of telling her something I knew would crush us both suddenly felt all that less appealing. Just like that, my already shaky will crumbled beneath me.

Even now, as we lie on a bed of blankets on the living room floor, reclined against the edge of the couch while we work on our very different careers side by side, I still can't bring myself to ruin the moment.

She's working on her laptop, editing a video and humming along to whatever song is running through her head. Her hair is twisted on the top of her head, and she's wearing one of my shirts. The thin blue material hides the pink paint still on her chest. A brand identical to the one I can't bring myself to wash from my skin.

The weight of what we exposed to each other today is heavy on my chest but freeing at the same time. It's what I've wanted confirmation of for weeks—that she feels the same way I do. Now that I know she does, things have shifted, clicked into place.

"Are you actually doing any work over there?" she teases, leaning over my lap to get a better view of my laptop screen.

"A little. You're distracting me."

She rolls her eyes, settling back in her spot. "I'm distracting you? You're the one who's half-naked. I think *you're* distracting *me*."

"Would you prefer I put my shirt back on? Oh wait, I can't. Not unless you plan on taking it off."

She scoffs. "Yeah, right. You'd like that too much."

I don't bother denying it. If we hadn't needed to finish painting the bedroom before we both passed out from the fumes, I would have taken her right there on the floor, paint-tipped fingers and all. My need for her is at an all-time high tonight, but being with her like this—being normal together—is more than enough.

"There's not much you could do that I wouldn't like," I tell her.

"I'm sure I could find a few things."

After pressing Save on my messy first draft of a university syllabus, I shut my laptop and set it on the floor beside our blanket bed.

"Like what?"

"I don't think you like it when I forget to put my box of Lucky Charms away in the morning."

I bite back a laugh. "I guess not."

"Or when I don't stack my shoes on the rack by the door."

"You do have a lot of shoes."

She pinches the outside of my thigh. "Cooper."

"What? Do you really think I care about those things? Because I don't. Not enough for it to be a big deal. Does it bother you that I always bring a basket of dirty clothes to the laundry room and then forget to put them in the washing machine?"

"No."

I lean over and kiss her cheek as I say, "Exactly."

"Well, don't you just have an answer for everything."

"It's one of my best quirks." With my hand on the back of her laptop, I press it shut and then set it on the floor.

She watches me curiously as I grab her thigh and use it to urge her onto my lap. Straddling me, she sets her hands on my shoulders and hums, "Along with being humble, apparently."

"And patient."

Her smile turns goofy as she brushes her fingers over my forehead. "And what exactly are you waiting patiently for, Sparrow?"

I grip her waist and pull her closer, accidentally rocking her against my cock. It has a mind of its own around her and, apparently, doesn't need much more than a look at her to grow rock hard.

"Oh," she breathes. "That."

A laugh tears free from my chest as I shake my head. "No. That's just from being around you. All I need is to feel you close to me. Especially after earlier."

"You mean when I told you that I love you?"

My heart stills. Somehow, even after seeing it written on my skin, it's an entirely different experience to hear her speak those words out loud. I feel them settle deep in my chest.

"And I said that I loved you too," I rasp, cupping her nape and stroking the side of her throat. "You make it impossible not to fall for you. I should have known from our first day in Madrid when you stripped in front of me on the way to the pool that I never stood a damn chance. I've never been more grateful to be a replacement travel buddy."

"Shit, I was so nervous you were going to hate being around me every day. It still feels like a dream to have you here, telling me all of that."

"You better get used to it, love. I'm not going anywhere," I promise.

Suddenly, a pang of guilt hits me. I fight back a wince, knowing full well what I have to do but wishing with everything in me that I didn't. *We'll be okay*, I tell myself. We're in love, married or not.

"Addie, there's something I—"

Her eyes go wide as she speaks at the same time, and I immediately shut my mouth, listening to her.

"Oh! I almost forgot to tell you! We got invited to a Champagne Swim party tomorrow night. Well, it's not really a party. It's more of a get-together with the models from today and a few others who aren't featured in this new collection. It's tradition to celebrate after a killer shoot. Obviously, this is the perfect time to introduce my husband to everyone. What do you say? You don't have to come if you don't want to."

I don't even have to think about it. Of course I'll go with her. Regardless of my limited past with public events, I would never turn down a chance to spend time with her. Especially not when she's nearly vibrating on my lap, excitement rolling off her in waves.

"I'd love to come," I say.

"I can't wait." She grins and proceeds to drown me in kisses.

And for the second time, I don't tell her that we're not really married. I can't get myself to ruin this moment. Fuck. *I'm doomed.*

I WAKE the next morning to a cold, empty bed. Pushing up to sit, I look frantically around the room, taken aback by the bright stream of sun that slips over the bed. I'm never up after the sun has risen this high.

The tension leaches from my bones when I see a small, pink Post-it note on Adalyn's pillow. It's folded carefully, perfectly in half, almost missable amongst her fluffy pink pillow.

I open it and read it with a sleepy smile.

Good morning, handsome. Yes, I turned your alarm off because if I'm going to be keeping you up late tonight, I figured you're too old to be able to do that without sleeping in. I have a day of pampering planned, so I'll see you tonight.

I love you,
Xoxo Addie

Nerves fill my stomach, and my smile falls. Another day without coming clean. I scrape a hand down my face and groan. There's no way I can go to this party with her thinking we're married. The last thing I want is to embarrass her by introducing us to her colleagues as husband and wife, only to have to break the truth to everyone later on.

God, I'm an asshole. A selfish, greedy asshole. I'm always putting everyone else first, and now is when I decide to do the exact opposite of that?

With another inner scolding, I force myself out of bed and toss a shirt on before heading to the kitchen to make coffee. I'm hit with a shot of guilt when I find another Post-it on the counter beside a coffee cup I've never seen before. There's a picture of Jack Sparrow on the mug, and the writing on the note is the last nail in my coffin.

I remember hearing years ago that your parents

have cups with their nicknames for each other, so I figured why not? Let's carry on the tradition. Okay, now I'm leaving.

I love you, in case you forgot already
Xoxoxo Addie

I lift the mug and stare into the drunken eyes of Jack Sparrow. There's no possible way I could love Adalyn more than I do right now.

A knock on the door has me setting the cup aside before leaving the kitchen. My dad shakes a brown paper bag in front of him after I open the door and silently curse at his presence.

"Morning, kid. Hope you're hungry," he says, all pip.

"Hey, Dad. Did we have plans that I forgot about?"

"Nope. I just missed you."

He pats my arm and then walks right past me, heading right inside like my house is his. I swallow my indignance and close the door behind him.

"You just saw me."

"You keep saying that, and I'm not going to lie, it's starting to offend me."

"Sorry," I sigh. He's unloading the bag of food when I enter the kitchen after him. "What did you bring?"

He frowns. "Croissants, muffins, and those cute mini cheese bagels Addie was telling us about at dinner. I was hoping she would be here. Where is she this early?"

"We're going to a party for her latest photoshoot tonight, so she's out getting pampered, I suppose. Why don't you ever bring *my* favourite breakfast food in the morning? That seems a bit unfair."

"I'm still trying to convince her that the Whites are better than the Huttons. If it comes down to a bit of bribery, then so be it," he admits.

"What did you and Ava bet this time?" I ask, swiping a blueberry muffin and sitting at the kitchen table.

He grins. "You know me so well."

"I also know that mini cheese bagels aren't going to get her to switch to our team. She's a Hutton through and through."

"Have some faith in your wife, son. She'll stray from the dark side soon enough."

My appetite spoils at the reminder. I stop picking at my muffin and set it aside. "She's not my wife."

Dad laughs, brushing off my comment as a terrible joke. "That's funny."

"I'm not trying to be funny. There's nothing funny about it."

The mood shifts in an instant. Dad's expression twists with confusion. I nod, answering the question he has to be repeating over and over in his head.

"It wasn't real. Someone screwed with us." The words taste sour.

"When did you find out?" is what he asks first.

"Yesterday."

"How?"

He listens intently as I explain everything the lawyer told me on the phone. A vein pulses in his forehead, and I wince, familiar with what that means.

"Can we find out who did this? This is a cruel joke," he huffs.

"I doubt it. That night is still blank for me. Addie too."

"Shit," he breathes, collapsing on the chair across from me. "What are you going to do?"

"I don't think I have many options here. Tell Addie and hope she doesn't abandon ship?"

"She won't abandon ship. But telling her is definitely the right move. Especially before someone else does."

I swallow thickly. "Nobody else knows besides us, Braxton, Maddox, and the lawyer."

He gives me a disbelieving look. "Did you forget who Adalyn is? It won't be long until the truth weasels its way out to the public. You want to be on the right side of the reveal, Coop."

He's right. Shit, he's too right. It's easy to forget about the publicity that follows Addie when it's just us. I've never spent too much time thinking about it, but I should have.

"I was going to do it yesterday as soon as I got home, but she was so happy it felt worse to tell her and take that away. Then I woke up this morning, and she was already gone."

"Tonight. Do it tonight, whether you want to or not. Even if she's happy. Trust me, she'll appreciate the honesty more than anything."

Nodding, I decide to open up completely.

"I got the university teaching job. I start at the end of August."

Something deep and heart tugging flashes across his face as he swallows. "For real?"

"Yeah. For real. I'm sorry I didn't tell you sooner. I was nervous, I guess. Didn't want to jinx anything," I admit.

Without saying a word, he crushes me in a tight hug. I shut my eyes, soaking in the moment.

"I'm damn proud of you, Cooper. I knew you would get the job. You're my boy, after all. You've always accomplished everything you've set your mind to."

"Thanks, Dad." Relief rushes through me as the weight of carrying my secret slips away.

He squeezes me a final time before pulling back, patting my arms as he does. He grins at me and nods. I watch as he glances at the coffee cup on the counter. A new emotion flicks through his gaze this time before he's looking back at me knowingly.

"Did she get you that?"

My pulse thumps. "Yeah. I found it this morning. She said we need to continue the tradition you and SP started with your lame mugs."

He stares at me for a moment longer and then says, "Tell her the truth, son. Adalyn is your woman, wedding be damned. Look at that tattoo on your finger. It's not going anywhere. I knew Scarlett was meant to be my wife probably too quickly for some to understand. When you know, you know. But once you do, you have to work that much harder to prove you're worthy of that honour. Don't give her an opportunity to believe you're not."

His words strike deep. I tuck them away, keeping them somewhere safe.

"Thank you, Dad."

He smiles softly. "You're welcome."

"Just out of curiosity," I begin, nerves obvious in my tone. "If I were to marry her for real, would you approve?"

His answering smile is all I need to know how he's feeling, but I wait for his answer anyway.

"You don't even have to ask. She's already family in my eyes. Make it official."

37

Adalyn

GIDDY EXCITEMENT RUSHES THROUGH ME AS I RUN MY HANDS over my front and push down the last sequin that flipped up on my dress during the ride over. Voices and pop music slip beneath Sebastian's front door. Ivy knocks for us, a burst of her fruity perfume tangling with the flowery scent of mine.

"You're practically vibrating," she notes, laughing under her breath.

"I'm excited to see my husband. Sue me."

It took a lot longer to get ready than I had initially thought. With Ivy surprising me with a celebratory post-wedding brunch and a full day spent shopping and getting our hair and makeup done, the day flew by, and then suddenly, it was evening. I've never been one to turn down a day of pampering myself, but I've also never had anyone waiting at home for me either.

"Is he here yet?" she asks.

"No. I told him to be here a few minutes after us so he didn't have to be here alone."

"Smart plan."

The door opens a beat later, revealing a grinning Sebastian dressed in a bedazzled suit jacket, a matching shimmering dress shirt, and a pair of pink slacks. The white lights he's set up through the penthouse make him look like a disco ball.

"Was there a dress code we missed?" Ivy asks, stepping inside. I follow her, instantly feeling the heat from the throng of people wandering around.

"Why, are you feeling plain, Vee?" I tease.

"Next to you two sparkly bitches? Yes."

Seb chuckles, giving me a side hug. "No dress code. Great minds just think alike."

"You're lucky I don't get offended easily," she grumbles.

"Adalyn!"

Spinning toward the female voice, I find a group of women waving from the balcony doors on the opposite side of the living room. They're unfamiliar to me, but I smile and wiggle my fingers in their direction anyway.

"You've let vultures into your home," Ivy tells Sebastian.

"Vultures with killer modelling ability, I'm afraid."

"Should I go say hi?" I ask.

"No. You should text your husband and ask where he is. I'll cover for you," Ivy says, giving me a soft push.

I flash a grateful smile and nod. "Thank you."

She kisses my cheek and saunters toward the group of women, long legs eating up the space. She may not have dressed up in sequins and sparkles like Seb and me, but she shines bright enough on her own. Eyes are drawn to her wherever she goes.

A touch to my bicep has me looking up at Seb as he says, "I'm going to mingle. Come find me when your man arrives."

"Okay. Have fun."

He turns and greets a couple who just walked inside, turning on his dazzling charm. I leave him with them and slip into a quieter corner of the living room before texting Cooper.

Me: Almost here? I miss you.

His reply is instant, and I'm smiling as the message pops up on my screen.

Hubby: In the hallway.

A thousand wings flap in my stomach as I quickly pocket my phone in my clutch and head for the door. The following knock signals his arrival just a beat before I'm there, pulling it open.

My mouth goes dry as I stare at him. At *my* man. He stares right back, those pretty eyes of his slipping all over me from head to toe. I grin wide enough my cheeks burn, unable to keep my happiness at bay.

"I missed you too," he says softly, pulling his hands from the pockets of his black pants.

I don't wait for him to open his arms before I walk toward him and pull him in for a kiss. His lips part on mine instantly, a breathy groan slipping from between them. Hands cup my cheeks with the ghost of a touch, as if he's aware of how long I spent in a makeup chair today and doesn't want to ruin anything.

One day apart was all it took to have me missing him this intensely. It's almost scary to imagine how I might be if we were to be apart for longer than that. Maybe it isn't healthy to love someone this much, but I've never been much of a health nut.

"Come in," I breathe.

With his eyes still shut, he traces my bottom lip with his thumb. "You look beautiful. Stunning, really."

My cheeks grow warm. "Thank you." I pinch the open collar of his royal blue button-up, rolling it between my fingers. "I love this. I'm about to have the most handsome date here."

"It matches your eyes." He says it so casually, like it's second nature for him to match his clothes to the colour of my eyes.

"You're going to make me emotional and horny if you keep it up. Are you ready to make your grand entrance?"

After stealing another kiss, he taps my nose and slides his arm around me, tucking me into his side. "Yes."

We shut the door and move inside the penthouse. I'm the slightest bit nervous as I keep an eye on Cooper, waiting for him to tell me he doesn't want to do this the further into the crowd we get.

"I promise that it's not always this overwhelming. Sebastian is just really popular in Vancouver."

His fingers rub my bare arm reassuringly. "How many shoots have you done for Champagne?"

"Six. We have another two booked, but they aren't for a couple of months."

"And they treat you right? With respect?"

"Always."

"Then these parties can be as overwhelming as they please. I'll be here for every single one of them as long as I get to spend the night with you. So, relax, love. I'm not going to run out of here," he says.

I nod, sighing. "Okay."

"Do you always spend the day out before these parties?" There's not even a hint of judgment in his question, just simple curiosity. Fuck, that's nice.

"Not always. Ivy threw me a little bit of a newlywed brunch. It was really thoughtful. I think I ate far too many pancakes, though."

That's what the woman at the first of five dress stores told me this afternoon before I gave her the middle finger and left. It wasn't the first time someone has told me what I should and shouldn't eat, especially being in the modelling industry, and it surely won't be the last. But I've never appreciated hearing it. I don't believe you have to look a certain way to be beautiful, nor should you not be allowed to do something like modelling if you're not a size zero.

They can take me as I am or not at all. I will never change myself for someone else.

It means everything to me that Cooper loves me as I am.

"There's no such thing as too many pancakes," he says stiffly. The sudden change in his tone has my hackles lifting. It's closed off. Faraway.

"Tell me what did you do today. Something fun, I hope?"

His throat bobs with a heavy swallow, the arm at my back tensing ever so slightly. *Something is going on.* I know him too well by now to think otherwise.

"Not much. I just had breakfast with my dad and got a chunk of my syllabus done."

"What did you and your dad talk about?"

When he glances at me, the weariness in his eyes has me even more nervous. What is going on? Is his family okay?

"You know, if something is going on, I hope you know that you can tell me. I'm here for you always," I add, voice as gentle as I can make it.

He flinches at my words, and it's all the confirmation I need that something's really, really wrong.

"Let's talk about it later. Please? I want you to enjoy the party, Addie," he says.

I almost laugh. "I can't enjoy a party knowing something is upsetting you. Is it your family? Is everyone okay?"

He looks around the room, expression growing more and more nervous with each person he finds nearby. I watch him tug anxiously at the collar of his shirt, my stomach leaden.

"My family is good" is what he chooses to say.

"So, what's going on? You're worrying me."

"I'm sorry," he says on a wobbly breath.

"For what? What happened? Was it something I said?"

He shakes his head, jaw tight. "No. You're goddamn perfect. Please, can we talk about this later?"

It's an unfair request, but as our muttered conversation draws the attention of the people nearby, some of whom apparently aren't above trying to capture it on camera, I know I should grant it anyway.

When a hand that doesn't belong to either Cooper or me touches the back of my arm, I recoil, my mind too scattered to focus properly. Cooper's eyes flash over my head. The touch vanishes just as quickly as it appeared.

"Hello, I'm Sebastian. You're Cooper, I assume?"

Cooper nods stiffly, slowly looking back at me. I suck in a steadying breath, paint a smile on my face, and loop my arm through his much tenser one before facing Seb.

He does a good job of hiding his interest in whatever he saw happening between Cooper and me. It's an appreciated gesture.

"Yes, this is my husband, Cooper. Cooper, this is my favourite boss, Sebastian Bradford," I introduce them.

Cooper shakes Seb's already outstretched hand. "It's nice to meet you."

Sebastian flashes his teeth in a dazzling smile. "You as well. Addie here speaks highly of you."

"She's too good to me," Cooper says.

"She's too good to and *for* everyone," Seb corrects him, shooting me a wink.

"That's absolutely true," Ivy says, joining us now.

Cooper's nearly as good at faking being comfortable in a tense situation as I am because he doesn't hesitate before extending a hand toward Ivy. She takes it gracefully, giving him a firm inspection while they shake.

"I'm glad you could make it. Addie didn't stop talking about you all day," she says.

I roll my eyes. "Don't embarrass me."

Cooper tucks his hand into his suit pants. "Thank you for making her so happy today. If I was going to miss her all day, at least it was for good reason."

Ivy sneaks a look at me, approval bright in her eyes. I chew on the inside of my cheek to keep from laughing. *I know, girl. I know.*

"I figured it was better late than never," she says.

Sebastian goes to speak when phones begin dinging all through the penthouse, his included. Mine vibrates once in my clutch, and Ivy must feel a similar buzz in hers because she starts searching for her phone right away. Watching dozens of people all lift their phones to their faces at the same time would be funny if they didn't all turn to stare at me directly after.

It feels how I assume stepping onto a runway for the first time would feel, but instead of everyone judging me for my walk or the clothes I'm wearing, they're judging me for reasons I don't know.

"Why is everyone staring at me?"

Cooper shifts beside me, and one look at him has my stomach dropping. *Apologetic.* He looks sorry for something. *Really* fucking sorry.

I barely recognize my voice as I ask, "What's going on?"

"Oh, honey," Ivy whispers, quickly shoving her phone away and moving toward me. "Seb, you need to kick everyone out before someone starts recording her and this shit hits the fan faster than necessary."

Tired of not getting answers from them, I tear my phone out of my clutch and click on the most recent notification on the screen. I don't pay attention to them as they start to rush around the place and start barking orders at everyone. Not once I read the post.

"This isn't real," I declare. "Whoever posted this doesn't know anything. It's fine. You can all calm down."

I feel my eyes go wide at the number of comments and shares already rolling in before I tuck my phone away again. It's okay. These rumours are the kind of ones I pay someone to make go away.

"Addie, honey, let's at least get out of the way of these

damn piranhas before we start to figure this out," Ivy urges as she starts to lead me through the living room.

Cooper is close by, not leaving my side, and as I reach for his hand, I say, "Just ask Cooper. This tweeter has no idea what they're saying. We're married. We have been since Ireland. I don't know where they got their information, but they're wrong."

I can't find his hand. It's not until I turn to see why that I notice that the apologetic expression I saw him wearing earlier has only gotten worse. He won't look at me. Not even when I step closer, our chests nearly touching.

Around us, it's a jumble of loud curious voices and questions that I can't even register. Tears burn my eyes as I look up at him, silently begging him to tell me that I was right. That this isn't really happening. That he didn't know.

"Cooper." It's a broken plea.

"I'm sorry, love. I'm so sorry. I was going to tell you. Fuck, I swear I was—"

I stop hearing him. Someone bumps into me from behind, sending me falling against the man I thought was my husband, and I recoil, slapping his chest with my palms.

He spits something at the person who pushed me, but I don't care what it was.

"How long have you known?"

Flinching, he says, "Since yesterday."

"When yesterday?" I grit out.

His answer hits me like a ton of bricks. "When I was with your brother."

Before he came home and found me in the spare room. Before we painted each other's skin.

Before we said I love you.

God, I think that's what hurts the most. He shouldn't have hidden it from me and come here tonight knowing that I wanted to introduce him as something he isn't.

"Oh," I breathe. This is a nightmare. A party with my colleagues is not the place for this.

With the last bit of strength I have, I make the decision to pull my shoulders back and, without another word, turn and leave him standing there in the crowd. He calls my name as I slip through bodies, but I know that if I pause, I won't be capable of walking away from him again right now.

I need to think about this. About what to do and say. And I have to do that alone, without him distracting me and turning me into goddamn mush.

Right now, he's a complication that I don't need.

38

Cooper

The house is empty when I finally get home. Her absence only twists the knife in my gut.

Leaving her alone, not knowing where she is or if she's safe, feels like the absolute wrong thing to do, but I'm not sure I have much of a choice. She disappeared in a sea of unfamiliar people, and regardless of how long I spent looking for her afterward, my search came up empty.

Something tells me that if Adalyn doesn't want to be found, she won't be.

I could have spent my entire life never seeing her look at me with such hurt and betrayal. Knowing that I broke her trust and possibly her heart is worse than finding out we were never really married in the first place.

God, what I would do to know what she's thinking right now. Is she convincing herself that I'm relieved with the news? That I'm not so immensely in love with her that I wouldn't marry her right now, right here, in my living room? I don't care that it's only been a couple of months. Two months with Adalyn is the equivalent of two decades with anyone else. Nobody gets me the way she does. Like she sees me for all I am, and instead of finding parts she wants to tweak, she accepts them without a second thought. We may be complete opposites, but that doesn't matter anymore. I'm not sure if I ever really did.

Why would I want to wait when I feel as positive as I do about her and us and the future I want to have with her? We can't be through. I know that to my very core.

Sitting on the edge of the couch, I bounce my leg and pull out my phone. The lock screen image is one I stole from Twitter after our afternoon at the skate park. It was taken when I kissed her as we skated side by side. I've wanted to recreate this image on a canvas for days, but I don't think I could do the original justice.

I pull her contact up and type out what feels like a million messages before settling on one.

Me: I won't ask to see you, but I will ask you to tell me where you are so that I know you're safe.

I send it off before I can chicken out. The next few minutes drag. It's silent in the house, but I can't get myself to turn on the TV. Maybe I'm punishing myself. At this point, I don't know what I'm doing other than wishing I hadn't been such a selfish prick and withheld the truth from her.

Her reply comes ten minutes later, the contact name making me wince.

Wifey: My brother's house.

Me: How long are you going to stay there?

Wifey: I'm not running away. I just need some time alone. I'll see you tomorrow

Me: I love you.

Wifey: I love you too. Goodnight, Cooper.

Cooper. Not Sparrow. I've never hated my name more than right now.

Adalyn

Braxton is the sister I never had. She was always around while I was growing up, and while my brothers and their guy friends never gave me the time of day, she always did. She was always giving me advice on boys and clothes and how to pluck my eyebrows just right without overdoing it.

But she also broke my heart once, back when she left all of us behind. It feels like ages ago now when she and my brother had a falling-out that destroyed their friendship. They found their way back to each other, even though it took nearly a decade.

I never put much thought into how my brother was able to get over her betrayal and create a life with her despite their broken past. It seemed like something that would never happen to me. Yet, to some degree, I guess it has.

Cooper is my best friend. He's the one who, with only the hint of a smile in my direction, makes me want to kick my feet and giggle like a lovesick fool. He's the one who I find myself rushing home to just because I want to spend as much time with him as possible.

He's the one I can't picture my life without. Our time together hasn't changed me or what I want in my future—I've never needed anyone or anything to do that for me—but it has made one thing clear. Cooper is the one I want that future with.

It didn't take him keeping things from me to realize that. I've known that from the moment he went along with one of my ridiculous schemes in Madrid without a hint of hesitation. He's never judged me, never second-guessed me.

Not being married after spending weeks believing the opposite fucking sucks, but in all honesty, I didn't fall in love with him because I thought he was my husband. I fell in love with him because of who he is. A gentle, funny, loving man who would do just about anything for me if I let him.

It takes more than the title to make a man a husband and a woman a wife. It takes love and trust and compromise. *Trust.* That took a hit today. My stomach swirls at the reminder.

"You don't have to put on a brave face, Addie. It's just us," Braxton says, her hand rubbing circles on my back.

We're sitting at the edge of their spare bed, my sparkly dress tossed behind us. The baggy shirt and sweatpants I'm wearing now belong to my brother. The one standing in the doorway, his arms crossed as he watches us. His face is a mask of indifference that I want to tear right off. There's no way he isn't going to give me a hard time about what happened, regardless of how relaxed he's trying to make me believe he is.

"I'm waiting for Maddox to tell me that I should never have gotten with his best friend because if I hadn't, this wouldn't have happened," I mutter.

"That's not at all what I was going to say," he mutters, that mask slowly slipping away to reveal something even worse than indifference. Sympathy.

"Don't look at me like that. You can't honestly tell me that you're not the least bit happy about this? You didn't want Cooper and me married to begin with. In fact, it pissed you off enough that you punched your best friend in the face. Have you and Dad planned a *congratulations you're not married party* yet?"

A line forms between his brows. "That was because I felt betrayed, Adalyn. You're my baby sister. Was I just supposed to let him get away with marrying you when he was supposed to be keeping an eye on you instead? The both of you should have known better, and I've apologized to him for what happened. We've moved on."

"Okay, and what about me? Have you even once thought about talking to me, or have you been content letting me sit in a heaping puddle of guilt because of what I thought I did and how it hurt you?"

The words just tumble out of me. Feelings that I didn't know I had shoved down rumble back to life. Silence falls over us. Shit.

I clear my throat. "I'm sorry. I shouldn't be taking my emotions out on you."

"No, it's okay. I should have spoken to you about this. I didn't even think . . ." he starts before cutting himself off with a frustrated sigh. "I guess I didn't think about how you would be feeling after everything that happened that day. I'm sorry."

"I hated knowing that I hurt you. That I hurt everyone," I admit.

Braxton gives me a soft squeeze. "Everyone knows that. And despite their initial reactions, I know for a fact that they're hurting with the both of you right now."

"I appreciate that, but if Cooper were as upset as I am about this, he would have told me instead of keeping it to himself." Maddox chuckles under his breath, and I glare at him. "Why are you laughing?"

He unfolds his arms and then sits beside me. "Is that really what you think?"

I nod. "The Cooper I know doesn't hide things from people. He wouldn't keep secrets he knew would end up hurting someone he loved if they were exposed."

"Before a couple of weeks ago, I would have said that I know Cooper better than anyone else. Now, it's obvious that's changed. You know him better than anyone, yet you're the only one thinking that he kept the truth from you because he doesn't care about you. If you put aside your hurt feelings for a minute, you would be able to understand why he did what he did."

"If I could do that, I would have already," I say, frowning.

Braxton rubs my side and presses the side of her head to mine. "I think Cooper didn't tell you the truth earlier because he loves you and he worried he might lose you if he did. For once, the most selfless man I've ever met chose to be selfish, even if it wasn't the right thing to do. The last thing he would have ever wanted to do was hurt you."

"Love does crazy things to a person, Addie. It can turn you inside out and upside down. Take it from us," Dox adds.

I know they're right, but that doesn't make all of the hurt go away. I'm not as upset with Cooper as I am with the knowledge that he's not really my husband. My emotions are all mixed up inside of me, making everything foggy and hard to understand.

"I really liked being married to him," I whisper, rolling my lips and sniffling angrily when tears well in my eyes.

It feels like a breakup without the actual breaking up. Like someone ripped a part of me away for the hell of it. Disappointment settles in my belly, making friends with the hurt already there.

"Oh, honey," Braxton whispers, but it's Maddox that wraps his arms around me and hugs me so tight it feels like he's trying to take my pain away and keep it for his own.

The thought makes my tears fall.

"Don't cry. Fuck, I've always hated seeing you cry," he murmurs, stroking my hair.

I bury my face in his shoulder and choke out, "Sorry."

He doesn't reply, but I hear him swallow. Another hand rubs my back, and I know it's Braxton's. I'm incredibly grateful to have so many people in my life who love me so deeply. A wave of sadness slips over me when I think about how Cooper's doing right now. Does he have someone with him to comfort him the way I do? If he's hurting the way I am . . .

My voice is scratchy when I say, "I should go home."

"You can stay as long as you want to," Maddox grumbles stubbornly.

"I know. But . . . if he's hurting too, he shouldn't have to be alone. That's not fair."

"You know, Adalyn, I think you might be the best person Cooper could have fallen in love with," Braxton says. "He deserves someone who will take care of him the way he's been taking care of us our whole lives."

Her words are all the confirmation I need. I pull away from my brother and wipe my wet cheeks. With a straight spine, I ask them to walk me to the door before I lose my edge.

"Thank you," I tell them both. "I know I just kind of showed up here, but I appreciate you letting me talk this through with you."

Maddox shakes his head and pulls me in for another hug. "Come here whenever you want. We don't see enough of you while we're here."

"It's not my fault you're parents now," I tease.

Braxton snorts a laugh. "You're right. That's all on your brother."

"I don't hear you complaining," Dox throws back. "Actually, you're usually doing the opposite—"

I push out of his hug, nose scrunched. "That's my cue. I'll see you soon. Promise."

My brother just laughs while pulling open the door and ushering me out. "I love you, Addie."

"We love you," Braxton corrects him.

I smile, waving as I head down the porch stairs. "Love you back."

As I slide into my Jeep and crank the A/C, I feel a bit more settled. A bit more sure and confident. Ready to tackle the obstacles waiting for me at home.

39

Adalyn

The lights are on when I get home. I'm not surprised. I wasn't going to sleep tonight either.

It's a hot and muggy night, which only makes me feel even more sluggish on the walk up to the door. When I twist the knob, it's unlocked, so I walk inside. Slipping off my shoes, I take my first look into the house and gasp, my hand flying over my mouth.

Cooper looks as surprised as I feel when he spins to face me, eyes wide. The paint roller in his hand clatters to the floor, pastel pink paint splashing over the linoleum and the edge of the couch.

The wall where the TV was mounted is bare and wet and *pink.* What were once plain beige lampshades are now pink with silver beaded fringe. A leopard-print fuzzy throw is slung over the armchair tucked by the foyer, and a grey shag rug is in the hallway. It's a decorating disaster—my favourite kind. I spy the opened boxes across the room and release a tight breath.

"What are you doing?" I ask, bewildered.

He's shirtless, dressed only in a pair of sweatpants. His toes are pink, speckled with paint to match his pant legs. The glow I've come to expect to see in his gaze is gone, dulled. My heart starts to ache.

"I didn't think you were coming home tonight," he rasps.

"Me neither."

Running his fingers through his messy hair, he cautiously asks, "Why are you here?"

"I asked my question first."

He sighs, looking around the room. It feels like forever before he finally answers me.

"We didn't get a chance to finish unpacking your stuff yesterday."

"And the paint? It was never the plan to paint the living room pink."

"The painting was a selfish decision. It seems I can't stop making those when it comes to you."

"I don't understand, Cooper. Please, just come out and say what you're thinking. No word games or dancing around my questions."

He wets his lips and nods sharply. "I wanted you to come home tomorrow and see that whether we're married or not, I want you here. *With me.* Pink walls and all. I'm in love with you, and there isn't a damn thing that could happen that would change that. I'm sorry I didn't tell you the truth the moment I learned it. It was a jackass move."

My chest is tight, each inhale stressed. My first instinct is to run to him and jump into his arms, to tell him it's okay. But I hold myself back, knowing damn well it shouldn't be that easy.

"I love you too. That's why it hurts so bad that you kept this all from me. Did you really think that I would just leave? After everything?"

He laughs humourlessly. "I was scared, Adalyn. Fuck, look at you. You're gorgeous, not to mention hilarious and brave and outspoken and ridiculously driven. You hold the world by the balls in a way I've never seen anyone do before. And somehow, you ended up with me. We said I love you to each other after I had someone telling me that the thing that brought us together in the first place wasn't real. Of course I thought there was a chance you would be relieved not to be tied down to me.

"I was going to tell you last night. I had my entire speech planned out, knew what I was going to say down to the final sentence. But then I saw you turning my house into a home—our home—right in front of me, not because you had to but because you wanted to. So, I took the easy way out. It wasn't the right thing to do, and I'm so damn sorry that I hurt you. I'll do fucking anything to make it up to you, love. Anything." He finishes on a heavy breath, devastation heavy in his stare.

I swallow the ball of emotion in my throat and slowly walk toward him, half-heartedly avoiding the drying paint on the floor. He watches each step I take, as if he's waiting for me to spin around and take off in the opposite direction. If he could read my mind, he'd know that wouldn't be possible for me.

The moment I press my palms to his hips and glide them around his back, he sighs in relief. I nod, knowing exactly how he's feeling. Like the past few hours apart have felt like days, and with this simple touch, something heals inside of us.

Tipping my head back to look up at him, I find his eyes and say, "No more keeping secrets. I'm here to stay. Of course I'm sad that we're not married, but you're still mine, aren't you? This is our home, our life together. I'm not going anywhere unless you give me a damn good reason to."

His hand cups the back of my head as he bends and slides his nose along the length of mine. "Never. I'm yours. And you're mine. And all of this is ours."

"Then that's that," I whisper and then tug him toward me, slamming my lips to his.

It's not a gentle kiss. It's an *if I don't kiss you right now, I might die* type of kiss. His lips meet mine with the same intensity, and it makes flutters fill my belly before travelling down, settling between my legs.

In one quick swoop, he has me in his arms, my legs wrapping tightly around his waist as he begins to carry me through the house. I nip at his bottom lip and run my hands down his naked chest, letting the warmth from his skin burn my fingertips. I'm a greedy bitch when it comes to Cooper. I can't get enough of him, and I don't see that ever stopping.

Bringing my mouth to his neck, I plant soft kisses over the scruffy skin and let his following soft groans send me into a lust-drunk spiral. It goes dark around us when we move into the bedroom. I'm toying with the waistband of his sweatpants, trying to tug them off, when he laughs and drops me onto the bed. My smile is wicked as I move backward and prop myself up on my elbows by our pillows.

I tug my lip between my teeth and watch as he sheds his pants, eyes never moving from where they hold my stare. My skin grows hot, the blood beneath boiling from how badly I want this man. It's always like this with us. *All consuming.*

He doesn't tease me this time. It's like he feels as desperate as I do because he climbs onto the bed and settles between my legs without hesitation.

"I don't think I could have slept tonight without you," he whispers, kissing his way down my neck and chest. One hand smooths down my body while the other palms my tit, giving it a soft squeeze. "You belong here with me."

I smile lazily, humming. "How very caveman of you, Sparrow. What's next? Are you going to paint your name on my skin next?"

His eyes heat and drop to my baggy-shirt-covered chest. I barely have a chance to blink before he has it off me and his hands over my naked tits, fingers teasing the nipples pointed at him.

"Would you like that?" he asks coyly.

"I think I would."

Groaning almost painfully, he tears my pants off and then glides his thumb through the wet flesh between my legs. I hiss between my teeth and buck into his touch, legs spreading wider for him.

"So wet for me," he breathes before sinking two fingers deep inside me. "So perfect."

I'm so beyond foreplay that I wrap my fingers around his wrist and tug, hoping he understands what I need. He does. With a nod, he curls his fingers once before pulling them free and using them to spread my arousal over the length of his cock.

"That's so hot," I blurt out.

His laugh is strangled as he glances down at himself. "Thank you?"

Winking, I say, "You're most welcome."

He shakes his head, smiling to himself. It's the smile that does me in. I'm an awkward, sometimes hard-to-handle woman, yet for some reason, I have a feeling that those might be his two favourite qualities about me.

I reach for him and settle my hands on his shoulders. "I love you."

His expression softens. Lowering his body over me, he kisses all over my face, spending extra time with my lips before he's lining himself up and pushing inside, filling me slowly, gently.

"I love you," he whispers.

I drag my nails over his sides and up his back at the first proper stroke, my breath hitching at the stretch that follows. He drops his forehead to mine and puffs a breath across my lips.

"Want to feel you like this for the rest of my life."

Biting down on my lip, I wrap my legs around his hips and cross my ankles at the middle of his back, pulling him as deep as he'll go.

"Only like this?" I ask breathlessly.

He doesn't even have to think about it. "No. In every way possible."

The confirmation fills me with bliss. I feel like I could explode from both pure happiness and the growing pleasure stretching me tight. It's a deadly combination, but I accept it with open arms. I'm one lucky fucking girl.

My climax approaches so quickly that I struggle to keep from losing control of myself as I reach across my body and grab his left hand, bringing it to my mouth. Tattoo to my lips, I hold it there as I come, filling our bedroom with my cries.

A beat later, he freezes inside of me and groans long and hard as he flips our hands where they rest across my mouth and kisses my finger. I'm still pulsing around him when he pulls out, cups my cheeks, and takes my mouth in a soft kiss.

We stay in a sweaty, lazy embrace for what feels like hours before he pulls back and traces my bottom lip with his thumb.

"I want to marry you, Adalyn," he admits on a soft exhale.

My heart skips. "For real?"

"For real."

"You know that means absolutely no take backs this time?"

He laughs, stare growing heavy with humour. "I wouldn't have taken it back last time."

"Me either. I was so close to telling you a million times not to bother with a lawyer."

I grin when he drops his face to my neck. His smile brushes my skin.

"We'll do it right this time," he says.

"And what exactly does that entail?"

Rolling off me, he pushes himself up with his elbow and rests his cheek in his palm. With a waggle of his brows, he smirks.

"Sorry, love. These lips are sealed."

I roll over and straddle his hips. He barks out a laugh when I flatten my palms on his chest and tilt my head.

"You say that now, but I know exactly how to get them to open," I coo.

He spits a curse when I slide down his thighs and grip his still-hard shaft in my fist. I swear his eyes nearly roll back as I give him a gentle pump.

"You're going to drive me crazy," he grunts.

"Yet, you'll love me anyway," I sing.

"Damn right. Till the day I die."

And as crazy as it may seem, I believe him.

40

Adam

TWENTY-NINE YEARS AGO

I've never felt so sick to my stomach. Fear and worry turn my blood to ice as I open the back seat of my car and stare at the boy sitting in the car seat that I hope I installed properly in my haste to get home.

His blue blanket is tucked over him as he sleeps with his neck craned at a horrifying angle. Every curse word known to man tumbles through my subconscious. I don't know a goddamn thing about children, let alone toddlers.

Is he hungry? Probably not because he's sleeping. Do they wake up when they're hungry, though, or do I just have to feed him in the morning? Does he sleep all night, or should I stay up and watch him? Fuck. Where does he even sleep tonight? I don't have a crib. The only bed in my place is mine.

Rolling my lips, I reach into the car and slowly lower the blanket enough I can unbuckle the car seat straps. He looks so small . . . so breakable that I hardly apply any pressure to his chest as I undo the clips and, with my heart in my throat, start to pull his arms out of the straps.

A soft noise falls from his tiny pink mouth, and his long lashes flutter for the briefest second. My chest grows tight. He's so precious. And he's mine. My son, Cooper. His pajamas have Monsters Inc. characters on them, making him look that much cuter. I take in a steadying breath and focus. It's the last one I take until he's settled in my arms.

I abandon the diaper bag Beth gave me where it sits on the front seat and start up the sidewalk to the house. It's a warm, quiet night, at least. No nosey neighbours or curious passersby to stare at us.

Cooper appears to be a heavy sleeper because he doesn't fuss even as I accidentally let the front door slam shut behind me. I don't bother with the lights and head straight for my bedroom. It's late, and he needs a bed.

"Time for bed, bud," I whisper and stretch one arm to the covers, pulling them back. Tossing the pillows to the floor, I carefully set him in the bed and cover him to his armpits with the blanket.

He looks far too small for this big bed, and fear sparks at the thought of him rolling off in the night. With that image in my mind, I slowly shift him toward the centre of the mattress and stack the extra pillows along the edge of the bed. It looks like a terrible solution, but I try and calm myself with the reminder that I'm going to watch him all night.

Tomorrow, I'll get him a proper bed.

God, he's going to be so terrified waking up in such a new place with someone he's never seen before. Probably as terrified as I am right now. I never thought I would be a dad yet, let alone to a son I never knew existed. But it's the weirdest thing because I don't have a doubt in my mind that he's mine. I recognize him down to my core. This is my son, and while I don't have a fucking clue what to do, I'm positive that I'll do right by him. I'll do everything I can to give him the best life.

My fingers shake as I brush messy brown curls from his forehead and stare down at him with a feeling I don't recognize. Something beyond love and care. Something both healing and terrifying.

I press a kiss to his forehead and whisper, "It's you and me now, Coop. I'm your dad, and I swear to be the best one there ever was."

PRESENT

"What are you thinking about right now? You just got the pouty puppy look," Ava says from across the coffee shop.

We're at Starbucks for our weekly gossip session, as Scarlett and Oakley call it. I think they're just jealous we never invite them, but that's neither here nor there.

"I don't have a pouty puppy look."

She pulls a piece of her muffin apart and tilts her head at me. "Yes, you do."

"I brood. I don't pout."

"Don't argue with me. Out with it. What's up?"

"Do you remember when I brought Cooper to your house the first time?" I ask, tapping the side of my mug of lemon tea.

"Um, yes. It's hard to forget a shock like that."

"You've never told me what you thought that day. Did you think I could do it? Raise him on my own?"

She frowns, sitting forward in her chair. "Is that a real question? Because I've never doubted you. Not once. You took your boy in without a second thought and did everything in your power to give him a damn good life. He was raised with more love in his life than both you and I ever had. Bounds more of it. What has you thinking about the past?"

"Thanks, Ava. I think it's just the reality of his relationship with Adalyn. He might be thirty, but that's my boy. It's weird to see him so grown up. I guess I just want to make sure he's going into this new chapter of his life knowing what it takes to be a good husband and father. I want to have left that example for him."

Her smile is soft, understanding. "You did leave that example for him. There's no way either Oakley or I would have given him our blessing to marry our daughter for real this time had we not known how amazing of a man he has grown up to be."

"He asked you already?" Pride sparks to life inside me.

"This morning. I don't know how he got Adalyn to let him leave her side after what happened yesterday, but I found him on our front porch, looking like he was going to pee his pants."

"That's my boy."

"I'm so excited to plan the wedding. Do you think they'll have a big or small one? Selfishly, I hope big since Maddox and Braxton had a small one, but I'm not picky."

I take a swig of my tea and then say, "I think we could try and coerce them into something bigger. Cooper would marry Addie anywhere as long as he got to call her his wife once they were done. It's up to your daughter, I think."

"We're such gossips," she giggles, drinking her tea.

"Are we gossips or just simply over-involved in our children's lives?"

"Is one really better than the other?"

I laugh. "No, I guess not."

"Oh well. It's not every day that my best friend's son decides to marry my daughter and make us family. I refuse to apologize for my meddling."

"You make a strong case. I think I agree with every damn word you said. Cheers to being unapologetic gossipers," I sing, lifting my mug in the air.

She clinks our mugs together, grinning. "Cheers."

Ava

It's been months since my second son has been home, and now that he's home, I know I'll struggle to let him go again in a few days. Tears fill my eyes the moment I wrap my arms around him and hold him tight. He hugs me back as I softly cry into his shoulder.

Noah has never been affectionate to many people, but I'm grateful to be one of the chosen ones. I wouldn't be able to handle it if I weren't.

"When did you get back?" I ask, but the words are muffled in his shirt.

"Just this morning," Tinsley answers for him when he doesn't reply.

His silence isn't unusual, but I choose this moment to pull back and wipe at my cheeks. When I see him glaring over my shoulder at Oakley, I want to cry for an entirely different reason than just seconds ago.

I give Tinsley a smile and grab her hand, squeezing it. "How are your parents?"

Her silver eyes glow with an easy happiness that perfectly matches her personality. She has always been a sweetheart, even when she was just a little girl. I've always considered her the light to Noah's dark.

"They're good. Keeping busy. The new gym is opening in a few months, so Dad's been there practically twenty-four seven. Mom's trying to keep up with all of my brother's baseball games and fundraisers."

"Oh, we know all about sports and how taxing it can be to plan around. I'll have to give her a call this week," I say.

"She'd like that."

"Word on the grapevine is you've been training Noah too?" Oakley asks. He's slowly migrated to my side in the time I've been speaking to Tiny and wraps his arm around my back.

"Is the grapevine Addie?" She laughs softly before reaching toward Noah and flicking him in one of his bulging biceps. He stares intensely at her, just like always. "But yes. He's one of my best clients."

"You better be paying her," Oakley tells Noah.

I lightly jab my elbow into my husband's side. "I doubt Tiny wants him to pay her."

"I don't!" she rushes out. "He tries to, though."

Noah's eyes tighten at the corners, obviously not liking her having to come to his aid. I barely have time to prepare myself for the inevitable bickering that always breaks out between Noah and Oakley.

"Why does it matter if I pay her? Are you trying to see if I'm actually as broke and unsuccessful as you think I am?"

Oakley's arm tenses. I frown. "We don't think you're unsuccessful, honey."

"You don't. Dad does." It's a calm but heavy accusation. And it breaks my heart.

"I don't think you're unsuccessful. I think you're wasting your talent and, in turn, your life," Oakley says, far too honestly.

Tinsley sets her hand on Noah's shoulder in a calming but also protective gesture. She's chewing on the inside of her cheek, and I'm unsure if it's to keep herself from telling Noah to drop it or from coming to his defence again. By the slight gleam of anger in her eyes as she stares at Oakley, it's probably the latter.

I step in before things can spiral the way they tend to. "How about we don't talk about this right now. You just got here, sweetheart. I'm going to be cheesy and say that I missed you so much I may need a solid two days straight of your time to refill my Noah meter."

He nods stiffly.

"I think that's a great idea. I've been missing my Addie girl something fierce and need to visit her ASAP," Tiny adds.

"That's right, you haven't seen each other since before she

and Cooper got together. Oh, are you ever in for a treat," I exclaim, grinning.

Oakley chuckles, kissing the top of my head. "Here we go." I roll my eyes.

"I'm probably too excited. I nearly started crying when I found out they thought they were married in the first place. Have mercy on me when they actually do this time around."

"*If*. Not when, Tiny," Noah grunts.

She scowls at him. "No, it's a when. Your opinion is irrelevant right now."

The closest thing to humour I've ever seen on Noah's face appears as he shifts closer to her.

"And Maddox already punched Cooper?" Noah asks bluntly.

I bite back a smile. "Yes. There will be no more punching."

"Shame."

"Noah," Tiny squeaks through a laugh. "Don't go all protective big brother now. I asked you if you were going to fly home to have a talk with Cooper, and you said no. You rightfully lost the chance to beat your brother to the punch."

"Did Maddox make him cry?" he asks.

I shake my head. "No, he didn't."

"I would have."

"Have mercy," I breathe. "Not everything is a competition between the two of you."

"Yeah, right," Tiny says, laughing.

At least my two boys are getting along. That's better than the alternative, so if competing over everything works for now, then I guess I can't complain.

It's not often I have the whole family in the same province, let alone city, so I'm going to make the best of it. Starting with Adalyn and Cooper and what I hope is an upcoming wedding.

EPILOGUE

Adalyn

"ARE YOU GOING TO TELL ME WHERE WE'RE GOING YET?" I ask.

Cooper's hand is warm on my thigh as he drives us out of town. It's a beautiful day, and the sunroof is open, letting the warm wind blow my hair around.

"You haven't figured it out?"

"I know that the turnoff to my parents' house is coming up."

"It is."

"So, that's where we're going? You could have just told me that."

"I prefer making you squirm a bit." He moves his hand inward and squeezes my inner thigh.

I grin out the window. "Oh, I know. I'm pretty sure you have a kink for making me beg."

"I think I just have an Adalyn kink."

I turn my head to look at him, batting my lashes. "Aw. That was sweet."

"It's true. There are a million things I never thought I would be interested in until you introduced me to them."

"Like?"

"I never took myself for an exhibitionist, but with you, I just can't help myself the majority of the time."

"I'm happy to be of service when it comes to broadening your horizons, Sparrow," I proclaim.

"Should I be worried about what you have in mind for me for the rest of my life?"

My heart flutters at his promise of a future together. He's said things like this a million times over the past week, but I could hear him promise me forever a million times more, and it would never be enough.

"A little, but that's what makes it fun," I reply.

He shakes his head, smiling softly. An easy silence falls between us as we continue down the backroad, my Jeep kicking rocks and dust behind us. The metal gate that stands at the forefront of my parents' acreage appears after ten more minutes of driving. It's already open, and we drive through it and up the winding driveway.

The number of cars in front of the house is surprising, but not because it's unusual. I just wasn't expecting so many people to be here today. When it comes to my family, a full driveway means a whole shit load of fun and craziness.

"Did I forget someone's birthday?" I ask when he parks between my uncle Tyler's SUV and my dad's truck.

Turning off the vehicle, he shakes his head. "No birthday, love."

"So . . ." I arch a questioning brow.

"So, you'll see when you stop asking questions and come inside."

"Is it a surprise for me? Because if not, I'm going to feel a bit teased, not gonna lie," I say before hopping out and rounding the hood to meet him.

He hooks an arm around my waist and brings me in close as we start toward the house. The warm breeze rustles the material of my skirt, making it swoosh along my ankles. I hope I'm not overdressed, but Cooper picked this out for me himself. A matching white ruffled skirt and cropped tank set weren't what I expected him to choose, but it's one of my favourite outfits, so there were no complaints from me.

The front door is already open when we reach the porch, with my dad waiting for us. I smile at him and quickly kiss his cheek.

"Hey, Dad. I feel so special getting such a personal welcome, but we can let ourselves in on our own." I laugh.

"I know, sweetheart. Come in." He steps to the side, and Cooper and I follow him inside.

The silence inside is all sorts of suspicious. I look around the empty main room, confused. "Why is it so quiet? I know everyone is here."

"They're in the backyard," Dad answers. Cooper's fingers ghost my spine.

"Are Tiny and Noah still here?"

Dad nods. "They are."

"Jamieson and Oliver?" It's been forever since I've seen my cousins.

"So many questions," Cooper murmurs into my ear, the words just for me. "Patience, Adalyn."

"They came with your aunt and uncle," Dad answers me.

"Ooh, this is so exciting. Did you buy me a car? Or—shit, did someone die?" I suck air through my teeth. "Tell me someone didn't die."

Dad barks a laugh. "Nobody is dead."

I blow out a big breath. "Good. Okay."

We stop near the kitchen, and the lack of heat at my back has me spinning to look for Cooper, only to not see him. When I face forward again, the look on my dad's face is one I've only seen once before—during Maddox's wedding when he walked Braxton down the aisle and handed her over to my brother.

"Why are you looking at me like that?" I ask, my chest constricting.

His smile is so soft, so warm. I glance around in search of my family, but it's still just us. Dad grabs my hands and holds them between us. His palms are sweaty, and I'm positive mine are too.

"Did you know that the day you were born, I drove my truck into a fire hydrant?" he asks, voice barely above a whisper.

I giggle. "What? No."

"I did. I was in the middle of practice when my coach at the time pulled me aside and told me your mom was in labour. You would think that after going through it twice before, I would have been calmer, but that couldn't be further from how I felt. I knew long before you came into this world that you were going to change everything for our family. We needed your spunk and attitude. Your sunshine and out-of-this-world humour. So that day, I lost my head to excitement and fear and drove my truck into a fire hydrant.

"I know now that the feelings I had that day were only a sneak peek of the ones I would have every day for the rest of my life. You're my baby girl. My risk taker and world changer. I'm so unbelievably proud of you and everything you've done up to this point and what you have yet to do. The thought of you getting married has always terrified me. You deserve the best this world has to offer, and I think you've found that with Cooper. If you agree, then follow me to the backyard. If you don't, then tell me right now, and I'll help you get the hell out of here runaway-bride-style."

I squeeze his hands back far too tightly. My father is an emotional man, but he's never told me all of this before. Tears collect in the corners of my eyes before I dab them away.

"I love you, Dad," I croak.

He tugs me toward him and wraps me in a strong, secure hug. The kind that used to settle my mind when I was younger. "I love you too, sweetheart."

"Did you say runaway bride?" I ask with a rough laugh.

Gently, he wipes a tear from my cheek and nods. "Yes."

Everything dawns on me then. The lack of people in the house but the substantial number of vehicles on the driveway. Cooper's disappearance. Dad's speech. This damn outfit.

"There aren't many people who would know you well enough to be confident surprising you with a wedding," he adds.

"No. There aren't."

"So, am I walking you out there, or am I helping you run?"

It's the easiest choice I've ever had to make.

I make a show of primping my hair and drying my eyes. "How do I look?"

"Beautiful, Adalyn."

"Then, shall we?" I ask. He extends his elbow, and I take it.

We walk through the rest of the house, and then Dad pulls the back sliding door open. Soft music drifts toward us, and the smell of flowers fills my nose. Stepping outside, I laugh in disbelief.

It's a pink hibiscus paradise. They're everywhere. In baskets, bouquets, weaved through an extravagant wedding arch that Cooper is standing under, watching me with such a love-filled expression that I feel my heart still under the weight of it. The corner of his mouth tugs into a small smile, adoration flickering across his face.

"It's beautiful," I whisper.

Dad sets his hand over mine and swallows so heavily I hear it. "You deserve this and more."

"I don't want more." I have everything I could ever want already.

A sniffle at the end of the front aisle pulls my eyes from Cooper. It's my mom, a tissue held to her nose as she weeps. Adam is on her one side, an empty seat on the other. I'm grateful when he rubs Mom's back soothingly.

Beth is on the opposite side of Scarlett, a similar emotional expression on her face as she watches me walk toward her son. I nearly break out in a sob when she nods at me ever so slightly, an approval I didn't know could mean so much to me.

Across the aisle, the rest of my family sits. Maddox, Braxton, and Liam. Jamieson, Oliver, and their parents, Tyler and Gracie. Tinsley and Noah and even Tinsley's parents, Braden and Sierra. Ivy lifts a hand in the air and waves excitedly from her spot beside Braxton, and I giggle, not surprised she found herself with an invitation.

Everyone I love is here. It's small and quaint and intimate. It's everything I could have asked for, all planned by the man I can't wait to spend the rest of my life with.

I feel like I can't breathe when Dad kisses my cheek and hands me over to Cooper. There's too much love in my chest. Too much happiness.

The minister is watching us with a gentle expression, smiling, but he fades to the background when Cooper whispers, "You are a vision."

"I knew there had to be something important happening for you to venture deep into my side of the closet and find me an outfit."

His smile is blinding. So fucking bright. "I took a risk today with this, but I figured it fit the theme of our relationship. Loving you was the greatest risk I've ever taken. I would take it over and over again if you were the reward."

I let out a watery laugh and lean my forehead against his chest for a moment. "You're so damn poetic. Fuck, I've already cried too much, and I'm pretty sure the bride isn't supposed to be crying before the ceremony actually starts."

"This one can do whatever she wants. This is your wedding."

Looking back up at him, I say, "Our wedding. Our proper wedding. God, I love how that sounds."

He glides his knuckle over my cheekbone. "You know what I love the sound of?"

"What?"

He leans close, lips touching my ear. "Mrs. Adalyn White."

My cheeks flush as I giggle and nod eagerly at the minister. "Let's move this ceremony along, then, yeah? I have a last name to take."

And twenty minutes later, I take that last name with pride before letting my husband carry me down the aisle as our loved ones fill the yard with cheers and congratulations.

Today marks the next chapter of our love story. And if the first one was any hint as to how the rest of them will be . . . I'm in for a lifetime of bliss.

The End

BONUS CHAPTER

Cooper

sparrow

Frantic knocking on the front door has both my wife and I jumping off the couch, rushing toward the noise. I attempt to keep Adalyn behind me, but she shoves past me with an annoyed twinge of her lips.

The knocking continues, and Adalyn yells, "We got it! Calm your tits!"

A small smile twists my lips as I urge her to the side despite her huff of frustration and open the door. It's raining heavily, and thunder rumbles through the wet streets. I double blink at the image of a soaked Tinsley on our front porch.

She's practically vibrating, but from what, I'm not sure. Fear or anger? I don't think I've ever seen her truly fear anything, though. She's too similar to Adalyn in that regard.

"What happened?" Addie gasps, making quick work of urging her friend inside. "You're soaked."

"I noticed that," Tiny replies. She shivers.

Adalyn wraps her arm around Tiny's back and rushes her through the house, toward our bedroom. I close the door and silently follow the two women.

"What happened?" Addie asks.

I grab a thick towel from the bathroom closet and hand it

to Tinsley. She gives me a small, thankful smile and then lets Adalyn move her into the bedroom.

She sits on the edge of the bed and starts to dry her soaking-wet hair. Colourful ink peeks out from the neckline of her tank top as it clings to her upper half. Her legs are bare besides the tiny shorts that have long since ridden up her thighs, leaving the intricately coloured designs that start at her knees and work upward exposed. Everything she's wearing looks tight and uncomfortable, and I'm positive the rain hasn't helped much. She must have been working out before she came here.

Her words are rambled, so quick I can hardly understand them. "I had to come before Noah had the chance to convince me to leave it alone. I need you to tell me what to do, Addie."

"With what?" Adalyn asks cautiously, crouching in front of her.

Tiny exhales. "There's a producer interested in him. A real-time producer, and Noah wants to turn him down."

I suck in air through my teeth, but the two girls are so focused on each other that they don't pay me any attention. It's like being a fly on the wall. Braxton would be so jealous.

"Are you kidding me right now?" Addie squeals, grinning.

"Yes! Like make your dreams come true kind of real."

"Please tell me that stubborn asshole isn't actually thinking about turning Reggie down."

Tinsley shakes her head before pausing, realization flaring in her eyes. "How do you know the producer's name?"

Adalyn licks her lips and shrugs, but there's no taking back what she's accidentally exposed.

"Lucky guess?"

"What did she do?" Tinsley's looking at me now.

I swallow, unsure of what to say. Looking to my wife for help, I find her chewing nervously on the inside of her cheek.

"I think we should be focusing on whether or not Noah turned him down," I say.

Tinsley narrows her eyes on me before slowly moving them to Adalyn. "Spill it. Did you have something to do with this? He hasn't met with him in person yet, but he will *absolutely* say no if you had anything to do with it, Addie. You know that, right?"

Adalyn releases a frustrated laugh. "Of course I know that. Why do you think I haven't said anything? But come on. You know just as well as I do that Noah was never going to do this on his own, and it would be a complete waste of his talents if that were the case. It's not like I did anything more than use a few contacts and let Reggie listen to some of Noah's music. I didn't tell him to offer Noah anything. He did that all on his own."

She pushes to a stand and pulls her hair over her shoulder. My gut tightens when she frowns.

"You have to convince him to take whatever Reggie has offered him, Tiny. You're the only person he will listen to. This could make his career," she adds softly.

Tinsley blows out a tight breath. I can see the game of tug-of-war going on inside of her head right now, and I don't envy her or this situation. When Adalyn sets her mind to something, there's no chance of changing it, so I hadn't bothered trying when she whipped up her plan a couple of days ago. She does these things with the purest intentions, and I took a vow to stand by her side through every situation like this, as her husband and partner.

She places her hands on her hips and stares at her best friend. "You can tell him this was all me. But just try to get him to at least meet with Reggie. If he says no after that, I'll let it go."

Tiny rolls her lips, considering that. "I'll try and get him to meet with the producer. You're right—this is a once-in-a-lifetime experience for him, and he does deserve it. I've always thought that he would get on a stage someday in front of more than a few rabid drunks with no appreciation for his music. I want this for him just as much as you do."

Adalyn's relief is obvious. Her shoulders drop, a fierce breath coming out in a woosh. "Thank you."

"You should have told me about this plan of yours," Tiny mumbles.

"Would you have told me not to do it?"

"Probably. Would you have listened?"

Addie chokes on a laugh. "No."

"Exactly. So, just give me a heads-up next time," Tiny pleads.

"Deal."

Done with the space between us, I move behind my wife and cup her elbows, bringing her back to my chest. She relaxes in my hold, and I fight back a smile.

"And you, Cooper. You are not supposed to enable her," Tinsley scolds me.

I grin, not bothering to look apologetic. "What would you have me do? She's my wife."

Addie awws and snuggles back into me. "Exactly. Now, get off my bed before you leave a big wet stain, you wet dog."

"Maybe I want to give a little shake onto your pillow."

"Try it. See how long it takes me to throw your ass back onto the porch," Addie sings.

I kiss the side of her head and laugh at the two of them. Despite everything that's changing in our lives and families, the friendship between those two never will. I'm just happy to be by Adalyn's side for everything that's about to happen soon.

Coming Soon...

Book three in the Greatest Love series is coming by the end of 2023, and I have included the prologue on the next page.

Noah and Tinsley's story is unlike any that I've written so far in my career. There will be several triggers as their story is on the dark side. Noah is not my typical hero, which hopefully has been made clear to you during the course of this series thus far.

Noah is an anti-hero in its purest form. His actions can be selfish, harsh, and borderline unforgivable at times. I want everyone to be aware of this before reading the next book, as this is a story so different from all of my work thus far in my career.

For those who are not interested in this type of story, please know that I absolutely understand. Book four is coming in early-ish 2024 and will be back to my light and cheery work with the first of the Bateman boys in a single mom, firefighter romance.

Thank you. Noah's prologue is one flip away. xx

PROLOGUE

Noah

When I was ten, my father took me to a therapist.

He said it was because I was different. That I was just hard to understand. That he and my mother didn't know how to reach me.

I knew he was lying.

My parents took me to a therapist because they were scared of me. They feared me because they didn't understand me.

I've never been like my brother or sister. There's something wrong with me. Deep, deep down in the shadowed crevice of my soul. Where there should have been light, there is darkness; a massive black pit of emptiness.

They've never understood why I lacked the glimmer you should have found in the eyes of a musically gifted young boy with a bright future ahead of him, and they never believed me when I tried to explain.

They chalked it up to some illness that must have festered in my brain, but they were wrong.

I held no light because I had given it to her. The moment I laid eyes on my golden girl, I tore myself open and handed her piece after piece of me until there was nothing left but that eery darkness that scared my family.

It is because of the girl with the glossy brown hair I imagine wrapping my fists in and pale, unblemished skin I want to decorate in bruises the shapes of my lips and fingertips.

The owner of the charred, bloody organ that beats like a kickdrum in my chest at the mere idea of her existence. Tinsley Lowry is my obsession. The reason I'm still here, living a life that gives me no joy, no satisfaction.

She is happiness personified. Everything fucking good on this earth.

She is mine.

And after all these years, it's time she knew what that means.

Thank you for reading Her Greatest Adventure! If you enjoyed it, please leave a review on Amazon and Goodreads.

This second-generation series is far from over!

His Greatest Mistake – Maddox and Braxton (Out now)

Her Greatest Adventure – Adalyn and Cooper

His Greatest Muse – Noah and Tinsley (Pre-order now)

Book 4 – Oliver Bateman and ? (TBA)

Book 5 – Jamieson Bateman and ? (TBA)

To be kept up to date on all my releases, check out my website! www.hannahcowanauthor.com

If you have not read all of the original love stories in this world, now is the time to do so!

Lucky Hit — Oakley and Ava
Between Periods (Novella and BH prequel)
Blissful Hook — Tyler and Gracie
Craving The Player — Braden and Sierra #1
Taming The Player — Braden and Sierra #2
Vital Blindside — Adam and Scarlett

Acknowledgements

I'm not going to lie; Cooper and Adalyn were hard for me. With each book I complete, the pressure to create something perfect grows. I'm so lucky to have the support system that I do, full of people who motivate me each and every damn day. Without them, I don't know if I would have gotten over the hump I faced at the beginning of this novel.

To my alpha readers, or my best friend's, rather, you are my heart and soul. You are my motivation, my courage, and my biggest protectors. Hayley, Megan, Becci, and Rose. This one is for you.

To Taylor, my best friend of over a decade and the best assistant a girl could ask for, thank you for taking most of the load off of me before I can crumble. You make everything behind the scenes run so much smoother. If I didn't have you . . . ugh, I can't even think about it. I love you.

To my beta and ARC teams, you are always such an amazing group of people. I can't thank you enough for taking the time to consistently read my work and be there for me during and after my releases. I am so grateful for each and every one of you.

When it comes to my editor and my cover designers, you guys know the drill by now. My appreciation for you doesn't have an end.

I owe a massive thank you to my hubby for being such a massive support during the most stressful of times. You are my rock and my stability, and I love you endlessly.

And to my readers, I owe everything to you. Every read, every book sold. Without you, I wouldn't be here living my dream. I will spend every day thanking you for what you have given me.

Xoxo, Hannah

About The Author

Hannah is a twenty-something-year-old indie author from Canada. Obsessed with swoon-worthy romance, she decided to take a leap and try her hand at creating stories that will have you fanning your face and giggling in the most embarrassing way possible. Hopefully, that's exactly what her stories have done!

Hannah loves to hear from her readers, and can be reached on any of her social media accounts.

Instagram : Hannahcowanauthor
Twitter, Facebook : Hannahdcowan
Facebook Group : Hannah's Hotties
Website : www.hannahcowanauthor.com

Printed in Great Britain
by Amazon

23616733R00187